International praise for Susan Johnson's

HUNGRY GHOSTS

"This novel is so well-crafted it exudes a breathless quality."

—*The Australian*

"*HUNGRY GHOSTS* is magnificently controlled, thoroughly worked and courageous in its aims."

—*Sunday Age*

"A novel that combines emotional power with assured artistic polish."

—*Who Weekly*

"*HUNGRY GHOSTS* is psychologically perceptive, resonant and full of suspense . . . gratifying."

—*Sun-Herald*

"Impossible to put down."

—*She*

D1469068

Also by Susan Johnson

A Better Woman

SUSAN JOHNSON

HUNGRY GHOSTS

WASHINGTON SQUARE PRESS
PUBLISHED BY POCKET BOOKS

New York   London   Toronto   Sydney   Singapore

All characters in this novel are the invention of the author and none are identical with any person living or dead. While Hong Kong exists, occasional historical facts and details may have been re-arranged to suit the purposes of fiction. The city as described has been imaginatively reconstructed by the author.

A Washington Square Press Publication of
POCKET BOOKS, a division of Simon & Schuster, Inc.
1230 Avenue of the Americas, New York, NY 10020

Copyright © 1996 by Susan Johnson

Originally published in 1996 in Australia by Pan Macmillan Australia Pty Limited

ISBN: 0-7434-3777-2

First Washington Square Press trade paperback printing April 2002

10 9 8 7 6 5 4 3 2 1

WASHINGTON SQUARE PRESS and colophon are registered trademarks of Simon & Schuster, Inc.

For information regarding special discounts for bulk purchases, please contact Simon & Schuster Special Sales at 1-800-456-6798 or business@simonandschuster.com

Cover illustration by Eric Dinyer

Printed in the U.S.A.

For Les,
the point on the map

'When we look at a rock, what we see is not the rock, but the effect of the rock upon us.'

BERTRAND RUSSELL

'To be permanently in exile is to be permanently in disguise; it is an extreme form of self-protection.'

MARY GORDON

··

A CITY BUILT ON FORGETTING

S OMEWHERE in a room in the colony, a pile of stones is growing ever damper. They are made of sandstone of a rare, lucky colour, a buttery cream laced with pale, whitish veins. The sandstone came from China, beyond the colony's borders, and the bringing of it involved many arduous journeys. In the room, the stones are probably stacked neat as stones can be stacked, according to size and weight. Possibly they stand in impressive piles to the roof, forming labyrinthine canyons. The stones once formed Bonham House, one of the first and most impressive of the colony's structures, built to house imperialist army officers. These men must have thought that the stones beneath them, above them and around them on all sides would last forever, longer than their own bones. They must have stood on verandahs of creamy grace looking out at ships, confident of the future's cargo. Instead, Bonham House and its verandahs were later dismantled stone by stone and the stones carried purposefully to a room, while ruling men decided where they should be reassembled.

One hundred and fifty years later, the stones are

still lying in the same room. No less than six different buildings have been erected and demolished on its old site, which once overlooked ships in a fresh harbour.

Nowadays of course the water is foul and no building is abiding. In Hong Kong it is believed that memory itself is dead, and that the past has no truck with the future. In the city of the new there is no room for ghosts and it is believed that history cannot follow you far. The colony's burghers have built a space museum to announce their faith in this belief, a splendid building situated on one of Hong Kong's most visible sites next to the harbour. Inside its strange timeless dome, visitors can make imaginary trips into space, into unplundered galaxies, to places with no human memory at all. At the museum's opening, a leading burgher announced with tears in his eyes: 'I hope to live to see the day when such space museums will be found in every district of our colony.'

As expected in such a place, its people live as if in perpetual fever, straining to arrive at the future. The present exists as a stepping stone only, a convenient spot to position your foot in readiness for movement. Indeed, the people of Hong Kong have a way of walking pitched slightly forward, as if leaning into a coming breeze. They picture themselves travelling unfreighted, unchased by earlier selves. Certainly they believe themselves unshackled from the past, from mothers and fathers, from memory.

Around their heads the city of the new is in constant renewal, a permanent reminder of change. The concept of heritage has no coinage in a world proud to have no visible reminders of decay.

But even in Hong Kong the past has a way of rising up. The earth has a way of reminding you it has a memory, remembering seasons, the incipient leaf within the blackened twig, the tilt of its axis. The earth below the colony is in fact nothing but the past itself, layer upon layer upon layer. The triumphant city of the new is actually built on expired granite, a coarse crystalline rock particularly susceptible to disintegration and rot.

And do not forget that the very first of the city's buildings, a crude governor's residence built on a hill, was blown away at one stroke by the earth's breathing. This wind lifted ships of many tons high above the water, randomly dropping them onto city streets below. The governor's residence did not last the night, only the faintest outline of its foundations remained.

The rare stones of Bonham House escaped such a fate. They lie stacked in their cool forgotten room somewhere in Hong Kong, while once ruling men who considered them are long dead.

What is to become of the past's heavy stones, in a place which only acknowledges the future? What of memory, where does it go, in a city built on forgetting?

RACHEL: THE OBLIVION OF BEGINNINGS

I REMEMBER the exact moment I believed myself to be stepping out of my life. It was morning, peak hour in Hong Kong to be precise, and I was standing on a traffic island overgrown with fume-choked plants, with red taxis and chauffeur-driven cars speeding past me taking important businessmen downwards into the city. I could see their fresh suits through the windows, the slant of their ties, their cursory glance towards me and away again as they took in my unimportance, my unstockinged legs and lack of a feminine business suit, the general disarray of my demeanour. Behind me the street rose and rose, winding up and around the mountain till it reached its pinnacle, its peak. Above my head were tower blocks tall as the clouds only more numerous. On both sides of the road where the cars sped up and down an anachronistic rainforest was stubbornly rooted, its massive trees wound with thick, aggressive vines, clutched tightly as if ready for defence. Hundreds of birds survived there, their uproar fighting other noises: government buses using the full force of their brakes, jackhammers at maximum throttle, taxi engines straining in return hauls for more businessmen. Still, the sound of the birds swelled in my ears, shrill, overwhelming. I remember it was already hot, a little cloud of steam rose from my shower-damp head as the sun cooked it. The air around me was water-logged, heavy, and smelt of incense, exhaust fumes, open drains, summer mould, escape. I was wearing a loose cotton dress which kept slipping off one shoulder and a hot breeze lifted it away from my body and blew over my belly and breasts. A trickle of water followed the indentation of my spine and my feet were slippery in their shoes. Between my legs were the dying sperm of the man I already knew I was going to marry, although I had only known him one night. I felt braced for some coming thing, difficult, profound; my old skin dropped away effortlessly. Everything before me was new, unrecognizable, and I relished a world wiped clean. I was leaving the predictable without a backward glance, all I knew was the oblivion of beginnings. Before me was the lifeboat out of my own dead sea and I would have trampled faces to reach it.

It is only now that I can ask myself this: how ravenous was my heart that I was ready to abandon the drowning? How empty, how fathomless?

I first met Anne-Louise Buchan when she was twenty and I was almost nineteen. Her reputation preceded her: we had both been at the same high school in Brisbane, but at different times, and I already knew she was intimidatingly intelligent, with a clever tongue and a famously insouciant manner. I also knew she had pert, high, Italian-statue breasts because she revealed them so readily, and that while in the fifth form she had established a club with some other fearless girls advocating the concept of Lawrentian free love. Apparently this involved a lot of nude dancing and the hugging of trees, with boys from the boys' school next door being roped in to watch and have garlands of vines intertwined with frangipani flowers laid across their brows. She was suspended for two weeks when this activity was revealed but later, when she was unexpectedly elected school captain, made a brilliant inflammatory speech about the needs of the body.

I heard her voice before I saw her body. In the office of the fashion magazine where we worked as trainee artists, little cubicles had been erected to give the illusion of privacy and she was hidden from view. Her voice rose up from her cubicle towards the ceiling, towards the sky, towards the ears of everyone who could listen. It was the most compelling voice I had ever heard, naturally loud and authoritative, capable of being thrown across rooms. It soared up, exciting, dangerous, and I was instantly enraptured. She was on the telephone talking about someone, dismissively, even with contempt, and her tone was thrillingly confessional. She had a born-to-rule accent which somehow managed to sound louche, rule-breaking. Her voice carried with it the spirit of transgression, of journeying to some richer, darker place. The fact that her voice was loud did nothing to distract from its confessional quality, for Anne-Louise Buchan sounded as if she alone had some matchless knowledge she might at any moment choose to reveal.

'He's completely indolent,' she was saying. 'His concept of hard work is adopting the missionary position.' This was followed by the most alarming laugh, unwieldy, grazing the hysterical, disproportionately huge in the wake of such a minor witticism. My hands began to sweat and my mouth fixed itself into a lewd, unnatural grin.

'Anne-Louise,' said our boss as we turned into her cubicle and Anne-Louise Buchan swung around. She was smoking a bright pink cigarette which she used to wave us away. Her desk was strewn with newspapers, pencils, dirty coffee cups, overflowing ashtrays, decaying orange peel, packets of contraceptive pills, dozens of packets of Sobranie cigarettes.

'I'm busy,' she said, covering the mouthpiece, returning immediately to her call. I could not believe that a twenty-year-old would have the gall to dismiss her boss, but I could also see that our boss, a nervy woman who was perhaps five or six years older than ourselves, was clearly intimidated. While Anne-Louise continued her conversation into the phone I inspected her. Her face was immediately arresting, being big, mobile, fully alive, a kind of figurehead for the rest of her. It sailed above her graceful upper body flat like an ornament, wide, almost Slavic, with flattened cheekbones and intelligent, blazing black eyes. Already at twenty her eyes had an arty smudge around their sockets, incipient circles which made her look world-weary, seasoned. She was wearing all black, at that time completely unfashionable, and yet gave the impression of a haughty chic beyond fashion. Her hair was collar-length and dishevelled, a murky blond, and had obviously only barely survived a permanent wave.

At some point while she was talking Anne-Louise Buchan began to look directly at me: I was unprepared for the resolve of her glare. Her stare was excessive, her black eyes had a charged, merciless focus. I immediately blushed and looked away, wanting at once to be cruel and dismissive like her.

'Well, well,' she said, still looking at me as she put down the phone, 'what have we here?'

I had no reply, no repartee, and stood with my eyes on the carpet while our boss introduced us.

'You'd better say boo to this goose,' said Anne-Louise Buchan. 'You never know when I'll come in handy.'

What is it that compels us to choose one person over another and ensures that we will keep coming back? What lost, desired part of ourselves do they declare for us, that we long to reclaim for ourselves? I only know that when I saw Anne-Louise Buchan I chose

13

her for myself as deliberately as I might choose a colour which suited me, a food for which my tongue longed. She was everything I was not: socially fearless, infinitely careless, weightless. Nothing settled on her shoulders for long, not regret, not doubt, not fear. She was like some sheer garment flowing in the wind, streaming, effortlessly fluid. Since I myself was weighed down by self-consciousness and had rarely performed a spontaneous act, Anne-Louise Buchan's carelessness struck me as serendipitous, nothing less than a talent for life. If her nonchalance meant Anne-Louise occasionally rode over people, she did not appear to notice and it was this more than anything which attracted me. I could not get over the fact that she did not seem to care if other people lived or died. She did not seek out anyone's good opinion either, and never recognized when she gave offence. I myself was constantly attentive and found it burdensome, but Anne-Louise rarely noticed anything which did not immediately concern her. Anne-Louise was my best friend for fifteen years and yet if you had asked her at any time over those years she couldn't have told you the colour of my eyes. She rarely knew when I was saddest, when I was in flight, she could not have told you my history of want.

If I was only ever an unkind person in private, Anne-Louise Buchan was unkind out loud. In this I considered her to be a better person than myself, clearer, more authentic. I would like to redeem all the times I have smiled in my life when I would have preferred to draw blood. I was well trained to be obedient, compliant, to sniff out other people's intentions before they even realized them themselves. I am the alert, nerve-wired child of an alert, nerve-wired mother and an overanxious, bad-tempered father. My mother feared the insides of elevators, tunnels, locked toilet cubicles, the human heart, my father feared his own self. My mother in fact preferred her human beings speechless, without fully functioning sexual organs. A fresh, unfurled baby fulfilled entirely her idea of an agreeable person: it never answered back and was incapable of orgasm. Babies to her were symbols of perfection, unsullied by the dirty hands of life. To my mother they represented the body incarnate, mindless, without history or regret, oblivious to the implications of feelings. My mother obviously preferred life best in its controlled nascent state, before chaos and ruin forced the door. She would have kept us all wordless and dependent if she could, in a fug of milk-innocence, beyond yearning. When we defied her and reared up on two legs to indulge in masturbation and free will, she brought a succession of perpetual infants into the house, the produce of teenaged unmarried girls marooned in hospital beds elsewhere. While these girls considered adoption my mother tended their babies, cocooned, barely conscious, forming. They lay in their baskets like dumb, grasping plant-life, all biology, all need. She could answer such needs unambiguously, certainly: it was our own murky, uncontainable adolescent desires she found untenable. She made it clear that we were the personal embodiment of her disappointment, altogether too sexual, too complex, too *large*. Meanwhile fresh babies continued to lie there, our replacements, eternal reminders of our downfall.

My mother must have thought that if she bolted the door, adult chaos and ruin might turn away. I know she believed allowing evil in was a kind of moral choice which only the weak permitted.

Is it any wonder that when ruin came my first instinct was to close my eyes like her? And what defences could I have possibly had once I found malevolence was already within?

....

MARTIN: HIS FUTURE, ARRIVING

I T happened to be a flawless October day when Martin James Bannister first arrived in Hong Kong and the sky was open and forgiving. The famous city of chance was spread out below him, detailed as a map, yielding. As the plane descended, he saw the inlets of faultless islands, the bite of the mainland, container ships lying in a gleaming, obviously prosperous harbour. It was late afternoon and the setting sun struck the city's towers, which were denser, more prolific, more splendid than he had anticipated. The city of the new reared up, alive, teeming, its perilously tall buildings puffing out their newly born chests. Enormous cliffs of marble and glass were ablaze with the reflection of the sun, turning them into one mighty man-made shield, flaming. This shining shield was like a deflective armour against the natural world, a challenge held up to God. Martin Bannister's eyes were hurt, fended off, and retreated to the great mountain rising up behind the towers as if in God's defence, competing with the city, and failing. As the aircraft dropped lower it appeared to him that the buildings had won, that human cleverness had triumphed over nature.

The plane almost grazed the tops of apartment blocks in its descent and as it did so Martin Bannister took one final airborne look over the colony, his possible kingdom. It was the city of chance and he was feeling lucky, as if the winning deal was in his very hands. He unconsciously swung his lower jaw gently in its socket, a barely noticeable gesture, but indicative of deep excitement to anyone who knew him.

Martin James Bannister was not expecting anyone to know him. He was cast off, adrift, his own God, answerable to neither parents, siblings nor a wife. Like the city below, he was freshly invented, a weightless thing with nothing to hold him. He was the only surviving child of parents he considered lost and an early wife had long since been thrown off. He was still young, not yet thirty, and certainly did not consider himself even close to middle-age. He was of the generation that had indulged in a long, extended youth and which would have trouble coming to terms with the finite nature of life and its unfortunate habit of ageing the body and narrowing choices.

He had spent his boyhood in a dark flat in an unattractive street off Wandsworth Bridge Road, London, before moving to an uneventful town in New Zealand with his mother and second step-father when he was sixteen. If anyone asked him now he said he had grown up in London, deleting his New Zealand years entirely, for if being alive meant anything to Martin James Bannister it meant mutability, re-invention, which sometimes translated into simple, old-fashioned lying. He was of the school which believed ears needed appropriate conditions before information could be correctly heard, that like an alternative form of vegetable life they needed to be properly nurtured.

Fortunately for him, Martin Bannister was startlingly handsome, beautiful in an original way, which generally ensured a good supply of women willing to fall in love with him. He had a finely wrought face, sensitive, with a full mouth cleverly carved, and very pale luminous green eyes. His eyes were strangely beautiful, so oddly coloured as to seem a genetic impossibility. His cool, marbled irises frequently caused young women to stop in mid-speech when he turned their full glory upon them. Impressionable young women imagined he could see right through them and were frequently overcome with embarrassment until his charm and disarming stutter soothed them.

Martin Bannister had a vague, unclassifiable accent, capable both of assuming English, upper-class tones when necessary or of falling into flattened New Zealand vowels when he was drunk or angry. His stutter too made him seem endearingly vulnerable, particularly when he was trying his hardest to appear cool and unruffled. He did not know that his stutter betrayed him, implying as it did some broken, yearning quality, an inner hesitancy. His general manner too was soft and somehow feminine, despite

21

years of cultivating what he believed to be a tough, unyielding exterior. Yet the whole effect was surprisingly seductive, his voice low and exciting: when he was at his charming best, both men and women leaned a little closer.

Martin Bannister had in fact once been a slightly built effeminate boy, fearful of hard, bone-knocking sports, delicate in his movements. He had grown to love music, to develop a keen, lyrical sense of the beauty of words, of the numinous. As a tender and beautiful fourteen-year-old he had been approached by hopeful men in Hyde Park while reading Wordsworth and pondering nature. His body still remembered this earlier lost self in gestures which resolutely remained: when drunk his hands turned graceful on loosened wrists, his hips assumed a kind of sway. His speech too became more lilting, his stammer girlish and soft.

Before he moved to New Zealand, Martin was briefly famous for being the cleverest teenager in Parson's Green, the only one at his bully-boy comprehensive to achieve a string of brilliant 'O' levels. At university in Wellington a succession of girlfriends attempted to get him to notice them but he was too busy being surprised to discover he was not the cleverest boy reading English. He entered a short period of decline, an extended sulk, in which for the first time in his life he saw that he was being forced to assume the role of second best. He saw himself coming second to colonial second-raters, enduring a lifetime of standing in front of a blackboard in a classroom in some backward town in the middle of nowhere.

It was at this point that Martin James Bannister began his long climb upwards. He applied and was accepted at the London School of Economics, packed his bags, and did not look back. He put aside his love of music and nature and unearthed in himself a will to succeed, to smash anything second-rate which might get in his way. If this included his own self he did not waver, and set about to crack his own bones.

His first job in the City after leaving the LSE was with Coutts and Co., one of the Queen's banks. He quickly learnt that young men with a future wore satin spotted ties and smelt freshly washed so he took to wearing an expensive but subtle after-shave and throwing expensive deodorizing talc under his arms. Although he was only doing backroom clerical work for the first couple of years he was conscious of trying to fit in as comfortably as possible. He had not been to the same schools as his colleagues from wealthier families and certainly no-one seemed to have heard of him when enquiries were made but Martin managed to be suitably vague about his background, implying schools in more glamorous European countries, absent parents. Luckily at that time in the City banks were filling up with young men and women from families much like his own, the children of builders and postmen and East End taxi drivers who twenty years previously would not have got a look-in.

Martin's evasiveness about his background was his introduction to the possibilities of re-invention, his first lesson in the nurturing of ears and the skilful art of growing what is fed into them. He felt the exhilarating breath of chance, all his possibilities rushing in at once.

Flying into the colony that first afternoon Martin Bannister felt the same breath. As he stood on the tarmac after leaving the plane he had smelt petrol, the soft Asian air, a stench possibly coming from the harbour or an open sewer. But he had also smelt success, the whiff of money, chance headed his way. He thought that it could only mean the onset of blessings, the lucky ruffle of his future, arriving.

ANNE-LOUISE: WITHOUT PEER

G R O W I N G up in the subtropical heat of Brisbane, Anne-Louise Buchan rarely thought of Asia. Her imagination leapt entirely over such sulky, swarming places to land in Paris, New York, Rome. It was in those cities she imagined you lived a fully stretched life, plump, gleaming. In an apartment in Paris your best self might emerge and life might shimmer as it was meant. From books and paintings and indeed from her own family Anne-Louise conceived the idea that life was elsewhere, most certainly not in the comatose suburbs of Camp Hill or Clayfield. In these places life existed as a half-cooked thing, clumsy, insubstantial. She intended a life baked to perfection, a life lived at full heat.

She grew up the only child of an adoring, indulgent father, already older than most fathers at the time of her birth. He fed her chocolates, coconut ice, flattery, his elderly love, to the cost of her younger and beautiful mother. It was her mother who had wanted a child, who had pleaded for one but who had not foreseen the unfortunate implications. Margaret Buchan had fought a long and bloody battle to win her husband from his first childless wife, a struggle which had eaten up her youth. She had been twenty-one when she fell in love with the dashing South African forty-five-year-old Harry Buchan; it was wartime and Brisbane had never been so exciting. Handsome Americans roamed the streets and it seemed to her that every night she danced at the City Hall or up on the hill at Cloudland. She could still remember the feel of the beautifully sprung wooden dance floor beneath her feet, kissing now-forgotten soldiers under the stars outside Cloudland. The city lights were strewn below, distant, dreamily radiant. She had felt in full possession of herself, confident, gorgeous, and could not have imagined it would take almost thirteen years for her own war to end on becoming Harry Buchan's second wife.

The year after they were finally married their only child was born. By then Margaret was thirty-five and believed that Harry would only value her all the more. Instead, he unexpectedly fell in love with the infant at the expense of herself, forgetting that her own beauty was meant to be his undeserved reward. He was ridiculously proud of the child, stupidly boastful, as if he were the only sixty-year-old man alive to have achieved such a feat. She was secretly relieved, however, to note that Anne-Louise would not grow into an obvious beauty as she herself had been: while Anne-Louise's attractions were undoubtedly great, the growing girl had merely an interesting face rather than a beautiful one. What she did have was an outstanding natural voice, booming, bossy. Already at seven her daughter's voice issued orders to her more passive playmates, bellowing instructions to the wayward. She had too an alarming temper, a cyclonic fury if she believed herself thwarted. Her mother was sometimes frightened of her, of the unswerving will evident in her eye, of her overheated, dramatic passions. While Harry Buchan laughed at his daughter's wilfulness, enjoying its obvious displays of her spirit and talent, Margaret Buchan feared Anne-Louise would come to a bad end, that one day she would come across somebody stronger than herself who would finally say no. She would learn in fact that the world itself could say no as clearly as any person, that in life you did not get everything at will.

Margaret Buchan herself had once wanted to go to Paris for example, to drink champagne out of a new shoe. When she was eighteen an uncle working in London had suggested to her mother that she travel over and help him paint theatre sets. This uncle had left years before and was now well established building sets; Margaret was at art college and desperate to go. But her mother had hardly set foot outside Brisbane environs (not counting a frightening holiday as a sixteen-year-old to Sydney) and she had hummed and haaed until it was too late, until the war had started and it was too late to go. For a while Margaret had been appeased by the excitements of wartime and the attentions of Lt Harry Buchan and her own personal battle. She had loved listening to his stories about coming to Australia when he was twenty-five, how he fell in love with it and became naturalised at the beginning of the war just so he could join the Australian army. It was only years later, after Anne-Louise was born and Harry's attentions had wandered, that she began to think again of what might have been, of the alternative life she might have led. Harry had not even taken her back to Cape Town as he had promised. It was this unlived dream life which fed into her daughter's, this sense of lost chance which permeated Anne-Louise's own aspirations, unconsciously propelling her forward. In this way dreams are catching and some children follow, like sleepwalkers, paths laid down by former dreamers, seamless and indistinguishable from their own.

From her much-loved father Anne-Louise got the dangerous notion that she was unique, capable of anything, indeed that she was something divine. Her drawing he immediately declared without peer, and predicted she was destined for greatness. She absorbed this knowledge along with the sweet things he fed her, she was his angel, his personal saviour. To sit on the knee of a man who adores you is intoxicating indeed, to watch his face alight at simply moving your lips is to achieve home rule. Anne-Louise learnt early that she could make her father laugh like no-one else could, tell him the rude jokes her mother did not allow. Her dad told even ruder ones back and the two of them laughed in delicious conspiracy against her mother. When she was very small her father uttered shocking words like 'wee-wee' and 'bum' out loud and Anne-Louise collapsed into frightened giggles. When she was older and came home starving from school, calling out as she walked in, 'What's for tea?' her father always replied, 'Poo on toast,' and she always smiled, no matter how many times she heard it.

Anne-Louise believed early that her desires alone controlled the house, that she had long ago usurped her own mother. As she grew she looked upon her mother with a vague pity, knowing that her father preferred her, his special love. At fourteen, when she wanted to wear a pair of hotpants made of purple satin to a party, her mother refused outright but her father simply clapped and whistled and said, 'You'll win a few hearts in that, darling.' By this time Harry Buchan seemed to Anne-Louise to be a very old man indeed, doddery and fading. He sometimes held her hand too long or pressed her tightly against his chest so that she became conscious of her still-swelling bosoms. She had recently achieved her first Tweeny First bra and was embarrassed to see it hanging exposed on the clothes line with the rest of the washing. When she disposed of her sanitary napkins she did so like a criminal, keeping them stashed in her upper drawer until she could dispose of them in the dark when everyone had gone to bed.

One night she snuck into the kitchen with a bag

full of used pads, knowing that the rubbish was due to be cleared the following morning. As she turned into the kitchen she ran smack into the large, unmoving body of her father, standing moonlit by the door.

'Angel,' he said in a dreamy, far-off voice, 'what are you doing up?'

She swung her criminal's bag behind her body, conscious of the smell of used blood which drifted upwards. 'I was thirsty,' she said, pushing past him, clutching the bag to her belly.

As she stood pressed against the sink, the bag squashed against it, her father came and stood behind her. He placed his large, heavy arms around her shoulders; she could smell his old man's odour: soap, freshly laundered pyjamas, cigar smoke, and decay, from deep inside, blowing up the pipe to his mouth.

'You know you're my special girl,' he said. 'Give your old man a kiss.'

She swung around, kissed him briefly on the cheek, and moved swiftly to the door.

'Night, Pa,' she said, stopping to turn around. 'Oh, I forgot,' she added, walking back to the bin, 'failed drawings.' She quickly stuffed the evidence deep inside. 'Sweet dreams,' she said, leaving.

What impulse made her stay by the door, certain he could not resist the urge to snoop? After a while Harry Buchan did in fact turn towards the bin, raised the lid and rooted around inside. Anne-Louise Buchan did not wait to see if he lifted anything out but spun on her heel and ran back to her bedroom, turning the light straight out. She lay in the dark, her heart beating hard, her eyes ceaselessly roaming the room.

From then on she kept her diary, her drawings, her letters, her very self under lock and key. She knew she must protect herself from invasion, that to defend a private self she must use the full force of her will. She never again willingly touched her father and he never touched her; her sexual self stood between them like a wall. If her mother noticed she did not say but sometimes Anne-Louise caught her watching her with a searching expression, as if she was about to ask a question, except she never did.

When her father inconveniently had a stroke while at the pictures watching his favourite film *Doctor Zhivago*, Anne-Louise did not at first realize the implications. When he finally came home from hospital, her father had clearly gone and a drooling fool had taken his place. She tried never to go near him and when her mother asked her to look after him one afternoon she stayed in her room and turned up her stereo, never going in to his room once.

'Has he been alright?' her mother asked when she got home.

'Fine,' she replied.

But he was not fine and when Margaret Buchan opened the door she found him sprawled where he had fallen.

After this Anne-Louise felt guilty. One afternoon

not long after she came home early from school to find her mother prostrate on the lounge. It suddenly occurred to her that her mother might be suffering too.

'Mum,' she enquired as gently as she could, 'is there anything I can do?'

Margaret Buchan turned to her and her face was contorted, her mouth a lipless black pit. 'You? What could you do? You stole his best years from me, that's what you did. What more could you possibly do now?' She flung herself upon the pillows, letting loose a terrible howl. Anne-Louise stood watching until once again her mother turned her head. 'Get out of my sight, you stupid girl!' she screamed. 'Now!'

Anne-Louise stood drawing up all the bridges into her fifteen-year-old self, pulling shut every entry she could find.

It was not long after this that she began to grow thin, to starve her previously plump teenaged rump into submission. She did not eat cake or coconut ice, she did not eat flattery or chocolate. She ate instead the insides of tomatoes, the whites of eggs, the top halves only of celery stalks. She could soon feel her own bones coming to the surface, her own power calling them at will: her flattened cheekbones appeared, the bones of her adult face rose. She knew her eyes to be more prominent, shining and ferocious, her stare to be chilling and pronounced. She took up smoking, Sobranies by preference, and began to plan her faraway life. She planned to take great leaping strides away from Brisbane, away from suburbs, away from everything familiar. She read Lawrence and Fitzgerald and biographies of great artists and planned to escape just like them. She never went near her father and when he was finally put into a nursing home visited him only when forced.

At sixteen and ten months she lost her virginity and with it her desire to starve. She read *The Female Eunuch* and stopped dieting and shaving her legs: this was the beginning of her body-as-God period, her Lawrentian rejoicing, her fame as a schoolgirl revolutionary. For the rest of her life Anne-Louise Buchan would fall in love with wildly inappropriate men and sleep with many others, discovering herself disappointed in all of them. Never again would she find a man who loved her more than anyone in the world, who would sit her on his knee feeding her chocolate, happy to keep doing so for all time.

Against all odds her father lived on and on, a living witness to her most private crime.

RACHEL: THE ART OF BLITHENESS

THAT first summer when I came to Hong Kong people were marching in the streets. A great city of people, locals mainly with a sprinkling of expatriates, all marching and chanting. There were hundreds, thousands, moving as one mass, their dark heads raised, their mouths open and howling. The noise permeated the walls of restaurants, the insides of cars, incessant, lamenting. I seemed to hear it in my bed at night, rising up from the streets, floating skywards. I once asked a passing Chinese girl to translate the words they were chanting. She looked at me before speaking and said, 'They are saying, "Satellites have already reached heaven but democracy is still stuck in hell."' She turned away before I could ask another question.

The marches were in fact a wake of sorts, for students freshly killed in China. In the hot glamorous light of the Hong Kong summer I could not picture the fall of their bodies, I could not see the dark spill of their blood. When I spoke to an Englishman at a bar in a hotel he said such crude methods of dispatching discontent were typical of barbarians and that the colony should watch out.

But it was myself who should have kept a vigilant eye, myself who should have seen the warning. The local people would surely have told me that fresh blood is the worst kind of omen.

Anne-Louise Buchan quickly became my best friend, on whom I could try out new selves. I knew she had lots of other friends and I was flattered to be chosen. I do not know why she picked me to add to her list, only that she did. It was an unlikely pairing and yet surprisingly we complemented each other: she seemed to find me endlessly amusing and at the beginning of our friendship she referred to me as 'happy little Rach'. If she was inclined to be patronizing I did not mind, for in her company I *did* feel happy, and loved. Like all friendships destined to be close, I remember slipping effortlessly into intimacy: although we were very different personalities, we somehow recognized each other. Perhaps she saw in me some willingness to accept her most glamorous version of herself, for she certainly inspired me to feel all my possibilities. In Anne-Louise's presence I believed myself funnier, wittier, less tongue-tied, as if her own attributes were too abundant and I profited by the overspill. I *was* funnier when she was around: because she believed me so, I became so. When we were together we spent a lot of time laughing, at silly things usually, often decipherable to no-one else. I felt myself becoming the foolish adolescent I had never been, giggling helplessly. We quickly developed a girlish language of private jokes and sayings: once, for perhaps six months, we irritated everyone by prefacing everything with the words 'profoundly' or 'superficially'. 'Now that's a profoundly gorgeous boy,' Anne-Louise might say. 'Superficially gorgeous,' I'd reply. It was embarrassingly silly yet we found it hysterically funny. Sometimes Anne-Louise inserted one of these words into conversations when I least expected it: I remember a dispute in our office once between Anne-Louise and the art director. 'I find your argument profoundly flawed,' she said and winked at me.

She had a way of making everyone rise to the occasion so that you became your most shining self. I felt fearless in her company, dangerous, charged, as if I was capable of magnificence. She enlarged rooms, lives, happiness itself, her own excitements catching everybody up, desperate not to be left out. It was exciting being around her, as if she had been given a larger dose of vitality than everyone else. When she sat at a large restaurant table those farthest away from her thrilling voice felt beached, removed from the action.

I remember sitting with her once on a footpath outside a party not long after I met her, both of us slightly drunk, our heads tipped back to an enormous moon. It was summer and the air was rich and wet against us, dense, breathing.

'You are a striver,' she announced in her deep, commanding voice. I was already used to her

disarming habit of making direct personal pro-
nouncements and always felt obscurely flattered. I
liked her rich, curly vocabulary too, and could have
listened to her making speeches about me all night.

'A striver?' I asked, not turning towards her but
aiming my head at the moon.

'There are strivers and accepters and you are a
striver. What are you striving for?'

I turned to look at her. 'I don't know. I only
know I don't want to wake up one day and find my
life has escaped me.'

She smiled at me, her big alive face vivid in the
light. 'Ah, you see, Rachel, only strivers know about
the stealthiness of time. No matter how young they
are.'

She looked up at the moon, shadowed yet bright,
and all at once it seemed that I was on the brink of
my life, and that everything wonderful was before
me. I could not have said exactly what I expected
only that it involved taking life by the neck and
wringing out all that was possible: great joys, great
sorrows. A fever to start rose in my chest, to understand, to claim splendour. I must have made some
sound because Anne-Louise covered my hand with
her own and when I turned to her I thought that she
understood the swell of exultation, that she shared
my desire to run at life full tilt.

'It's less ruinous being an accepter,' she said in
a low voice, 'but not as spectacular.'

I smiled and it seemed to me that we had made

some unspoken pact, fateful, hazardous, that we had come to an understanding without words.

I realize now that all understandings are personal, that different ears do not always hear the same meaning. I no longer know if at the end Anne-Louise still believed in the superiority of the spectacular, if she still clung to the dignity of ruin.

We had both moved to Sydney independently, Anne-Louise getting out of Brisbane as soon as she could by applying to the National Art School at East Sydney Tech, myself after leaving Seven Hills College of Art in Brisbane. When I first went to Sydney I shared a house in Darlinghurst with several Marxist artists I knew from college committed to workers' rights and women's liberation. Since I had just started my first job as a trainee artist on a fashion magazine featuring glossy girls worrying about boyfriends and lipstick, I tended to hang my head a lot and sneak out the door hiding my freshly waxed legs. Of course Anne-Louise, who worked at the magazine too, was instantly treated with mistrust by my housemates, suspected of being too frivolous. If she noticed she did not care and continued to announce herself loudly at our front door, sometimes wearing elaborate false eyelashes or alarmingly long silver false nails. 'Don't worry, sweetie, I'm a feminist at heart,' she might say on passing the most disapproving member of the household.

I loved her for it, her carelessness, her dash, her

lack of regard for other people's opinion. As someone overly concerned about what other people thought, indeed terrified lest I do the wrong thing and fall short of my housemates' political standards, I felt rested in her company, as if I too did not care, as if I too could learn the art of blitheness. I was still young enough not to know the word's full implications, its attendant lack of empathy, indeed its very insensitivity to others. Had I known would I still have thought that blitheness was worth gaining at any cost?

I knew of course that Anne-Louise was not frivolous and her party-girl act only a minor amusement. I knew that she had secret great aims, to draw as if tracing a plan laid by God, to paint a picture whose value no-one could dispute. I had seen the mad, determined glitter in her eye when she talked, the fierce way she attacked waiting paper. 'I have to get better,' she said once, furiously tearing out the page on which she was drawing. She was already better than all of us, her eye was astute, her hand steady. The bedroom in the house she shared in Newtown was covered in drawings: life-drawings, buildings, faces, outlines for intended paintings. When she used colour she did so fearlessly, nothing she touched was tentative, all her work from the first stroke was fully born. She had none of the fear of approach I suffered from, what to put first, where to go next. She plunged straight in with the instinct of genius, and I envied her for it. While I worried that I might never be better than mediocre, Anne-Louise put her head down and did not look up. Sometimes she became dangerously over-excited and stayed up all night drawing, covering the bed, the floor and every surface with used paper. 'I prefer the night,' she said, 'people's dreams are so noiseless.' I stayed up with her for long hours while she raved, listening to her lay out her plans. She spoke of how painters, like writers, must develop a vocabulary, vivid, teeming. 'Only by training can we learn to be more articulate,' she announced. I loved her dense, contrived language, the way she spoke in whole poems. Her dark, compelling voice in the night was hypnotic, her speech disjointed and yet strangely lucid, in the way of lunatics or fanatics. Yet sometimes in the mornings I could not remember exactly what it was she had said. I remembered only the sensation of her voice, deep and flowing, the sensation of having been expanded, of having touched upon some dark, central mystery to do with life itself. She was like an explosive gas carefully bottled, dangerous when close to a flame.

Everyone claimed Anne-Louise and soon she was lunching with all the most important people on the magazine, charming them with her lack of obsequiousness, her disregard for their importance. Some of them were famous enough to find disregard refreshing, her cool young eye a welcome change. She asked me along to a lunch once but I was intimidated and struck dumb in the anecdotal competition, without even one name to drop. Anne-Louise was, of course, sensational, laughing her seductive, near-hysterical laugh, telling stories everyone admired. She was very blond then and manic on hunger, her eyes slightly wild in her head. I remember she ordered a salad and ate one curled leaf; for the main course she toyed with a fish. She was devastatingly cruel about our home town and told an elaborate, embossed tale about how she made good her escape. She referred to it as 'The Planet Brisbane' and ridiculed its unpleasant combination of smug self-satisfaction and provincial defensiveness. 'It's proud of its blandness,' she said, letting out a scornful snort, 'as if being safe is all there is!' While it was true that at the time a conservative, ham-fisted politician had banned street marches in the city and was frequently declaring states of emergency, Anne-Louise gave the impression that she was a political refugee, a comrade of Chilean leftists fleeing the slaughter of Pinochet. 'I've claimed asylum,' she said and everyone laughed. I thought of Brisbane's somnambulant heat, its dazed, empty streets, its innocent pride as a place of health and safety for children. I did not hate it in the pure, unobstructed way Anne-Louise did but felt something more knotty, like familial love, a fierce attachment shot through with bitterness.

That day at lunch I sat back to watch Anne-Louise perform. It wasn't as if she told bare-faced lies exactly, more that she gave facts an added sheen, buffing them until they resembled something better. I was never sure how much of this was intentional, how strong her need was to play to an audience, to prove herself shiny and bright. The whole time I knew her I was never sure whether the public self I saw was in fact her real self, naturally exuberant, unconscious of its own display. I could not help feeling that it was all an elaborate show which afterwards exhausted her so that she longed for nothing more than to be alone in a quiet room. I believed she saw social interaction as a kind of competition which the loudest and wittiest person always wins. I noticed too that when we were together in public she was sometimes vaguely dismissive of me, as if I alone had witnessed some private flawed act she regretted.

'Rachel won't hear a word against Planet Brisbane,' she said that day at lunch. 'In her secret heart she believes in clean streets and children standing up straight and shooting graffiti artists on the spot.'

Everyone laughed and, of course, I did too but I noticed that Anne-Louise wasn't smiling.

Brisbane to me was a damp, underground place, the smell of soil beneath the raised wooden floor of our house. Under the house it was cool and secret, a place where adults rarely came. We concocted home-made poison there and murdered ants and drew up plans to run away. Later, when I was involved in a deadly power struggle with my father to claim my human rights, I retreated to that underworld place with my paints and my anger to plot my revenge. By then my mother was upstairs with her replacement babies and our adolescent selves were cast out. I sat beneath my parents in their heaven, raging like Lucifer below. I wanted my rights, I wanted to claim my own life. In our awake upstairs life my father had the only rights: the right to be angry, the right to be loudest, the very right to be right. He squashed our emerging adult selves like insignificant animal life beneath his feet, denying our emerging grub-like selves.

I had once loved him in a clean, unadulterated way, with the overheated passion of every little girl. Until I was eleven or twelve I offered him nothing but unqualified admiration, and he offered clean, uncluttered love in return. I cannot say at what precise moment this unadulterated love became spoiled and the easy swing of my father's arms grew stiff and self-conscious. I know only that it seemed to me that one morning I woke to find my father my captor, a stone in the entrance blocking out light and escape. Perhaps his bully's tendencies had simply lain latent, waiting to announce themselves only when he had something tangible to fight. While we were still children and technically incapable of defiance we had proved unworthy opponents, and he had been able to move us around like pieces on a games board, portable playthings, light and inconsequential. It was only when we began to answer back, to question and demand, that he became frightened. He drew himself up to his full height and began to wage his defence against the undermining of his authority. He used sarcasm, scorn, ridicule, shouting; when all else failed he used a more physical weapon, the strap. Even at more sedate moments he never seemed to be listening properly to what we said, his eyes seemed perpetually elsewhere.

For a long time afterwards I loved only men whose eyes did not look into mine. My father's imprint was my only guide and I'm ashamed to say I followed it instinctively. I was deeply etched and my route to disaster was embarrassingly direct. I was blind and homing, insensible to everything except impulse.

. . . .

MARTIN: HER ROYAL BLOODY HIGHNESS

T HE beautiful Martin Bannister took to the colony as if it were made for him, and him for it. Hong Kong did not permit indifference: people either loved it or loathed it on sight. Martin Bannister loved it straight away, its blaring neon signs, its never-ending noise, its constant push of faces, its general extravagance. If he regularly ate dinners worth hundreds of pounds and drank bottles of wine worth a week's rent then he also handed out large notes indiscriminately to beggars. The beggars always looked at the notes in disbelief and would have fallen at his feet if pride had not prevented them.

In his job as a futures dealer for a merchant bank he was known as one of the 'golden bachelors', a quaint expression apparently common amongst the local Chinese. Groups of pretty secretaries, Chinese girls with bad English, giggled behind their hands when he walked past; his own secretary, Queenie Wong, blushed each time he looked at her.

'Take this to Mr Coulsen, Queenie,' he might say, only to watch her wide silly face become engulfed by waves of blood lapping all the way to her hairline. 'N—N—Now, please,' he added and she would scuttle off, blood still slapping against the shore of her face.

In his office on the twenty-third floor Martin had an insurmountable view of the harbour across to the space museum and the hills on the other side. Originally there had been eight distinct hills which the local people believed to be inhabited by dragons but two or three hills had since been razed to make way for new buildings. Once, when a new hotel was being constructed on a prime site next to the harbour, the Chinese became frightened that the dragons would have their view blocked off and would not be able to make their way down to bathe. An expert in *feng shui* was called in and a glass atrium added to the building's plans so that the remaining dragons could continue to have a clear view of the harbour. The local people were not sentimental but they were superstitious and certainly believed in covering their backs.

Martin took all this folklore in but was not impressed, any more than he was flattered by the secretaries' giggles. He declared himself fond of the Chinese though, even going so far as to take language lessons. He had learnt German at school and reckoned himself a dab hand at languages but the harsh, strangulated sounds of Cantonese were beyond him. He knew a few words to flatter local businessmen, men who continued to burn offerings to Gods but who still knew how to make a million.

These were the Chinese who truly impressed him, rich men with smooth unmoving faces, who opened their mouths to reveal the decaying teeth of one-time poverty. Some had gold teeth of course, the more sophisticated wore shining false choppers made in England or Japan. Martin lunched with them in clubs, former enclaves of the conquerors and only recently open to Chinese. The original clubs had long since disappeared and were now relocated in shiny new buildings. These businessmen kept their own private stocks of brandy and rare wines in their new cellars, labelled and claimed. Over lunch Martin advised them whether to put money down on the price of crude oil going up or whether to take a punt on wheat.

'You married, Mr Bannister?' one of them asked him unexpectedly over coffee and brandy, and he took a moment to gather his composure. Normally the parameters of conversation were strictly patrolled; for the purposes of business an emotional life was deemed non-existent.

'D—D—Divorced actually,' he said and immediately regretted it, for the locals took a dim view of divorce.

'I see,' said his business contact but Martin saw that he didn't, Martin saw that he didn't see at all.

Martin's current girlfriend, Joanna, was a model who mainly did commercials for local Chinese television. She was not pretty like models are supposed to be; in fact, she was rather toothy and inclined to fat. Her bum was large. 'Old big bum,' Martin called her, which he supposed was a term of affection. Joanna, who was a kindly girl, smiled. She had red-blond hair down to her waist, which the Chinese adored.

He rarely went for confident, beautiful girls. He considered them vain and self-important. He pre-ferred girls who were a little unsure of themselves, fetchingly insecure, pleased to be the object of his attentions. He took out women other men might call plump, girls a fraction or two on the wrong side of prettiness. Whenever he did take out an outwardly loud, confident girl he soon found out she had never had a proper boyfriend who had lasted more than three months, or that she was privately tortured about the alarming breadth of her thighs. He believed all women were very good at advocating feminism and self-reliance while in their bloom but as their attractions faded every last one of them aimed to scuttle back to the safety of marriage and a man's solid bank account. Joanna, at thirty-four, was at this dangerous age now and he could clearly see the heat of desperation in her eyes.

Not so very long ago he had imagined himself in love with her, or at the very least infatuated. He remembered a brief, incendiary moment when he believed he had finally found the woman who would love him hard, all her inner doors flung open. For a few glorious months Martin had lived wrapped in love's cocoon, as if blind and mewling. It seemed to him that he had simply opened his mouth like a needful infant and Joanna had known what to do.

But this blissful state had not lasted and soon Martin felt the cold drizzle of disappointment. He had been in love before, and had once even married because of it, but each time he had ended up disillusioned. Yet it did not stop him from believing that each new fall towards love would have a different outcome: he was living with Joanna but his eyes were open, he still believed a better love was waiting. Even though he did not always like women, and indeed sometimes felt a simmering contempt for them, he carried a hope that was like the memory of something lost, of a love rich and whole. This wistful vein of romanticism mostly lay buried but now and then broke the calm surface of his adult self to surprise him.

Martin was only half-listening to Joanna's dull conversation now, preferring to watch the woman at the next table. She was pretty, laughing into her partner's waiting face, clearly in love. Martin turned his head away from the sight, picking up the bottle of 1982 Chateau-Lafite and refilling his glass. A Chinese waiter immediately appeared at his elbow.

'Sir, please allow me,' he said, taking the bottle.

When the waiter had gone Martin said to Joanna, 'E—E—Everyone here talks as if they're in a 1960s m—m—movie.'

She laughed, gratefully, inappropriately, showing her large teeth. 'I think it's sweet,' she said.

Martin rolled his brilliant eyes and looked out the window at Hong Kong harbour. He supposed he couldn't expect a model to avoid using nonsensical words like 'sweet'.

'Martin?' she was asking now and he turned his head away from the view. 'Martin, what are you thinking?'

It seemed to him that women were always asking him this. The more his eyes wandered, the more they pestered him, demanding back his lost attention.

'I—I—was thinking which currency I should buy tomorrow,' he said. 'Satisfied?'

He loved his job, the adrenalin-charge of it, the risk, the rewards. Although he was a good ten years older than the other traders he felt at the peak of his form. Every day he felt like he was walking a tightrope across a perilous height with no control over the wind. If he looked down he would lose his nerve: the trick was to keep his eyes on the other side. In the air Martin felt invincible, as if he could not make a wrong move. On certain days he felt a sure power course through his body, steadying his nerves and limbs. On those days he was able to move markets by his skill alone, to make bets that were sure to come through. If he took a gamble that the Japanese stock market would rise it invariably did, netting his investors millions. He soon had a reputation as a futures trader to watch: in his second year his senior directors were so pleased with him they gave him a bonus of half a million.

If Martin had ceased to be frightened of money he had also come to affect a certain disdain for it. He liked to spend extravagantly, to eat Russian caviar and drink French champagne, to take holidays at expensive resorts. He liked having money, being a member of the Hong Kong Club and sitting in aged leather chairs with other rich men at his club whenever he was back in London.

Every day he dealt in figures of millions and the noughts had long ceased to represent an actual value to him. Money itself was no longer real but a symbol of tomorrow: he spent his days trying to guess the future, standing in the present throwing his rope out.

In bed with Joanna that night Martin lay on his back with one arm against her neck while she tried to loop her big body around him. The air-conditioner had just been turned on and the air was still hot and damp. It smelt of mould, frying food, the high rot of summer. Joanna was very close and began to curl one fleshy leg up across his thigh but Martin roughly pushed it off. 'You're too heavy,' he said and she lay instead with her body turned towards him. He could feel her warm air, smell her winey breath, her too-strong perfume. Against his will his penis began to swell until it lay hard against his belly; he began to stroke the nape of Joanna's neck. Very gently, in an encouraging way, he pushed her head down towards the tip of his waiting penis. He could feel the rosy drop formed at the lip in anticipation of the slick glide of her tongue. She resisted being pushed but only for a moment, before continuing her long slide down.

Once, the night before Martin left for New Zealand, his first girlfriend Robyn illegally drove her father's car to his place to say goodbye. She was only fifteen and parked crookedly in the driveway, where Martin held her in the dark as she sobbed. He kissed her hard on the mouth and as she cried he unbuckled his belt and unzipped his fly. Before she had a chance to protest he pushed her head downwards and she awkwardly took him in her mouth for the first time, still sobbing. At that exact moment a light was suddenly shone upon them. Robyn froze, her mouth still pressed against him. Instinctively Martin flung up his arm, blinded. 'Martin!' his mother yelled. 'Martin, what are you doing?' His penis bobbed, refusing to bow, Robyn cowed in a half-crouch: Martin grinned into the torch beam at his mother. 'W—W—What does it look like I'm doing, you stupid cow?' he shouted. 'Stop it at once!' she yelled back, hopelessly. 'Martin, open the door!' While his mother continued to batter he thrust deep into Robyn's mouth and orgasmed explosively. She gagged and semen ran down her chin; she reeled back with a look of panic. 'You wait till your father gets home!' his mother screamed. 'He's not my bloody father!' Martin screamed back.

His mother was like that, foolishly insistent, battering again and again at life's closed doors. She was pretty and vain and used men all her life, for comfort, for safety, for compliments. She had the temperament of a spoilt, wilful child and sulked if she did not get her own way. 'Her Royal Bloody Highness,' Martin's first besieged stepfather Teddy called her when he finally grew tired of trying to please her. She could control the temperature of rooms by her will alone: when she sulked the very air crackled with frost, when she laughed the room blazed. She wanted her own way at all times and saw herself as trapped by circumstance, a woman who should have led a different, glamorous life. After Teddy died of a heart attack while at the football, his mother took to placing lonely hearts' advertisements and began a series of romances with East End criminals who escorted her to swank West End nightclubs. She was forty-two but claimed thirty-four and luckily her genetic heritage colluded with her. She still looked young and pretty enough to be bought fur coats, to be an asset on a gangster's arm. In her vanity about her looks she took up slimming pills and bizarre health cures: she was the first woman anyone knew to have colonic irrigation, a practice largely unheard of at that time. She would have had plastic surgery too but couldn't afford it. Fortunately, in the nick of time, she met another man who wanted to marry her. He was a New Zealander who had made his money from a tractor dealership, no less than the Lord Mayor of his home town, who had once personally taken afternoon tea with the Queen. Patricia Riley, soon to be Bannister, was impressed and, as soon as she decently could, packed up her son and meagre belongings and moved with Mr Norm Bannister to a small town in the distant land of New Zealand. She supposed it might be romantic.

At forty-five she unexpectedly fell pregnant. She already knew she had made a mistake in marrying Norm Bannister but this was a disaster. If he beat up a surly sixteen-year-old stepson, what might he do to a screaming baby? She made discreet enquiries about terminations but there were none to he had. In a desperate moment she told Norm, whose thin mouth unexpectedly burst into a smile and who went around from then on looking as if he had swallowed the sun. When she told Martin the colour left his face and he walked outside without a word.

Martin was seventeen when his half-brother was born. 'Come and hold your brother,' his stepfather boomed at the hospital.

'No thanks,' he replied. His mother was cradling the child, her face unexpectedly blooming.

ANNE-LOUISE: DESTINED FOR HAPPINESS

I F truth be known it took Anne-Louise some time to fully notice Rachel Gallagher. She was used to summing people up at once and her initial impressions of Rachel were not promising. She struck Anne-Louise as coming straight off the assembly line: another predictable Clayfield girl, boringly pretty, suffocatingly polite. At first she seemed the kind of girl in whom any originality had been snuffed out: it was difficult to know who she was exactly, for her politeness had the effect of making her seem bland. It was impossible to know what her preferences and tastes were for even a simple question was never answered directly. 'What'll you have?' Anne-Louise asked the first time they had a drink together one lunchtime. 'Whatever you're having,' Rachel replied. 'Two Manhattans please,' Anne-Louise said to the barman and Rachel's eyes widened. 'Lead in the pencil, Rachel,' Anne-Louise said, ignoring Rachel's clear discomfort. 'But . . . but . . . we have to go back to the office,' Rachel finally said. 'I think I'd prefer wine and soda.' Anne-Louise laughed, 'Well, why didn't you say so?'

But Rachel's desk was opposite Anne-Louise's and

over time Anne-Louise grew to like seeing Rachel's anxious little face first thing in the morning. Anne-Louise soon realized that in fact Rachel was not conventionally pretty at all but merely gave the impression of prettiness: she had a small, pointed chin just this side of sharpness, a nose too small and inconsequential to be declared handsome. Yet she was elfishly cute, with a short boyish crop of black hair and a wide, sensual mouth, her white, even teeth expensively straightened. Anne-Louise noticed too that she was the kind of girl men liked: she smiled a lot and seemed willing to take men at their word. Beneath her stifling politeness was an animation not fully extinguished, some suggestion of restrained sensuality. Anne-Louise felt the brief wash of envy: she would like to be the kind of girl men liked too but felt herself to be too ungainly, too unwieldy. Unlike Rachel she did not flatter men and was most definitely not the type men wanted to put in their pocket. As far as Anne-Louise could see it had not done Rachel much good anyway: she was always getting tangled up with awful men, bossy types or loudmouths, men who sometimes put her down.

'He's a dreadful bore that Dick Wilcox, Rachel,' Anne-Louise advised her one morning, waving a pink cigarette in her direction. 'Dick by name, dick by nature.'

Rachel laughed, as she always did, which Anne-Louise enjoyed. Indeed, Anne-Louise enjoyed Rachel's general air of tribute, the admiration evident in her eyes. She clearly regarded Anne-Louise with a kind of awe which Anne-Louise found unsettling at first but quickly came to like. It reminded her of the awestruck Grade Eights when she was school captain, the way they gathered around her waiting to laugh.

Anne-Louise was not in the habit of choosing her friends carefully, preferring instead to gather up as many people as possible for the noise and comfort. She did not deliberately pick Rachel either and at first Rachel was just another body in the crowd. But Rachel's desk was close to her own and Anne-Louise began to address the odd remark to her: before long she found herself spending a lot of time leaning across the desk talking. What Rachel offered which her other friends did not was a certain sobriety, the freedom to talk seriously without having to be flippant. Flippancy did not come naturally to Rachel and when Anne-Louise was with her she found she could forego it herself to talk about her work and her ambitions. She did not trust many people with this side of herself and found it refreshing.

Over time Anne-Louise found that Rachel had a sense of humour too. Suprisingly, she liked to laugh; she was a quick learner, a mimic of sorts, and after a while Anne-Louise noticed that she had unconsciously copied some of her own mannerisms. She took to smoking Anne-Louise's pink Sobranie cigarettes and picked up Anne-Louise's habit of referring to men as boys. 'He's such a silly boy,' Anne-Louise overheard her remark once and it might have been herself speaking.

Anne-Louise began to ask Rachel around to her house in Newtown on weekends, where they sometimes stayed up all night talking and painting. She saw that Rachel's work was not as good as her own but that she had discipline and commitment. 'You have to free up your hand,' Anne-Louise advised, standing behind her, 'let your body guide you.' Privately she believed Rachel overintellectualized and if she let loose her senses she might flourish.

After several months Anne-Louise finally noticed that Rachel had become her friend. One Saturday morning over carrot cake in King Street, Anne-Louise looked at Rachel and suddenly realized that she had in fact become her best friend. 'What are you staring at?' Rachel asked, looking bewildered. 'Have I got a cappuccino moustache?'

Anne-Louise averted her gaze, uncharacteristically embarrassed. 'No, Rach,' she said, her eyes returning to the newspaper, 'you're still clean-shaven.' She could feel Rachel's eyes upon her and imagined her puzzled, worried look, of which she had unexpectedly become so fond.

Anne-Louise confided to Rachel her hopes and intentions, her desire to live a fast life. Together they made up girlish lists of everything they intended to do: Rachel's lists were always like battle plans while her own were the vaguest of dreams. She did not like planning, preferring instead to have life unfurl itself, to bless her with surprise. For Anne-Louise life was still a stream in which she was swimming upwards, bound for some unimaginable open sea. She supposed herself destined for happiness, as if happiness were a beautiful landing where you stopped and got out, eternally harboured.

What Anne-Louise did intend was to escape the ordinary. She did not want a life which ran straight ahead, she wanted detours and false starts and implausible destinations. She did not want a house and a mortgage, a safe husband and a superannuation package as her final reward. She wanted something exhilarating, even dangerous, but could not describe the exact shape of her forthcoming life, knowing only that she could not wait for it to begin.

By the time Anne-Louise turned twenty-four she could wait no longer.

'I'm going into exile,' she announced to Rachel one morning in the office and she saw at once that Rachel knew what she meant. Anne-Louise had already been to Europe twice: in her first year of work she had somehow managed to save or borrow enough for a six-week Eurail pass, despite being an erratic saver; being winter and low season the flight was cheap too. She had gone alone, her pack on her back, a sleeping bag strung to the bottom. She had travelled to Rome and Paris and stared at the sky, closer hung than Australia's, subtler. She froze in Berlin and drank strong coffee with cream; she wept at the beauty of Seville. Throughout it all she had sketched, filling twenty-three new books. She had stood in art galleries, transfixed by images, and finally understood Australian light. At art college she had been schooled in European art but saw that, until then, she had not fully understood its difference to Australia. Two years later she went back to Europe again, to new places this time, and realized that six weeks would not be enough.

'I'm resigning,' she said to Rachel that morning. 'Why don't you come too?'

Rachel looked alarmed at Anne-Louise's suggestion, as she did when anything unexpected was put to her.

'When were you thinking of going?'

'Tomorrow,' Anne-Louise replied.

Of course Rachel needed to plan, as she obsessively planned everything in her life. 'Do you plan your orgasms too?' Anne-Louise asked and Rachel looked offended. Anne-Louise never planned anything: she was always running out of money because she forgot to go to the bank, she was always rushing around madly at the last minute. She was a frequent guest in her friends' houses overnight because she had mislaid her door key and all her housemates were away or else she had forgotten to fill the car with petrol. Everywhere she went she left a trail of debris, overflowing ashtrays, discarded clothing, and once, a used condom in a friend's spare bedroom she had forgotten to discreetly discard. When she went through periods of arguing with boyfriends about the contraceptive pill being a male plot she was forever leaving her freshly washed diaphragm on the rim of the bath for her other flat-mates to find.

'What's this?' her flatmate Dan said the first time, coming into the room with Anne-Louise's cap perched on the tip of his nose.

'Oh, give it here, you tiresome boy,' she replied unblushingly. She did not understand why Rachel was so coy about such things, why she had looked so disconcerted.

'You're a prude, aren't you, Rach?' she asked and from then on deliberately left her diaphragm prominently displayed.

Anne-Louise negotiated the European trip in much the same way she did everything else: forgetfully, spasmodically, nonchalantly. When Rachel wished to enter into a debate about whether to take sterling or deutschsmark Anne-Louise rolled her eyes and patted Rachel on the head. 'You're profoundly sweet when you talk about money,' she said and Rachel replied, 'Anne-Louise, you're so *frustrating*!'

In truth Anne-Louise found talk of money boring and had no qualms about spending it, acting as if she were born to money and not hesitating to borrow it liberally. She was one of the first young people at the magazine to have a credit card and was always getting letters from the bank about being over-limit. 'Just increase the limit then,' she said to a bank official who telephoned and could not understand why he wouldn't. Nevertheless she always managed to pay before her card was cancelled, borrowing shamelessly from friends, ringing her mother in Brisbane to plead high Sydney rents. 'Be a darling,' she'd say to her mother, blowing kisses into the phone. She was a reckless, compulsive spender, who would return from her lunch hour with a bright red leather coat worth $500 or a pair of earrings which had consumed half her salary, expecting Rachel to admire her purchases.

Unlike Rachel she did not really care where they would base themselves in Europe, assuming that something would occur to them in time. So while Rachel planned and wrote things down carefully in her notebook (her blood group, her mother's name and address lest she be dismembered by an IRA bomb), Anne-Louise blithely waited out the days, barely counting. If she did not have money she expected some soon, if she was not exactly happy she expected to be.

By then Rachel had moved into the house Anne-Louise shared with Dan and Anthony, two gay men from the men's magazine one floor down. 'Yes, it's the two poofs and their fag hags,' Anne-Louise said at an office lunch and everyone laughed. In truth

Anne-Louise felt more comfortable around gay men, feeling none of the subtle anxiety she felt around straight men. Around straight men she was always conscious of not being beautiful or cute enough, of having to impress them. With Dan and Anthony and their friends and lovers she did not feel evaluated for her sexiness or her legs, that she was forever failing some private male test.

Whenever Anne-Louise did go out with a man she felt herself don protective equipment. She put on her wit along with her lipstick, a cavalier manner to cover her fear. She favoured loud, clever men, preferably of established celebrity, who asked no questions. She liked entering rooms and having people nudge each other; she liked to see heads turn. None of her boyfriends lasted long and tended to knock on her door at one o'clock in the morning after they had been somewhere else, expecting her peculiar form of comfort. Anne-Louise did not know that her deep impressive voice intimidated men, frightening them off and that her dismissive manner implied she had better things to do. She knew only that there was something about her which quickly exhausted men so that they only wished to stay a brief moment and no longer.

Her longest relationship was with a married sculptor who had been famous some years before but whose work had fallen out of fashion. He was much older than Anne-Louise and clearly not intimidated by her: instead, he was subtly patronizing and went about their affair as if he was in charge. He admonished her over her sloppy room, her disordered art work, and was always advising her which gallery owners she should be lunching with. Anne-Louise discovered that she did not mind and gladly sat back and let him direct.

'Ha, and you talk about me and men, Anne-Louise Buchan,' Rachel said to her one evening after the sculptor had left the room. 'What about you?'

Anne-Louise turned to her. 'It makes a change having someone fuss over me,' she replied, walking away.

While men came and went Anne-Louise expected something beyond continuity from Rachel. She was of the generation schooled to believe that a good female friendship was more flexible, more nourishing, indeed more viable than any romantic attachment to a man. Although paradoxically Anne-Louise did not entirely give up the contrary notion that she might one day find an interesting man, at the same time she believed in the perfidity of men, in their unreliability, in the dangers of investing too many hopes in them.

'At least *you'll* still be around in twenty years,' Anne-Louise said to Rachel when as expected the married sculptor returned to his wife.

They were drinking beer on the back steps not many weeks before their departure. 'Don't make it sound like the compensation prize,' Rachel replied.

Anne-Louise gave a great, unheralded sigh. 'You know, sometimes I wouldn't mind a brute of a husband shouting for his supper.'

Rachel heard something sad and low in her voice; she looked up at her from the step below but Anne-Louise did not meet her eyes.

'Only joking,' she said in a strengthened voice, 'I'm not turning revisionist.'

A wistfulness settled inside her. She felt Rachel's gaze as unexpectedly she reached out to give Anne-Louise's hand a sympathetic pat. 'He didn't deserve you anyway,' Rachel murmured and Anne-Louise stiffened.

'Sometimes you sound like the Avon Lady,' she snapped, pulling her hand away. She could not stand being pitied.

On evenings when the soft rain of melancholy fell upon her, whenever yet another boyfriend went back to his wife and Anne-Louise felt herself to be an instrument of departure, she played her favourite song over and over. It was a song about the faithlessness of men, a tender, funny song and she played it loud, singing along. It did not fail to lift her up, to make her life seem brave and daring. Often she woke Rachel and they sat together and drank a strong cocktail, then danced to the song with bare feet. Anne-Louise was a fluid, graceful dancer, even at her heaviest her little feet were light on the ground, her wrists slender and hands sinewy. She swayed and sang at the top of her voice, smiling at Rachel. Sometimes the two boys joined in too but mostly it was Anne-Louise and Rachel, swaying and laughing.

After only a short time Anne-Louise once again felt unbeaten, feeling the lightness of the present moment, as if she would always be young and undaunted.

RACHEL: A HUNGRY GHOST

IN Hong Kong, after I knew I had made my mistake, I took to walking the streets as if lost and wandering. I let my feet make their own direction, up hills with a thousand steps carved into them, into streets where the gutted and headless bodies of snakes still writhed. I stood on the pavement amidst their swarming, freshly slaughtered bodies, peering into the dark shops where men and women drank snake poison. Occasionally they turned to stare at me with expressionless eyes, willing me to go away and join the other ghosts. The Chinese believed all of us were ghosts, that anyone who was not like them was not human. Sometimes I felt myself to be walking among them as if invisible, a vaporous body no longer blood and water but cast off, weightless. Only when I walked for a long time did I feel the full assemblage of my flesh return, my heavy bones, my musculature.

I walked past butcher shops, past the slayed heads of pigs, the chopped tails of cows and horses. The hair trailed down to the floor, stiffening with blood. Everywhere the Chinese pushed against me and I knew my sour Western smell offended them, being fed as I was on milk and cheese, mucus-forming products. They looked at me without affection: sometimes I reached out a hand to stroke a child's hair and the mother stared at me without smiling. Perhaps she thought I would pull my hand back to reveal a private thought, a captured ear, an evil spirit. Once, tired of walking, I caught a red taxi down into the city from the mountains above. The driver's eyes watched mine in the mirror and he said I had a lucky face. His English was not good but he was trying to tell me he had learnt the art of reading faces. 'You have luck in your eyebrows,' he said, pulling the taxi over.

He stopped in a cul-de-sac by the side of the road, switched the meter off, then turned in his bucket seat to assess me. He looked solemnly into my eyes and reached out his hand, tracing the outline of my face. His hands felt hot and boneless and I closed my eyes as he traced my flesh, the shape of my skull, the curve of my eyebrows. He passed soft fingers over my lips and said, 'Your mouth is too greedy.' I opened my eyes at once. 'You are hungry,' he said, closing my eyes again with his fingertips.

When he began to trace the edge of my collarbone and move his fingers down towards my breasts I opened my eyes once more. 'Please, I have to go,' I said and he immediately withdrew his hand and turned around.

All the way down into the city his words swam in the watery air. All the way down the curling roads, past the shiny man-made cliffs, the roadworks, the construction sites, the Filipino nannies with children and shopping I thought of the consequences of being too starved. Through my own greed I had turned myself into a hungry ghost, loosed and dangerous, moving freely on the wrong side of the door.

I remember that when Anne-Louise and I got to London it immediately struck me as familiar, as if I had been there before. It seemed to me too that my eyes had switched to black and white to match the grey of the roads, the dull sweep of the sky, the yellowish-grey of the house bricks.

'Television has a lot to answer for,' said Anne-Louise, who had been there twice. 'It's just like being in an episode of "The Professionals".'

We were staying with an aunt of hers by marriage. 'God forbid that I should be related to them by blood,' she said in an aside shortly after we had been introduced. A late uncle of her mother's had married into the family some years before; they lived in a council flat on an estate near Wormwood Scrubs Prison, a pinched residence with heating in only one room. Anne-Louise and I were offered the living room couch on the first night, where we lay awake shivering in our sleeping bags, talking in whispers.

'Actually, I think this *is* Wormwood Scrubs,' she said, laughing. 'Did you see the bath?'

The bath had a wooden folding contraption over it so that it could be utilised as a table when the bath wasn't in use, which was often.

'They only bathe once a week!' she whispered. '*And* they share the bath water!'

I stuffed the end of the sleeping bag into my mouth. 'Luxury!' I said in my best Monty Python accent. 'We lived in shoe box!'

Anne-Louise giggled. 'She's like Andy Capp's wife. What's her name again, Mrs Capp?'

Anne-Louise's aunt came into the room just then without bothering to knock.

'All right, are you love?' she asked. 'Know where the lavvy is then?'

Anne-Louise said, 'Ta, Flo,' and I burst out laughing.

'Sorry, Mrs Greene,' I said, trying to stop, 'we've had a long day.'

'I'm sure you 'ave,' she replied curtly, shutting the door.

'We've offended her now,' I said, worried, but Anne-Louise was still laughing.

'Know where the lavvy is then, Rach?' she said between explosions.

I was no longer laughing. I found it disconcerting that Anne-Louise never knew when to stop, even when her teasing caused pain. I was thinking about Mrs Greene, how poor she was, how generous to offer us hospitality. I was lying there thinking how nice a person I was compared to Anne-Louise, who had the uncanny knack of honing in mercilessly on your weak spots. I resolved to buy Mrs Greene some flowers, to go with the jar of Australian honey we had bought as a gift.

'Hey, Rach. Where does an Englishman hide his money?'

I pretended to be asleep. 'Under the soap!' It was an old joke but I still smiled before falling asleep, nursing my saintliness.

London to me wasn't a generous city by nature, it didn't squander its beauty like Paris or Rome. You had to keep a weather eye out for its beauty, a well-proportioned park with a pleasing line of trees, an impressive building, a beautiful street or square, certain stretches of the Thames, a glimpse, no more. Its beauties were private affairs, for the rich or the lucky. Somewhere I guessed there was a more endowed, beautiful London but closed off, for private use only. The rest got council flats near Wormwood Scrubs, the ugly stretch of motorways, weary shops, littered parks, the cold down their backs and rattling their windows. The winter Anne-Louise and I were there was the coldest in fifty years; it was the year too of the infamous garbage strike and tonnes of black plastic bags were stacked high in all the public spaces of the city, in Leicester Square, up and down Charing Cross road. It gave the city a surreal quality, a broken-down look, of wartime or plague. For me London streets resolutely refused to sing; the city had a relentless, leaden air, its people looked tired and depressed. I had brought with me a thin, inadequate jacket and was forced to buy a duffle coat and a thick woollen scarf so that within weeks I looked like everybody else. I could feel a pinched look coming into my face, my shoulders beginning to hunch unattractively against the cold.

But if I turned small, Anne-Louise turned large, a creature immune to the seasons. It seemed to me that she took up more space, that her gestures were grander, that her startling voice had grown even louder. She strode London streets as if she owned them, a wild excitement blazing in her eyes. She did not appear to feel the cold at all and wore cotton dresses under the flimsiest of coats, tailored suit jackets or embroidered waistcoats for which she paid a small fortune.

'Your money's going to run out,' I warned but it was as if she felt hooked to some endless supply, as if I was the one who needed warning.

'I'd rather die poor but well dressed,' she replied, 'and never forget that whatever we build in our imaginations accomplishes itself in our lives.'

I smiled at her. 'Someone else said that.'

'Yes, but I've appropriated it,' she said. 'I'm building right now.'

I pulled my coat closer around me. 'Well, just make sure you're not building windmills.'

She laughed. 'Good old Rach, Miss Sensible to the last. Brisbane did a good job on you.'

I was pained for I did not want to be sensible, I

wanted to be reckless and daring like her.

'Oh, go root your boot,' I said, storming off. I heard her laugh even harder.

We lived by then in a large bedsitter in Bayswater, where we kept a supply of 20p coins to feed the gas meter. We sat huddled over the gas fire on the nights we did not go out, drinking endless cups of tea. 'This is the life,' Anne-Louise declared, 'civilization at last!' During the day we stayed inside the warm rooms of the National Gallery or the Tate, staring at our favourite paintings. At lunchtime we took our sketchbooks to parks and buildings, drawing until our fingers grew too numb and we could no longer feel our pencils. I was always tired and inclined to droop whenever I was warm indoors, often falling asleep in a chair by the fire, but Anne-Louise never did. Sometimes I woke with my mouth unattractively open to find Anne-Louise sketching me, her pencil passing noiselessly over paper. She was never tired, her enthusiasms seemed boundless, some private, restless energy propelled her without pause.

It shames me to admit that I did not notice when Anne-Louise's charged excitement fermented into something darker and more dangerous. I was so used to her extravagant speeches, her physical stamina for drink and for staying up late that for weeks, perhaps months, I did not recognize that anything was amiss. I only know that after a while it finally came to my attention that she was spending hours alone walking the streets and that when she did stay home she was drawing obsessively or staying up till dawn writing furiously in her diary. For several nights I lay in bed trying to sleep, sometimes turning over to watch her through my eyelashes. Once I said crossly, 'For God's sake, Anne-Louise, go to sleep!' but she did not even raise her eyes from the paper. Her large face had an intense absorbed look, her eyes were lit, her whole body was restless and expectant. As I watched, it finally struck me that her movements were too jerky, too rushed; she appeared as if projected on to a screen running on fast forward. I remember she was wearing an old silk shawl over her shoulders which kept slipping off; her hair, which was then long and cruelly permed, lay about her in a wild, frothy mass.

As I lay looking through half-closed eyes at her fanatical driven face that night, I suddenly saw that something was wrong. At the same moment I was struck by an overwhelming sense of foreboding, as if disaster lay just up ahead, looming, inescapable. My eyes sprang open and my hands began to sweat: I must have made some sound because Anne-Louise raised her head and looked straight at me. Her eyes were huge, their centres savage, and I saw that they were banished from the ordinary. I lay there, my heart moving noisily, every instinct telling me to flee. Yet I found I could not move, that my eyes were joined, fatally and unavoidably, to hers.

I lay awake for hours but must finally have fallen

asleep for when I woke it was light and Anne-Louise was standing over me. I let out a cry.

'You look so pretty when you're asleep,' she said with intensity, bending over and looking hard into my face. I reared back but she did not move away.

'We are all newborn when we lay down our defences,' she continued, 'innocent again.'

Her voice sounded strange, dreamy. I was on the verge of panic but instinctively knew I must remain calm. 'Yes,' I said, still staring up at her, 'innocent and dreaming of darkness.'

Her eyes were odd, as if she was not really looking at me but at something private, internal. She was looking into my face but her eyes were pre-occupied, elsewhere.

'Anne-Louise,' I asked, 'do you feel all right?'

She stood up and clapped her hands beneath her chin. 'I feel wonderful!' she replied in a passionate happy voice. 'Sublime!'

I raised myself cautiously onto one elbow. 'In that case can you please move so I can get up?' My heart was loud.

She stood aside with an elaborate bow and I swung my legs to the side of the bed we used as a sofa during the day.

'I think we should go to Richmond,' she announced. 'The sun's out.'

I pulled on my dressing gown and tried to make my voice sound normal. 'I think we should start looking for jobs.'

She swung around in a circle in the centre of the room, her hair and shawl flying.

'Oh, pretty please, little Rachel Gallagher, just look at the sky. It's blue!'

I went to the window and looked out. 'Well, blue-ish,' I said.

Despite my misgivings we went to Richmond and in my memory it remains the happiest of days. The sun did shine, the sky was blue, a few precocious daffodils daringly raised their heads for us. I remember that Anne-Louise was ridiculously happy, rushing about exclaiming over the beauty of swans, the tender green English grass, the tentative burgeoning of buds. Her eyes were still lit, her movements too fast but to me, bathed in sunshine, it seemed an ordinary happiness I could recognize, akin to the unburdened happiness of children. My sense of foreboding gradually gave way until I dismissed it as the learned, inherited reaction of overanxious genes. Lying on my back, the sun on my face, Anne-Louise like an unbound child beside me, it seemed that I had been mistaken, misled by the darkness, led astray by my own fears. Of course I realize now that the supposed happiness of children exists largely in the minds of yearning adults, pining for a world without tragedy, longing for the lost notion of safety.

MARTIN: HIS PANTHEON OF
PERFECTION

WHEN Martin was about to turn four, a strange woman came to take him away. He clung screaming to the fat warm bosom of the woman he believed to be his mother, terrified. Her bosom heaved and yet she handed him over, she placed him away from herself, away from her special creamed porridges with butter which she lovingly cooked just for him. He was carried screaming into a car with an unknown woman and driven away.

That this unknown woman should turn out to be his own mother was not reason enough to forgive her. She had been shamefully unmarried when she gave birth to him, leaving him in the sturdy care of her childless married sister while she went to London to marry the first of her husbands, a luggage dealer who specialized in fake crocodile and who did not have time for children. Martin did not care that when her marriage broke up she decided to come back and claim him. All he remembered for the rest of his life was the time when he was happy before his mother came. He remembered lying on a blanket in the Yorkshire sun, a large, cheerful woman blowing raspberries on his warm belly and making him laugh. After his mother came to take him away it seemed to him he was never as unburdened again.

As he grew he became increasingly obsessed with his real father. He pestered and pestered his mother for details yet she refused resolutely to speak. 'He disappeared as soon as he knew you were coming,' she said to him once and could not be coaxed to say more. 'Teddy's going to be your new father now.' When he was ten he found an old wartime photograph in the back of his mother's dressing table: he had been looking for money to steal but found the photograph more valuable. In it was a handsome man with eyes just like his own, smiling confidently into the camera. He took this photograph and placed it in his secret tin, along with his collection of coins and unexploded shells from the war. He wanted to ask Her Royal Bloody Highness about it but could not because then she would know he had been rifling uninvited through her things.

At night, using a torch beneath the bedclothes, Martin stared and stared into this photograph. It was black and white but he could see his father's eyes were as violently coloured as his own, startling, luminous. His father had a cigarette between his fingers, a careless air about him. He was dressed in an army uniform, or perhaps it was the navy, but unlike some men he was wearing the uniform rather than the uniform wearing him. He looked like he had put it on as an act of generosity towards something he knew to be intrinsically foolish and there was insubordination written all over him. When Martin looked into this photograph he felt emboldened too, as though the world he inhabited might yet assume a different shape.

In his awake daylight world Martin was always doing the wrong thing. When his mother got married to Teddy after living with him for two years, Martin picked the best roses for his mother's bouquet from a neighbour's fence, only to have her scold him and send him straight back to apologize. He shoplifted an expensive bottle of perfume to give her too, but she was suspicious and he was forced to confess. Martin spent his days trying to sneak within the radius of her sun, before she looked up and expelled him.

His mother was unpredictable, mercurial: she might take him in her arms and gather him up just when he thought she never would again. She gathered him up just enough times for him to live out his days in hopeful anticipation, for him to tremble with excitement on those nights when she swept in to his bedroom smelling of wine and perfume. 'Where, oh where is my beautiful boy?' she called in a high, tuneful voice, pretending she could not find him. She closed her eyes and felt around the bed like a blind woman and by the time she laid her warm hands on his face, Martin was quivering with joy.

But mostly his mother was cross with him, yelling at him to get out of her sight. She was always brushing him off as if he were dust, sending him from rooms because she wanted peace and quiet. 'Oh, go away, Martin,' was her favourite expression and years later, when he was grown, it was the main thing he remembered. He recalled the precise, weary tone of her voice and the hours spent sitting in the dark stairwell outside the front door, waiting for his mother's light to find him.

Years later, in New Zealand, after his brother was born, his mother seemed to forget him entirely. She swooned at the sight of her new son, coddling and cooing, and only ever spoke to Martin to ask for something. 'Go and put the kettle on for Jamie's bottle, would you, Martin,' she'd say, hardly bothering to look up.

When Martin left home his mother barely asked where he was going. On those occasions when he did come home it was Jamie-this and Jamie-that and Martin saw that his mother didn't even know the growing Jamie was rebelling. Although Martin himself did not know Jamie well, he saw that he was already getting into fights and was not surprised to learn that at the age of eleven Jamie was escorted home in a police car for trying to break into a house.

After Martin moved back to England, he only returned to New Zealand twice. Both times he cut short his stay, being sick of listening about Jamie. When Jamie ran away at fifteen, never to be heard of again, Martin quickly read his mother's inconsolable letters back in London before consigning them to the rubbish bin. He did not write back.

Yet Martin could not quite extinguish a desire to impress her, to get her to acknowledge all he had achieved. With his first bonus he sent her a first-class ticket to Bermuda where they sat together on a pristine beach and drank champagne. Later they ate in the best restaurant on the island, but his mother only smiled wistfully, making a toast to the absent Jamie, saying soon after that Bermuda was not nearly as beautiful as she had expected it to be.

While he was still working for Coutts in London, Martin ran into Robyn, his old girlfriend from his teenage years. He literally ran into her: turning the corner into Threadneedle Street he almost knocked her over. 'It's fate, my darling,' he said, laughing, steadying her and taking her by the arm for a drink.

'Well, Marty, you look like you're doing well,' she said, smiling attractively. 'Still messing about in cars?'

They laughed about it and until that moment Martin had not realized he was lonely. They went out for dinner that night and the next and after that Robyn never seemed to go home. Martin was alarmed to find himself so hopelessly and immediately in love and went with her while she collected her things from the flat she shared with two girls in Battersea. It was a bit downmarket for his tastes, for by then he was living in a large expensive flat overlooking a square in St John's Wood. Martin drove her home and looked into Robyn's eyes and it seemed that for the first time in a long while he did not feel abandoned. Robyn appeared to him a wide-open girl, ready to end all his wants: she cooked him breakfast and held him close, she took his penis and sucked softly. He thought he saw her both inside and out, that like glass she was transparent: he looked into her glass and saw only his own happy face reflected.

She was a legal aid lawyer but Martin did not really care what she did: in truth she did not exist for him outside his front door. She could defend hapless tenants against evicting councils all she liked, separate as many warring families. She was his nurse, his lover, his guide and he found himself wanting to marry her, indeed bullying her to say yes.

'But we've only been living together for two months,' she pleaded. 'Let's give it some time.'

So he waited and sulked and suffered a rabid jealousy on those nights she went out without him. He was twenty-four but felt like a child, helpless, at her mercy. He was overwhelmed in fact, completely in her power, and did not enjoy the sensation. At the same time that he longed for her to say yes he began to feel a surly resentment, the beginnings of revolt. If she did not say yes soon she could get out of his life, he would give her only so many chances and no more.

But one autumn evening while walking with Robyn on Primrose Hill she unexpectedly accepted his proposal. 'Darling,' he cried, scooping her up, 'we're going to be so happy.' She smiled into his face and he did not see one flicker of hesitation.

They were only young and after their marriage they continued to live the lives of young people. Martin continued to join his colleagues for drinks after work, Robyn went out to discos and dinners with her girlfriends. On summer weekends they often went for picnics, accompanied mainly by friends of Robyn's. Martin did not have friends in the same way Robyn did; he could not unburden himself upon unknown men, and to him all men were unknown. While it was true that he had a tendency to idolize certain men, he did not consider any man a personal friend. Every now and then he came across someone who impressed him but it did not occur to him to take the acquaintance further. There was a particular director at Coutts, for example, whom Martin referred to as a genius: it seemed to him that this man was far cleverer, more astute than any other he had come across. Martin went out of his way to impress him, to bring to David Tennant's attention his good work. Tennant seemed to respect him, even to be fond of him, in a manfully abashed way. He once asked Martin to lunch at his club and Martin worked very hard to impress upon him all the keenest attributes of his character. He asked intelligent questions and heard later that Tennant had put in a good word for him.

Soon after their marriage Martin was surprised to receive an invitation to supper at his house in Hampstead. 'Penelope would love to meet your new wife,' Tennant said gruffly. He raced home to tell Robyn, only to find she was not thrilled and did not view it as the coup that he did.

'B—B—But Tennant's a wonderful man. He's a genius!' Martin enthused, his excitement causing him to stutter.

Robyn looked at him sceptically. 'You know, I've never once heard you refer to a woman in such glowing terms.'

He thought this rather an odd thing to say but did not press her further. He was getting rather sick of that sceptical look on her face actually and would certainly not have included the new Mrs Robyn Coutts among his elected pantheon of perfection.

The sex between them quickly grew routine and Martin was forced to admit to himself his disappointment. He longed to feel again that flicker of danger, of famine. He wanted to feel more intensely, to snap something almost to breaking point. He had fantasies of Robyn roped, burning at the wrist, of pink welts rising on her back. Once, when she was wearing her dressing gown in bed, he managed to release the cotton belt from its loops and wind it up hard between her legs. 'Ouch,' she cried, 'stop it!' and he had been obliged to loosen his grip.

If he found Robyn a disappointment in bed he found her even more of a disappointment standing upright. It seemed she expected him to help her with the housework, even though he was paying all the rent. Her salary would barely cover the costs of their food and yet she was demanding he clean the bathroom and cook Sunday breakfast occasionally.

'Some women would be happy to do it every Sunday,' he said. 'Some women might see it as a way of saying thank you.'

Something like a smirk passed across her face. 'Oh, I get it. My domestic labour in exchange for my rent.'

He realized with some satisfaction that he hated her. 'No, Robyn. You're the one with the accounting mentality.'

He left the room before he could strike the smirk from her face.

She began to get on his nerves with her labour lawyer fervour, her left-wing ideas and friends who thought they could change things.

'These people are institutionalized,' he argued. 'You're defending third and fourth generation losers.'

'Losers!' she countered. 'They're only losers because they never got lucky. What chance did they ever have, born into an unemployed family on a council estate?'

Martin laughed. 'I tell you, my darling, if you offered them a job they'd run a mile. If you gave them half a million pounds they'd lose the lot.'

At some point during every argument she would accuse him of being a Thatcherite. Robyn was boringly predictable, a bleeding-heart liberal whose only personal experience of hardship was once having to go without freshly baked croissants, ground coffee and the papers on a Sunday. He felt a rising contempt, for her and all her self-righteous, do-gooder friends.

It seemed to Martin that very quickly his new wife had revealed her true colours. It was as if she had become someone else, an entirely different girl from the one he married. He could not understand it and felt unfairly trapped, yet at the same time could not bear the idea of being alone. He hated her and yet could not let her go: their arguments went round and round, growing more bitter and intractable. Before long each stood permanently braced, as if on either side of the ring. The time for reconciliation had already passed without either of them noticing. All that remained for them was to raise their fists, again and again and again.

When Martin came home one evening to find Robyn gone it could not have been more unexpected. Of course he knew that they were not getting on but his mind had not yet moved beyond that. He felt abandoned and rushed straight to the telephone. 'She doesn't want you to know where she is,' her best friend self-importantly informed him, obviously proud to be involved in the drama.

Immediately he felt a protective wall come down, dividing him from his own pain. He felt the sharp welcoming nudge of anger that his own wife should act with such violence towards him, that she should dare to leave him so publicly exposed. He swung his lower jaw murderously in its socket, fanning his fury. From this moment Martin retreated even further into the carapace in which he dwelt, from where only his longing was to draw him forth.

ANNE-LOUISE: THE BURGEONING WORLD

NOT long after Anne-Louise went to Richmond with Rachel she was walking down Oxford Street when she passed a sign in a shop window advertising for sales assistants. Straight away she went inside and announced herself.

'Good morning, I am here to assist you,' she began, talking her way in, dazzling her way through, a ferocious energy providing assistance. It took twenty minutes but she left with a job, having never sold a handbag in her life.

Ever since her arrival in London Anne-Louise had been struggling to quiet an inner turbulence. At first the slapping of her blood resembled the familiar excitement of being in a new country, of having been taken out of the known. Anne-Louise always relished being a stranger and imagined it suited her: from the first glimpse of the soft English dawn from the taxi window she had felt released. Yet this initial excitement had not subsided but had grown and grown until she could no longer look or listen or draw fast enough to take in the burgeoning world. As in a fever, Anne-Louise now lived in a state of perpetual restlessness, with time strangely expanding and contracting: a ten-minute wait seemed like eternity and what she supposed was a few moments of staring into space was actually two whole hours. She could no longer sleep and lay each night stretched and alert, exquisitely tortured. Yet this strange new turbulence did not alarm her, for she also felt immensely powerful, as if she possessed great physical strength and secret abilities. It allowed her to look into people's faces and see their most secret selves, their flailing hopes, all their sorrows. Walking down the street Anne-Louise took care to avert her eyes, lest she inadvertently catch a private howl, an inadmissible desire. She did not speak of any of this to Rachel, for she understood that the world was composing itself into a message meant solely for her.

There were six of them working at the shop, including herself and Mrs Pybus, the store manager. Mrs Pybus was a thin, wanting woman with halitosis and crushed expectations, and within weeks it was clear to Anne-Louise that Mrs Pybus did not like her. She was always asking Anne-Louise to keep her voice down and to refrain from asking Rachel and her other friends to the shop. Rachel had taken a waitressing job at a sleazy Italian restaurant in Covent Garden and, if she had time, dropped in. 'This is not a social club for your entertainment, Anne-Louise,' Mrs Pybus snapped, pursing her insufficient lips when Rachel came in the door one afternoon, causing Rachel to immediately scuttle back out. Anne-Louise only laughed, keeping the staff amused by imitating this undernourished curl as soon as Mrs Pybus turned her back. She knew that if she had not been so good at her job, frequently outselling every other staff member, Mrs Pybus would gladly have dismissed her. Because Anne-Louise did not particularly care, she began to take a perverse pleasure in displeasing Mrs Pybus.

One morning Anne-Louise turned up for work and as soon as she saw Mrs Pybus's face she knew something was wrong. Before she had even got through the door, Mrs Pybus called her over. 'I'm afraid that outfit is not suitable, Anne-Louise,' she said in an undertone.

'What's unsuitable about it?' Anne-Louise immediately retorted.

Mrs Pybus coloured. 'It's immodest,' she finally replied.

Anne-Louise looked down and saw that Mrs Pybus must be referring to her braless breasts: until that moment it had not occurred to her that her blouse was see-through.

'What is immodest about the female breast, Mrs Pybus?' she asked loudly.

Mrs Pybus looked quickly around, an embarrassed smile twisting her features. 'Please keep your voice down.'

But Anne-Louise was angry and fearless, ready to fight. 'I asked you what is immodest about the female breast, Mrs Pybus,' she repeated even more loudly.

By now all the staff and a couple of shoppers were watching. 'Follow me please, young lady,' Mrs Pybus said curtly, walking towards the store room.

Anne-Louise remained where she stood. 'I'm sure you can say here what you can say in there,' she replied.

Mrs Pybus turned around and in her embarrassment and fury even her ears had turned red. 'Miss Buchan, when I ask you to do something I expect you to do it.'

Anne-Louise felt a great rush of power. 'I am not your servant,' she said, looking around as if she expected applause. She saw the frightened face of a young junior, and smiled at her.

To Anne-Louise's surprise, Mrs Pybus began to walk back towards her. For a moment Anne-Louise thought she had won but then Mrs Pybus took her roughly by the arm and marched her to the door.

'Your services are no longer required,' she said, pushing her out.

'This is outrageous!' Anne-Louise cried. 'You can't do this!'

But Mrs Pybus kept pushing and Anne-Louise kept resisting, despite the fact that they were now on the street. Anne-Louise called over her shoulder to the other staff but none of them moved. At last Mrs Pybus dropped her grip and Anne-Louise almost fell to the pavement.

'You will regret this, Mrs Pybus!' she shouted,

suddenly noticing that their scuffle had attracted a small crowd. A group of people stood around watching her and she gave an impromptu bow.

'That woman believes breasts are obscene!' she called, theatrically pointing towards Mrs Pybus's retreating back. Someone in the crowd giggled.

'What's obscene about these?' she challenged, lifting her blouse to expose her high, white bosom. She looked around proudly and noticed that several people were smiling: she smiled back. At the same moment she happened to see two policemen approaching and instinct made her drop her blouse and break into a run.

It seemed to Anne-Louise that from this moment the turbulence inside her rose like a wave. She knew herself to be rushing headlong towards some crashing end yet all she felt was the shooting joy of movement. She was burning with happiness and knew herself to be incandescent, radiant with her own light. She could have led armies, charged headlong into open fire but instead she walked too fast down peacetime streets, swollen with joy. She saw her dismissal as a kind of test, of her bravery and ardour. She knew she had won the first of many battles and was impatient for further onslaughts: within hours of her sacking she tried to urge the other staff members to go on strike as a gesture of support but none of them would. Indeed, Mrs Pybus said she would call the police if Anne-Louise came anywhere near the shop. This only fuelled her sense of herself as a luminous combatant and when Rachel refused to join her in a picket she knew herself to be truly alone and blazing.

She began to draw pictures of Mrs Pybus, over and over. She drew her fleshless body, her thin, wanting lips, her dead eyes so full of blows. She could not stop and her only relief was walking the streets for hours and hours. Sometimes she walked all the way from Bayswater to the far end of Oxford Street where she spent whole afternoons in the coffee shop across the road from the shop. Once or twice she caught a glimpse of Mrs Pybus and her blood lurched. She remembered reading that if you put a drawing of your enemy in the deep freeze compartment of a fridge you would cause them irreparable loss and planned on doing this the minute she got home.

But on the way home Anne-Louise found herself standing in front of an art gallery window staring at a painting. She did not know how she got there, only that the painting had been waiting for her. She stopped in her tracks and felt her breath pass in and out: the painting contained a universe, every microscopic dot, every living thing, pulsing. Inside its centre, whole galaxies rotated, animals breathed, plants broke open. Anne-Louise began to tremble and then, like a sleepwalker, placed her hand on the glass door which would lead her closer to its pulsing centre.

Inside the gallery she walked from painting to painting. She recognized that she was looking into the colours of Australia, into its red centre, into Aboriginal dreamtime. She was filled with a sense of triumphant arrival and when a voice addressed her she turned towards it with an expression of infinite love.

Two hours later she walked out of the gallery with her second part-time job. That she was shining she did not doubt, knowing that no-one had the power to resist her.

In this way Anne-Louise found herself sitting in a large white room in Covent Garden, all thoughts of Mrs Pybus vanished. She was ablaze only with the idea of the paintings and regularly stood in front of them, staring into their mysteries. The more she looked the more she saw: stars, heaven, water, light, the process of creation. Inside their borders was a puzzle intended for her, a secret only she could decipher. She sensed some imminent answer, the unravelling of some central motive to do with life itself. Into their surfaces she fell and fell, dropped down inside like rain. There were eucalypt trees and wombats, goannas and spinifex, rivers, skies, the open mouth of heaven. Their colours and dots wrapped her up, enfolding her deep inside.

Soon the Aboriginal paintings gave Anne-Louise an idea: she began to conceive of paintings of London as the painters might, broken up, condensed like particles of matter, balanced by the laws of physics. She remembered when she was young practising half-shutting her eyes and peering out at a world half-seen: the room had dissolved into dots, tiny, miniscule, millions of them making up the whole. She recalled her amazement on discovering that the universe was made up of joined things, mere particles of colour and matter.

Immediately she was desperate to start and rushed out in her lunch hour, coming back armed with tubes of new paint, new brushes, paper. She intended to paint on paper not canvas, to hear it rustle like grass, to be nearer the legacy of trees. She sat squirming in her chair, burning for time to move. At six o'clock exactly she shut up the gallery and ran out into the street. She ran all the way to the tube and stood by the door, wild hopes breaking inside her. She looked at the faces of people trapped by their lives and felt a sharp stab of contempt. She, Anne-Louise Buchan, was different she knew, more alive, more willing. She was full to the brim and all the other faces were dead, their skin lifeless, their blood curdled and pale. She stood looking down on them, swollen with a mission, ready to break down the doors. At Bayswater she burst from the carriage, sending a young man flying; she did not look back and raced up the stairs.

Running down the street she dropped a box of paints in her haste: they scattered, brightly shining, around her feet. She stood transfixed looking down at them, admiring their pattern, before hurriedly gathering their silvery tubes into her arms and continuing, not stopping till she reached their front door. She flung herself into the room and Rachel turned around in surprise, spilling a saucepan of water in the tumult.

'What's wrong?' she asked, alarmed.

'I've got to start,' Anne-Louise replied, flinging her coat to the floor, dropping her heavy load in a chair.

'Start what?' Rachel asked, looking upset, reminding Anne-Louise of her mother.

Anne-Louise did not answer and proceeded to take off her clothes, stripping down to her bra and pants. She took her painting overalls from the drawer and began to set up, while Rachel stood still holding the saucepan. She did not ask anything further but merely watched Anne-Louise, who was pinning huge sheets of new paper to the least cluttered wall. When she had finished and at last stood without moving, Rachel came up behind her.

'You can't paint here,' she said in a soft voice.

'Oh, yes I can,' Anne-Louise replied. 'Just watch.'

She began to draw everything that was in her head: the underground, the faces of the people, the outline of trees in winter. She drew the heads of drunken tramps she had seen at the Embankment, a doorway she had passed on a cold morning, the rise and fall of water in the Thames. She was going to draw everything true and then break truth itself into atoms, into particles of light and matter. She was going to break up the world and then join up the dots; she was going to reinvent London through Australia. She felt the hand of God moving through her own and tears formed in her eyes.

First she had to reimagine the whole world: she lifted up her pencil and began.

Anne-Louise forgot to eat, as if she had forgotten the memory of food. In truth, it was not that she no longer recalled the smooth dissolve of chocolate against the roof of her mouth but rather that she had entered a period of intense concentration and did not want anything to distract her. She did not want the soft glide of butter against her tongue, the roll of creamed chicken down her throat. She wanted no competition for her concentration which she intended to be centred solely on her work. She pushed aside heaped plates of spaghetti with aubergines and mozzarella which Rachel knew was her favourite and which she made clear she had cooked especially for Anne-Louise. She felt strong and self-contained, master of her cells, in control of the ship of her life.

She was aware that Rachel was trying to call her but it was as if she was a long way off. It was as if her ears were no longer properly attuned to anything except her own private mission. She could not bear to stop, to turn around, to sleep, to listen. She lived consumed by internal fire, scorching, magnificent. Inside her head was a rich, peopled place, more than loud enough for her purposes. She heard Rachel calling but as if from a shoreline she had long departed and which she could only watch, being far, far out to sea.

....

RACHEL: THE ARROGANCE OF INNOCENCE

I N Hong Kong I began to take a boat to an island
full of other refugees. On the days that I sailed in
a free boat towards them, I could see from afar the
glint of their steel huts, the ring of wire around the
camp fences. Their small island was formerly the site
of a leper colony, far enough from the city of the
new to avoid contamination. Even so, lepers once
tried to swim back home, their wrecked bodies later
pulled into fishing boats like inedible sealife. The
people in the camps did not have the chance to strike
out to sea, being patrolled at all times, carefully
guarded.

When our boat reached their island, armed
guards met us in trucks to escort us to the camp.
There we were officially signed in, having been
granted clearance by some aid body or other. By the
time I got through to the concrete yard on the other
side the children were waiting and leapt and bounded
like dogs at the sight of me. I had come to take them
briefly to freedom, to walk them in a straight line
out of the camp down to a playground, to remind
them of a world unbound.

It was always hot and I tried to keep away from

the huts which smelt of stale food and urine. Thousands of people were housed there, families piled on top of one another, babies, old men. There were washing facilities of sorts down one end and the people in general were clean. Yet I could clearly see rashes on the faces of babies, the teeth of young men grown decayed and stinking, scabs forming beneath hairlines. The children were infested with head lice and scabies; I was conscious of worms beneath the skin, unseen migration, and always carried with me a cake of good soap and a clean towel. When one of the children held my hand too long I am ashamed to say I counted the moments before my hand was let go.

Accompanied by their teachers we counted children's heads both before and after leaving the camp's gates to ensure none had escaped. In an orderly fashion we made our way down to the playground, a conga line of desperation, momentarily travelling. The free sky wheeled endlessly above us, headed for China and beyond; the wet air rushed about our faces before moving on. We could see the world, the towers in the distance, the unreachable city of the new. We saw the rimless sweep of the sea below us, planes from rich cities coming in to land. The sun was fierce and pressed heavily upon our heads, all around us was open, empty land. I pictured the children running off over the bare, scrubby hills, their horny feet rushing over rocks. Yet not once did they try to escape but merely lowered their eyes against the sun.

At night in my own personal tower I thought of the people on the far island locked up in their tin buildings for the night. I imagined the collective swell of their breathing, their lost dreams floating to the roof. I was free of course and yet had built my own cage: unbound I had fashioned my own lock.

I remember well that night in London when Anne-Louise came bursting through the door and I could no longer shut my eyes to the fact that she was in danger. I had tried to ignore as best I could her obsession with Mrs Pybus and her ridiculous schemes for revenge and when she began working at the gallery I convinced myself that her obsessive behaviour had stopped. Now, as I stood watching her desperate rush about the room I felt the blood pulsing at my temples, dread choking my throat. I remember I was in the middle of something, washing up or cooking, and I stood for a long time holding some object in my hand while I calmed myself and tried to work out what to do. I felt bizarrely as if under attack, as if I were being bombarded: she crashed into the room like an invading army, scattering everything in her wake. I stood amid the noise and confusion and my first instinct was to cover my ears, to cower beneath a safe shelter.

While I watched it became clear she was setting up to paint, that she intended to use our bedsitter as a studio. I remember approaching her as if she was an undetonated explosive, fearful lest she go off. I was relieved when she ignored me and I stood silently behind her, watching her drawing with violently trembling hands. She was flaming, gripped by some wild, extravagant emotion, clearly gone from me. I backed away from her and stood with the rim of the kitchen sink pressing into my back, my heart thumping. She continued to draw and did not look up as I approached again, warily.

'You can't paint here,' I said in my bravest voice, anticipating the swing of her arm. She appeared murderous, capable of force and I felt my body prepare itself for attack.

'Oh, yes I can,' she replied, her voice rammed with purpose. 'Just watch.'

I had no choice and stood as if transfixed, knowing that disaster had finally arrived.

Anne-Louise existed in this frenzied, overwrought state for several nights and days. Standing in front of her drawing paper for hours at a time she obsessively worked and reworked the same details. As far as I know she did not eat or sleep but I continued to place bowls of food before her which she left to congeal on the floor. I pleaded with her to get some rest but she barely answered me. Once she took a long bath in the shared bathroom down the hall and only got out when a fellow resident knocked on the door to complain.

'Did you see that cat?' she asked when she came back inside.

'What cat?' I replied.

'It was very black with red eyes,' she said in a slowed-down voice.

'In the bathroom?' I continued and she looked at me as if I were stupid.

'In the street, just now,' she said with scorn. 'A black cat with red eyes. It knew me.'

I was totally at a loss, frightened. She was taller than me, stronger, obviously out of control, and I had no hope of persuading her to do something she had no intention of doing. She had already repulsed my suggestion of a doctor. 'What for?' she asked, surprised. Paolo, an Italian with whom I had just begun a relationship of sorts, was away in Italy and I had already left several urgent messages for him to call me as soon as he got home. Hilary, the director of the gallery where Anne-Louise worked, had been next to useless, saying she was just off to Wales and advising me to call a doctor. 'I'm sure there's nothing to worry about,' she said cheerily before hanging up.

Not long after I spoke to Hilary, two Americans Anne-Louise had met in a bar happened to drop in on their way to a late breakfast.

'Want to join us?' the girl asked Anne-Louise and to my surprise she smiled perfectly naturally and went to get her coat.

While her back was turned I attempted frantically to warn them but the boy only looked at me as if I was the one with a problem.

I waited anxiously for them to come back and

when they did all three were smiling. 'She's fine!' the boy said as they left. I realized that no-one in London knew her as well as I did.

I remember the next morning I was on the phone in the hall waiting to be put through to a doctor whose name I had got from the surly overweight medical student in the flat next to ours when Paolo walked in. I rushed towards him and fell into his arms; he reeled back against my weight.

'Hello to you, too,' he said, disengaging himself. 'Glad to see me?' He looked down at me and saw that my eyes were panicked, that I was clinging to him too fiercely. I looked anxiously towards our room and pulled him further down the corridor.

'It's Anne-Louise . . .' I whispered.

He smiled, being one of those men who was not frightened of her, enjoying her deep, uncluttered laugh, her dismissiveness.

'There's something wrong,' I continued in a desperate whisper, frightened lest she come out and hear me.

'What's she done now?' he asked, grinning.

I looked up at him. 'No, Paolo, she's sick or something. She's acting very strange.'

He brushed the hair from my eyes and held me, kissing the top of my head. 'Let's go and see, shall we?' He took my hand and I followed him back into the room, cautiously, as if entering enemy territory.

'Hi, Anna-Louisa,' he said without effort and she turned around and grinned.

'Paolo,' she said, smiling unreservedly, 'come and see what I'm doing!' Her black eyes were very beautiful, radiant with internal heat.

He walked up to her and slung an arm around her shoulder; she stayed smiling and looked up at him. After a moment he began to make sounds of approval. 'It's very, very good,' he said as if he knew, as if he wasn't a messenger boy with a flat full of Athena posters and Italian kitsch.

'Have you seen any Aboriginal dot paintings?' she asked not waiting for an answer. 'They paint the world as a logical combination of dots. Every dot has a meaning, a place. Every dot represents something. Every dot makes up a universe.'

He stood looking serious, his handsome eyes still on the drawings. 'But I see no dots,' he said, 'there are no dots here.'

She began to laugh, an hysterical, unstoppable laugh, loud, cruelly tempered. It went on and on until Paolo looked at me in confusion and I crossed the room and led Anne-Louise to a chair where we both stood over her. She was still doubled up, racked with convulsions: I finally went to the sink to get her a glass of water.

As I handed it to her she burst out again. 'Anne-Louise,' I said, 'stop it.'

She looked up at me, sobbing now. 'I can't,' she replied, choking. 'Oh, Rach, I can't.' I couldn't tell if she was genuinely crying so I kneeled down and stroked her hair. I looked into her face and my heart broke open. *Come back*, I willed, *come back to me*. I stroked her poor sobbing head and felt my own helplessness, the uselessness of my hands. Paolo came and placed his fingers gently on my shoulder; reluctantly I stood up.

'You stay with her,' he said. 'I'll be back soon.'

I watched him leaving and then turned to Anne-Louise. Her smudged blazing eyes were fixed pleadingly on mine, as if I could save her, as if I could even save myself.

Her mother somehow managed to get her into a good private clinic in Harrow; I still don't know how she did it from Australia. While I understood, of course, that it had something to do with money I was astonished at how quickly and smoothly it was arranged. The first time I went to visit Anne-Louise my palms were running with sweat; a large part of me did not want to go at all and I did not know what to expect.

She was sitting in the garden when I approached; it was late summer and I could hear bees. She did not see me at first and I stood for a moment looking at her big dishevelled face, the figurehead of her, so known to me and yet so unknown. As I watched she turned and smiled, gently, faintly.

'I'm not frothing at the mouth,' she said and I almost laughed in relief. I rushed up to her and placed yellow roses in her hands which, I noticed, were stained with paint.

'They're beautiful,' she said, her famous voice strangely tamed. When she looked up at me I saw that her eyes were no longer stoked, they had a hazy look about them, misty, becalmed.

'You look like a summer's day,' she said slowly. 'Elysian.'

I sat down on the bench next to her. 'And you look better, too.'

She patted my hand and I thought of how much she meant to me, how knowing her had made me feel free.

'The shrinks say it was an isolated psychotic episode,' she said in her new voice. 'It shouldn't happen again.'

I looked out over the flowering garden, at the dying lavender, the dog roses, the running vine drooping its head.

'It was terrifying, Rachel, like I couldn't turn myself off, like I was some machine being controlled.'

I wanted to offer words of reassurance but I knew none: she had sailed once again into uncharted waters, leaving the rest of us floundering in her wake. 'I've never been so scared in my life,' she said softly.

I felt useless, totally inadequate. 'Well, you've joined an elite club,' I finally joked, 'Van Gogh, Modigliani, Goya . . .' My voice trailed off pathetically.

I looked at her but she was looking out over the garden, a slow tear falling from one eye. 'You know what Groucho Marx said about clubs,' she said.

I sat with her while she continued to cry, silently, endlessly. She was swollen with sadness, rotten with it, slowly sinking. She cried and cried and I stroked her hand uselessly, sinking myself. It struck me that until this moment all our troubles had been small, sur-mountable, that we suffered only bad tempers and yearning. We had possessed the arrogance of the lucky, believing misfortune to be something which happens only to failures, to the unlucky, people who had somehow rendered themselves powerless. I saw now that there was no such division between the blessed and the unlucky, merely life passing over us all.

As I sat beside the blessed and sinking Anne-Louise I realized we had not anticipated a black hand placed upon our heads: we were supposed to swim forever upwards, never intending to be swept down. I stroked her hand and felt the warm beating blood passing through it, the pulsing life which must now encompass this new, unexpected diversion. I closed my eyes and turned my face to the sun, a great sadness within me. The grief of life cleaved to me and I knew it had come for good, settling within me, deeply, beyond light.

. . . .

MARTIN: THE FINAL DAYS

ONE day in Hong Kong a giant digital clock was erected, counting down the final days. The infamous hundred-year lease was almost up and when it expired, at midnight on a day towards the end of the twentieth century, the colony would be handed back to China. Triumphant officials from across the border came to witness the unveiling of the clock, on the very top of one of the city's finest new buildings and visible from many miles off. The governor attended the ceremony, of course, along with many other important burghers, nervous as to whether time was really running out. A few were gripped by open panic at the sight of the clock, as if they might not finish their dinner before the dinner plate was taken away.

Martin watched the unveiling from the top floor restaurant of a luxury hotel booked especially by his firm for the occasion. There were many luxury hotels in the colony but this was one of the best: carpets replaced every second year, telephones in every cubicle of the men's washroom, pretty Chinese waitresses dressed in long silk tunics slashed to the thigh. Martin was sitting next to the spoilt wife of a petrol company executive who had teenaged children capable of feeding themselves but who nonetheless still managed to sit around doing nothing all day, living thoughtlessly off her husband. She was twittering on about some murders which had saturated the colony's media for days.

'I'm *so* glad Sophie and Charles are at boarding school at home,' she was saying. 'Apparently the children at the school where it happened are *distraught*.' She leant closer to Martin, lowering her voice. 'They were buggered, you know. Both of them.'

Martin nodded his head in her direction, feigning the required solemnity. 'D—D—Do you think there'd be such an outcry if the murdered children were Chinese?' he asked before he could help himself.

The woman flushed and sat back in her seat. 'Of course!' she countered angrily. 'This is a dreadful thing to happen to anyone's child, Chinese or not.'

'What's this?' asked the woman's husband, joining in, a well-meaning smile on his jovial, alcohol-heated face. He was a rather stupid man with a penchant for the local girls. 'What are you getting so hot under the collar about, Di?'

His wife looked at him crossly and then glared at Martin. 'Mr Bannister thinks I only care about those two children who were murdered because they were English.'

Martin smiled at her. 'Now, now, my darling, I

didn't quite say that. I—I—I merely suggested that people are reacting with outrage when several Chinese children have been known to be murdered too but they rarely make page one.'

'Don't patronize me, Mr Bannister,' she said, standing up. Martin remained smiling as she walked away and he was relieved to see Gerald Kirby smile, too.

'She'll get over it,' he said as if bemused, his eye distracted by a passing waitress.

'Is she always so quick to bite your head off?' Martin asked, following the direction of his eyes.

'And your arm and your leg.' Kirby was still engrossed in the waitress, his wife obviously relegated to some distant corner. 'It's rare to see one as tall as that, Marty. Just look at those legs.'

The waitress was not to Martin's taste. He also disliked being called Marty by men he did not know and decided he had had enough. As he prepared to make his excuses he saw a young girl on the far side of the room, an attractive white blonde with an unusual face, slightly pushed in like a pug's. Yet it was an appealing face, sexy and vulnerable; he liked her white, flyaway childlike hair.

Martin excused himself and, as he stood, realized he was drunker than he had first thought. Moving across to the other side of the room he almost crossed paths with Mrs Petrol Company Executive Wife but she had obviously seen him first and changed direction. Nevertheless she gave him an unforgiving glare for good measure and he called out just to annoy her, 'Hello, Di!'

When he got to the table the girl was already waiting, looking up at him with her poor pug's face, ready and willing.

'I—I—I want twins,' he said. 'A boy and a girl.'

She laughed up at him, showing all her clean pretty teeth and he realized she must be American.

'Hi, I'm Trudy,' she said and sure enough he was right. 'I work for Coopers.'

'Hi, I'm Martin,' he replied in a perfect American accent. 'I work for myself.'

She smiled again. 'I know who you are. I'm a friend of Louisa's.' He had to think for a moment who Louisa was before he remembered she was an accounts executive he had found unexceptional after having dinner with her once or twice.

Martin pulled up a chair and put his arm around the odd-looking girl. 'S—S—Since we're old friends can I get you a drink? A baby perhaps?'

'I've got one,' she said, laughing.

'Which, a drink or a baby?' he asked and she laughed again.

'Would you like to accompany me downstairs to a room while we attempt to make one?'

She nodded her head, pushed back her chair and they walked straight out. He was unsurprised as it had happened before: in the colony all things were possible. Unknown girls handed themselves over as easily as a ringful of keys. Once, on a flight from

London, the girl sitting next to him sharing his champagne had proposed they join the mile-high club by retiring to the nearest toilet cubicle. Of course he had accepted and was later unperturbed by the sight of her fiancé waiting to greet her upon landing in the arrivals hall.

Possibly the white girl who was offering herself now was as drunk as him, for at the lift she had to rush back for her handbag. 'Don't go without me,' she called and Martin waited obediently by the door. He pushed the lift button and felt a deep familiar surge, an alertness in his blood, the sudden clearing of his fumy head.

'What a good boy,' she said upon coming back and he pushed her straight into the waiting lift and flung her against the far wall. As his tongue entered her mouth he rammed one knee hard between her legs and she let out a cry. When the lift stopped and the doors opened he was vaguely conscious of expressions of disgust but he carried on. Only when they got to the lobby did they disengage themselves; she patted her white flyaway hair in a hopeless fashion while Martin paid for the room.

Waiting for the lift again he saw Joanna coming into the lobby with a group of models. He had forgotten that she was due to fly back from a job and that the girls always had a drink together before heading home. He pretended not to see her although it was clear that she had seen him. As he stepped back into the lift he was left with the image of her hanging open mouth, her large teeth all in a row. It had to come sooner or later, Martin knew, and this way he was spared the excuses.

In the dark room he rolled the white girl onto the floor and ran his feet over her naked body. When he reached the moistness between her legs she sighed and arched her back and when he placed his foot over her strange flattened face she did not whimper. He forced open her mouth and she began to lick; the sole of his foot, his toes, his heel. He pressed down harder and she cried out, a pathetic sound, soon muffled. He got off the bed and squatted over her, his buttocks spread, and lowered his anus over her face. She tried to get out from under but she was pinned and reluctantly began to lick him. His penis rose up against his belly, forged, ready. He rolled her over and whispered into her blonde baby hair, *Would you like to be whipped now*? He took his belt off the bed and slammed it down against her buttocks. He thought he heard her crying but could not be sure and rammed himself up her from behind. As he came he pulled her flyaway hair back, hard, and there was no mistaking the sound of crying now, no mistaking the breaking of tears, freely falling.

When he woke she was gone, as he had supposed she would be. There was no note, no sign of her, indeed no evidence of her pale existence. Martin lay in the large bed and felt the weight of a headache and a familiar depression pressing down on him: he rolled over and began to sob.

ANNE-LOUISE: DARING TO HOPE

AFTER Anne-Louise came out of the clinic she felt as if she had been away from the world a long time. Everything seemed larger, louder, yet somehow more frail, made of insubstantial material. When she walked through the gates into the street the light was a strange, primeval colour and she clung tightly to Rachel's arm, trembling. She felt as though she had not used her limbs in a very long time, as if all her muscles were cringing. She had to concentrate on walking, on lengthening her stride. Rachel seemed to regard the occasion as one of joyous release and couldn't have known that Anne-Louise would have preferred to live forever unmolested. What she really wanted was to run back inside and live the rest of her life in complete safety.

'We're splurging on a taxi,' Rachel declared, 'and no arguments.' She was obviously nervous and had clearly forgotten that this had long been an area of dispute between them: in the past she always insisted on taking the tube and Anne-Louise was always hailing cabs.

Inside the large black heart of the taxi Anne-Louise stared out the window. Every face to her looked sad, broken by life. She felt weighed down herself, infinitely tired, and all she longed for was the oblivion of sleep. It was as if she could not rouse herself to full consciousness, as if a firm hand kept pushing her back under water no matter how desperately she struggled to rise. She felt saturated, blood and water, her lungs filled and sinking.

'Nearly there,' said Rachel, patting her hand comfortingly, as though she were talking to a child.

Anne-Louise was too tired to care and remained staring at the lost faces in the crowd on the street, floating like her, wavering.

In the weeks that followed she convalesced like an invalid, which in a sense she supposed she was. She felt exactly as if she was recovering from a physical injury, the same unclouded calmness in the wake of violent physical pain. Rachel, who was still waitressing, arranged for someone else to do her shifts and stayed home to look after her. She plumped up Anne-Louise's cushions and combed out her hair, she cooked nourishing soups and made her take her medication. Each afternoon she roused Anne-Louise from sleep and they walked briskly around Kensington Gardens.

'It's almost enough to make you want to stay,' Rachel said, chattering on aimlessly about the weather, 'but it's only a trick, isn't it? It's only like this for two months of the year.'

It was late September, a fabulous Indian

summer, and the sun still carried heat. Despite this, some of the trees were already turning, and the colours were brilliant. In the fading summer light there were golds and bright yellows, crimson bushes, burnt leaves. Anne-Louise saw all this but it was as if it were a miracle meant for someone else, a blessing no longer addressed to her.

She felt a sharp twist of bitterness. She looked across at Rachel walking beside her, so unaware of her own good fortune, so unintentionally insufferable, and a sudden vertigo gripped her. In an instant she saw that her illness had removed her from the ordinary, cruelly setting her apart from common life.

She could not stand listening a minute longer and, turning on her heel, abruptly walked off.

As the weeks passed and she did not feel gripped again by a sense of frenzy, Anne-Louise was left feeling vaguely depressed. While this tentatively reassured her that she was no longer mad, it did not help assuage a feeling that she was a form of debris, something broken and used up. She felt somehow quenched, as if partly extinguished. In those hours when Rachel was away she sat in the fleeing light staring into space, tears sometimes sliding down her face. She knew what was happening to her was a sort of punishment, though for exactly what she could no longer recall.

But as Christmas neared, Anne-Louise felt the first faint stirrings of animation. She woke in the mornings and could actually bear to get up, she read her first newspaper again. As her depression slowly lifted she took to probing her own mind as she would a sore tooth, regularly checking to see if she was hearing voices. One evening, lying on a cushion while Rachel was in the bath, she began to talk to herself, to see if her own voice sounded strange.

'Hello, you loony,' she announced to the empty room. 'Still mad as a hatter?' She stared into a mirror to see if her face had changed and was relieved to find it had not.

'As fabulous as ever I see,' she muttered to herself, hurriedly stuffing the mirror under the cushion when Rachel unexpectedly came back into the room.

Perhaps Rachel had heard Anne-Louise talking to herself because she looked over worriedly before grabbing her forgotten shampoo.

Anne-Louise had to laugh at the look on her face, so anxious, so ready to be alarmed. Of course when Anne-Louise started to laugh Rachel looked even more frightened, which only made Anne-Louise laugh harder.

'It's all right, Rach,' she said, controlling herself. 'I haven't lost my marbles again.'

Rachel smiled uncertainly and Anne-Louise smiled back. It was the first time in months she had found something funny and the notion pleased her.

The first time they went to dinner with friends at Paolo's, Anne-Louise noticed him casting furtive glances in her direction as if she might unexpectedly start howling. Helping him in the kitchen she could not stop herself, and growled when he passed her a full plate. The plate nearly shot from his hand and his wide brown eyes sprang open in alarm.

'And I left my muzzle at home, too,' she said, taking the plate and leaving the kitchen.

It was clear to her that as she relaxed back into the shape of her former self everyone around her relaxed too. By the end of the evening she had everyone in stitches, telling cruel stories about her fellow inmates.

'Yes, I promised Jesus Christ I would send him a postcard,' she said, 'although you'd think the Son of God would have his own express service.'

She momentarily felt the prick of conscience but brushed it aside: in her experience life had proved cruel and random and the rules of fair play no longer applied. Indeed, as far as she could see, happiness and pain were unfairly distributed, with the unworthy frequently getting more than their fair share of painless existence. She began to tell another story.

Hilary at the gallery turned out to be a brick, being a person totally uninterested in drama and certainly not excited by anyone else's private traumas.

'I'm so glad you're better,' she said, welcoming Anne-Louise back. 'I think it's best if we forget the whole thing and just get on with it, don't you?'

Anne-Louise could have hugged her but instead she smiled briefly and enquired as to what Hilary wanted her to do.

'You can start by helping me uncrate this lot,' she said. 'Here.'

She handed Anne-Louise a cutter and bent over a large parcel.

Anne-Louise hesitated only momentarily before stepping forward and plunging back into her life.

For a long time afterwards she worried when she became too excited, on the alert for any signs of sleeplessness or frenzy. Even after she had ceased all medication it took many months before Anne-Louise had the confidence to feel ordinary excitement, to let herself feel that joyful dizziness when something pleased her. If she looked at a painting for example and felt a quickening, a thrill, she walked away from it until she had calmed down. For the moment she left her own work completely to one side while she waited to feel absolutely sure. Occasionally, at night, she felt scared of herself and lay as if in panic, her heart beating noisily, terrified lest she lose control again. Yet she never did, and after a time she relaxed her grip and bit by bit her former carelessness returned. She even began to feel that on the scale of things what had happened to her was not that bad: people lived with agoraphobia, panic attacks, permanent anxieties far more disabling than hers.

As the long dark winter neared its end she felt the early tremor of spring, a sharp pleasure at the coming of the light. By this time she was confident enough to let herself feel joy, to let early buds flower in her blood.

She walked the streets admiring bursting trees, smelling the rich crack of opening flowers. She did not know enough about English trees but to her they all looked like apple and peach blossom trees in full flower, heavy with pink fairy floss.

She walked and walked, daring to be happy, risking the wrath of the Gods. She raised her large smiling face to the sun and when she was not struck down, dared to hope for herself again.

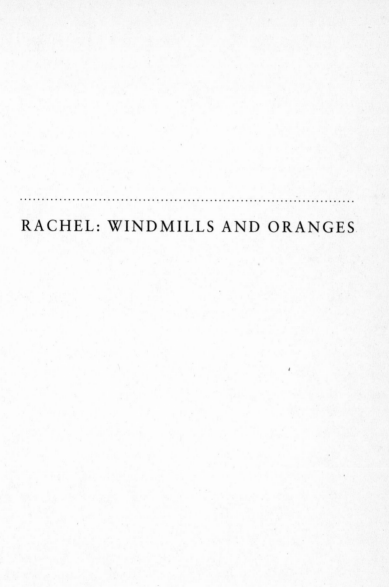

RACHEL: WINDMILLS AND ORANGES

I HAVE never been a superstitious person but in Hong Kong I became one. After living there a while I began to suspect there might be something in notions of fate after all, in the punitive and random acts of unknown Gods. I learnt that the ancients believed the fate of love was sealed at the moment of the first kiss. Above the heads of the kissing lovers the heavens decreed either happiness or despair. I thought of the first kiss between my husband and myself and knew that bad luck had entered our bloodstreams. We had kissed over the heads of the drowning calling for help from below.

I knew that on certain days of the lunar calendar, soothsayers and fortune-tellers gathered around Lovers' Rock. This rock was situated on one of the high, winding roads curling up behind the city, perched as if admiring the view. On special days girls and women came to place offerings to Goddesses, in the belief that the rock had certain magical properties which would ensure happiness in love, and luck in finding and keeping a good husband. The soothsayers and fortune-tellers gathered on these days to give counsel for a price, to sell incense and little plastic windmills symbolising a change in fortune.

Believing myself cursed by bad luck I decided to visit on one of these special days. While a large part of me recognized that I was being foolish, I could not quite shake off the idea that since I had nothing to lose I might as well give it a try. I walked all the way and as I walked I wondered how my life had come to this, how I had come to find myself dragging my unhappiness to the feet of an inanimate mineral. I felt ashamed and broken but pressed on, only stopping to buy a single stick from the incense sellers along the way. I felt for the box of matches in my pocket and kept my head down in the hope that no-one passing would recognize me. Lovelorn Chinese girls walked in groups around me, giggling, carrying windmills and oranges. I told myself that of course I did not believe in such nonsense, and yet I did not turn back.

At the rock I could not get close enough to wedge a single stick of incense into the ground. I watched as girls, middle-aged women, the infertile, the abused, placed their sticks in the crevices of the black silent rock. Smoke from a thousand incense sticks rose from its hunched form so that it resembled nothing more than a sleeping dragon, coiled, powerful. Little windmills blew in the air, their pinks and reds spiralling like fireworks. Oranges like golden balls were stacked here and there in balanced pyramids.

I stood well away from the crowd, sheltering beneath a tree while I wiped the sweat from my face. It was the first of October and the air was supposed to be cooling and fresh, like I was supposed to be a new bride glowing with fresh love.

I waited to cross the distance to the magical rock, a lovelorn, newly superstitious woman.

I remember in London after Anne-Louise came back to the flat, I could not stop furtively observing her. Her breakdown was like evidence of some incendiary quality I had suspected all along, as if she might burst into flames. When she came out of the clinic she was clearly doused and it did not take long for me to recognize she was no longer flammable.

Yet even as I watched she slowly returned to herself, much like a painting being filled in, growing sharper, more deeply coloured. I watched her colouring herself in, making uncertain moves like a child might, growing in confidence. By the spring following her illness it seemed to me that the work was completed, with only the paint left to dry.

I was growing disillusioned with Paolo by then, by our inability to move in the same direction. If I occasionally had romantic fantasies about being the wife of an Italian living in a small Etruscan village I was always sharply reminded by the reality of him, the reality of us. Although he was charming, a wonderful cook, an attentive lover, I could not bring myself to fall in love with him, no matter how hard I tried. There was something in him I couldn't take seriously, he felt too flimsy, as if I might pass my hand right through him. In truth I regarded him as a kind of well-meaning fool, diverting, but I did not want to settle for a clown.

I had always imagined running towards love with my arms wide open, speeding towards it without a backward glance.

I did not particularly like London. Oh, I liked it well enough when it was well-lit and blooming, when the city's parks and squares turned their faces to the sun. I certainly did not like its more common short, bleak days when the streets appeared as if lit by the moon. I was beginning to feel restless and unsettled; with the coming of spring I longed for change. I took to reading the travel pages of newspapers, comparing ticket prices, dreaming of Italy and France. I supposed vaguely that Anne-Louise would come with me but more often I traitorously imagined myself unencumbered, striding off alone. This was largely because as she slowly got well and was at last returned to her old self, once again making smart remarks and using her clever tongue, I was reminded of how she sometimes annoyed me. It was as if while she was ill I had forgotten how she took me for granted, how she assumed she knew without doubt my internal dimensions. Some part of me was already in rebellion for I had begun to imagine flexing my limbs privately, testing my own span. While I was not yet sure what form this stepping out of my own boundaries might take, I did not want anyone around to remind me of who I was supposed to be. I was growing increasingly bored with Anne-Louise's old jokes about me being the Avon Lady: in my secret heart I knew myself to be the Avon Lady with a trick up her sleeve and an uprising massing in her blood.

In late spring a friend from the restaurant where I worked asked if I would like to join her and a group of friends at her mother's house in France for the summer.

'I know it's late notice but someone's dropped out,' Lucy said. 'It'd be lovely if you could make it.' She suddenly gave an embarrassed little laugh and blushed prettily. 'How rude of me, Rachel. I didn't mean to imply you're our last resort.'

The house was in southern France but not in a touristy area she informed me: in the stony hills of Languedoc, not far from the Spanish border.

'It's very dry and treeless, more like Greece,' she said. 'The Corbière vineyards are nearby and there are lots of ruined Cathar castles.'

I was surprised and flattered to be asked and did not hesitate to accept. Lucy and her friends were slightly younger than me, fresh out of university, indulging themselves in their first year out. I calculated how much money I had, and figured I could just about do it.

'No, no, you go right ahead and don't worry about your oldest friend in the world,' Anne-Louise said, collapsing into mock-sobbing when I told her of my plans.

'I feel guilty about the rent,' I said. 'Can you get anyone in?'

'That depends on whether you're coming back,' she replied. 'Are you?'

I hadn't until that moment given it any thought. 'No,' I said, 'I don't think I want to come back to London.'

'Well, that's that then,' Anne-Louise said, 'I'll have to fling open the doors to unknown lodgers.'

'You really don't mind?'

'Actually I mind very deeply. I might just go and blow my brains out,' she said idly, turning away from me and picking up a magazine.

I watched her face, locked up, unreadable. I knew I would never fully understand her.

In France I lay as if in a stupor, the sun going straight to my head. I felt dazed and mildly happy, as I had not felt in a long time. Somewhere I still carried the terrible knowledge of frailty, and yet I still risked feeling happy. If I thought about Anne-Louise or Paolo at all it was in the same way I thought about Australia, some-where distant, far off. For the first time in months my blood felt fully warmed, and my limbs unfurled like plants in spring. I realized I was a person formed by the sun and my body at last felt at home.

At those moments when I roused myself sufficiently to re-enter the cool dark of the stone house I lay on crisp white cotton sheets and dreamed. I dreamed of crumbling castles and treeless plains, of flying astride some enormous creature that resembled a stingray. I was dreaming my life and felt as if I were waiting for my real life to arise. I was growing restless to begin, to feel that keen unhesitating propulsion towards my fate.

This is how we come to collude in our own destruction, this is how we come to long for the invading army to appear.

....

MARTIN: EXOTIQUE HOUSE

THE first time Martin engaged the services of a prostitute he felt the thrill of a dare. It had long been an idle wish of his, an occasional fantasy, as he assumed it was with all men. But then a colleague had come back from a holiday in Bangkok, renowned for its night-life and bar girls. 'I had two different girls every night,' he drunkenly boasted to Martin at yet another endless party on a junk in the harbour. 'I tell you, there was nothing they wouldn't do.' He cast a glance in the direction of his wife and seemed about to divulge to Martin all the things they would do. 'Really,' said Martin, 'how lucky for you,' extracting himself from his colleague's drunken scrum and walking away. 'I tell you, Bannister, by the last night I couldn't even be bothered to fuck 'em. I just lay back and let them do all the work.' All at once he seemed to realize he was speaking in a loud voice and his head retracted into the neck of his shirt like a startled turtle.

As Martin walked away he noticed he was carrying in his hand the beer-sodden name card his colleague had been dangerously waving about earlier.

Exotique House, it read, all girls with AID clean certificate.

He kept the card and looked at it occasionally, wondering if he would have the nerve. He had heard of men who had gone to prostitutes only to find they could not get it up. Their penises shrivelled and hid in their hoods, their pink heads could not be coaxed out. He did not enjoy the idea of this, the chance that it might seem tawdry or pathetic. He wanted to go in with all guns blazing and emerge with no regrets. Sometimes, early in the morning when he woke with an erection, he made himself come. He thought about girls strung up by rope, helplessly twisting. In these fantasies he experienced all the power of the world residing in himself and none of its weaknesses, all its strengths and none of its pity. In these fantasies he was always in control and full of authority, with no sadness or helplessness in him at all.

Everyone in Hong Kong needed to take holidays away from it occasionally. The colony devoured you with its ceaseless noise and crowds, its work ethic which never let up. All businesses traded six days a week, the more eager sometimes seven. Everyone was unceasing in their dedication to betterment, in their rush towards the release promised by money. The Chinese were renowned for their hard-working nature, their thriftiness, their tireless pursuit of gold bars. Ordinary workers spent their lunch hours reading the neon-lit shares index posted just inside the window of the stock exchange, some restaurants and most clubs had computer screens in their foyers, constantly scrolling through share indexes.

Martin himself regularly had to travel to beaches in nearby countries where he could switch off, well away from the blare of Hong Kong. He preferred luxury hotel complexes with poolside bars, where he could lie beneath an umbrella and have neatly groomed dark-skinned young men bring him iced drinks. He liked large, well-furnished rooms, knee-deep in carpet, fresh fruit, flowers and the best champagne. He liked enormous king-sized beds with stiff sheets and thick brocade bedspreads, bathrooms with wide baths and spas.

By now, he had been to most countries surrounding Hong Kong and had a few favourites. Coincidentally one of them happened to be Bangkok and Martin got Queenie Wong to make a booking for him at the Oriental. The hotel was old and famous and sat in its polished white and green splendour above the banks of the city's brown rushing river. Martin thought fondly of long breakfasts of fresh exotic fruits, French pastries, eggs and smoked salmon under a sharp clean sauce. He remembered the air feeling soft and pure against his skin, that there were many trees and flowering sweet blossoms and somewhere the soothing sound of tinkling water. Everything had looked pristine and glistening and he had immediately felt pampered.

Arriving now at almost midnight he strolled through the famous hotel gardens. Sweet air stroked his skin, tiny lights had been sprinkled here and there in the trees, unseen geckoes issuing their reassuring clicks clung to stones still warm from the sun. Martin walked as far as the river, which under the night sky appeared inky and dangerous, flowing swiftly towards the open sea. On the opposite bank he saw the lights of a temple, the gold head of a Buddha gleaming in the moonlight. Small boats rushed past him in the river's moving grace, borne homewards towards houses and families.

Inexplicably, as he watched, a feeling like home-sickness passed through him. In the rushing Asian night all at once he felt unaccountably alone. He had not made contact with his mother in years and his own father was gone from him. It suddenly seemed that he was lost, having travelled too far, or in the wrong direction.

Quickly, he turned around and headed for the hotel, feeling hollow from too many losses.

The foyer was still brightly lit and bustling, with guests arriving, and beautiful dark-skinned girls in short dresses having drinks with businessmen. As soon as Martin was back inside the light and noise he was returned to himself and his orphaned mood instantly vanished. He crossed the foyer purposefully and strode out the front door, which was opened for him by a neat boy in a bell-hop's uniform, complete with braided cap. Because Martin was relieved to feel back in control of himself he impulsively tipped the boy a large note. He watched with some satisfaction the boy's look of surprise, the quick rearrangement of his features into happiness. The boy raced out the door and personally hailed him a taxi, obviously wondering if this was his lucky night and whether any more bills would be forthcoming. But Martin climbed in without looking back and directed the driver to the girlie bar district.

When he arrived the streets were just waking, men and women advertising shows appeared fresh at their posts. 'You want girl, sir? Boy?' one of them asked, before he had even paid off the taxi.

Martin shook his head and brushed the man off, walking up the brightly lit street. All the way along men, women and teenagers tried to entice him into rooms, from which music could be heard booming. Occasionally he turned his head and saw girls in white bikinis dancing on tables, or wrapping themselves around poles on a raised stage. The air was hot and no longer smelled sweet but stank of beer, rotting food, vomit. Young boys passed selling cheap watches and cameras: on impulse Martin stopped to buy a camera and a roll of film. Groups of men passed him, some with their arms entwined around young girls, who chattered to each other rather than to the men. 'Take my photo, sir!' one of them called and the other girls dissolved into giggles. 'She very pretty, sir!' another cried cheekily.

He ignored them and kept walking. Halfway

along the street Martin saw a bar with tables strewn outside on the pavement. He sat down and ordered a beer, which he drank straight off before ordering another. Somewhere close, music was being played but only the bass could be heard, a rhythmic throb, which vibrated through his chair. He sat drinking, watching the midnight crowd, busy as peak hour in Hong Kong. He was aware of his own odour, of sweat and fear mixed, rising. Sunburnt English and Australian tourists wandered past dressed in skimpy shorts and T-shirts, their money bags slung low around their midriffs, their eyes wide open. Women dared their husbands to take them inside, to watch shows with girls doing unusual things with their body parts to ping-pong balls, razor blades, cigarettes. The night was noisy, brightly lit, the street dirty, smelling of the poor.

Martin took the card from his wallet and placed it on the table in front of him. He ordered two more beers just for good measure, drank them quickly then stood up and headed for the whorehouse.

Inside the room there was a flock of girls, a whole school of them. Plump girls, tall girls with long skinny legs, girls with bad skin and too much make-up. There were two televisions on and somewhere a radio; a thin, unattractive European man was sitting on a pink leather sofa draped with girls. The man avoided Martin's eyes as if he were in a sexually transmitted diseases clinic, which Martin fervently hoped he was not. He checked his pocket again for his pack of three condoms and at the same time noticed a condom vending machine promising fruit-flavoured varieties.

Two girls, wearing pink baby-doll negligees of a kind he had not seen since the 60s, approached him with a drink. One of them looked about thirteen at most and Martin ran his eye over her. She still had the gawky limbs of a child and no breasts to speak of. She smiled at him in a lascivious way and Martin instinctively turned away. His eyes landed on a plain girl with outsized glasses reading a magazine in the corner, apparently uninterested in touting for business. He peeled the two girls from his neck where they had settled like infants and made his way towards her. There was something ordinary and comforting about her, he liked the way she kept pushing back her glasses which continually slipped down her broad flat nose. Her nose, in fact, barely seemed to have a bridge at all but slid down towards her mouth where it ended abruptly in two flaring nostrils.

'H—H—Hello,' he said, standing over her and she looked up in some surprise. For a moment he wondered if she wasn't a cleaner or the house nurse, a woman not on offer.

But she smiled at him and stood up at once like a well-trained dog. Immediately Martin felt powerful, commanding, and a flicker of sexual excitement passed through him.

'You want to go to a room?' she asked in curling English. 'I show you my certificate.'

He knew at once he did not want to go into any pink polyester room decorated with plastic flowers.

'Come with me,' he ordered, turning around, and she obediently followed. After some debate at the front desk he was allowed to take her from the premises, but only after he had opened his wallet and produced several more bills.

She did not talk on the way to the hotel, which is what he wanted. When the same bell-hop opened the taxi door Martin tipped him again, more modestly this time. The girl followed him into the lobby, her eyes on the ground, seemingly unimpressed by opulence and wealth.

In the room he ordered her to have a shower and watched while she undressed. She had a small bosom and wide, broadening hips with stretchmarks across her belly from a child. She was squat and functional and Martin made sure she cleaned herself well. All the time he stood there she did not meet his eyes once and soaped herself as if her body did not belong to her. She had placed her large glasses carefully on the closed lid of the toilet, resting them on a clean, folded handkerchief.

In the bedroom Martin loaded the camera, then flung his own odorous clothes off and waited for her, fully erect. When she came back into the room huddled in a towel he instructed her to drop it. The towel collapsed around her feet and she stood naked, trying to cover her breasts.

Martin walked towards her holding the camera and without warning slapped her backwards to the floor. She looked up at him in fright as he took his leather belt in his other hand and brought it down upon her unprotected breasts. She let out a cry, but only once, then controlled herself, and he began.

....

ANNE-LOUISE: LIVING WITH BEAUTY

WHEN Rachel left London Anne-Louise did not feel bereft, not even momentarily. By then she knew lots of people, restaurants to go to, bars in which she could drink. Besides, she knew without question that she and Rachel had the kind of friendship that would not go away, despite time and distance and occasional bad behaviour. It seemed to Anne-Louise that Rachel was in her life like the moon or the sky, a permanent fixture with no chance of fading.

Yet after Rachel left for France the flat for a few days seemed intolerably large. Anne-Louise rocked around in it, listening to the sounds of neighbours through the wall, recalling how kind Rachel had been, how she had not fled when she could have. Anne-Louise might have shed a tear but had long ago schooled herself to believe she was not that kind, and got up from the sofa brushing sentiment from herself like fluff.

She had no trouble in finding someone to share the room and very quickly it once again became too small. Her first room-mate was a six-foot-four male saxophonist from Trinidad called Beauty she met in a bar one night. He was lean and indeed beautiful and instantly dubbed her Slim, for reasons she could not immediately fathom.

'Hey, darlin', it's because you're like that beautiful girl in that Humphrey Bogart movie,' he said when she asked, shining his saxophone and smiling up at her.

She gave a sardonic smile back. 'Yeah, right,' she said, lighting a cigarette, 'I bet you use that line with all your white chicks.'

He laughed, showing his perfect white teeth and she laughed back.

But living with Beauty did not turn out well. He quickly exhausted even Anne-Louise's legendary capacities: she could not remember smoking and drinking so much in her life. Together they went to bars, to clubs where he played with various bands, to endless parties which they never left before morning. They slept together once when they were both drunk but sanity had returned to them by morning.

'Hey listen, Slim, about last night ...' Beauty began and Anne-Louise leant over and pulled his handsome nose.

'Hey, Beauty, it's all right. I don't want to be your girl.'

She left the room before he could say anything too embarrassing.

Six weeks later, after Beauty had moved out, Anne-Louise discovered she was pregnant. She contacted a feminist abortion clinic straight away yet some part of her was secretly pleased. She had grown so used to thinking of herself as unlike other women that the pregnancy struck her as the opening of a gate into a previously closed world. For one wild, irrational moment she even considered keeping the child but immediately realized she would not.

She went ahead with the termination without a tremor, taking along a woman friend and cracking jokes. Later she spent the afternoon in bed reading trashy magazines and drinking sweet tea.

But in the weeks which followed, Anne-Louise was unexpectedly felled by occasional bouts of weepiness. She intuitively understood that she was forever going to be denied access to that most ordinary of worlds and for brief moments this knowledge proved too much.

After Beauty, an uncharacteristic caution overcame her. She felt slightly bruised and chose as her new room-mate the safest and dullest person she could find. Cassie was a friend of a friend, a Canadian who was doing some sort of archaeology course at the British Museum.

Anne-Louise liked her well enough but very quickly found her boring. Before long Cassie's pink and white innocence got on her nerves and she began to make cutting asides. Cassie would not go into Leicester Square after dark for instance and believed Soho to be teeming with danger.

'No doubt some Arab is waiting to stick a needle into your tender flesh, Cassie, and drag you off to the slave trade,' Anne-Louise said with disdain. 'You can't be too careful.'

Cassie was an easy blusher and clearly intimidated by Anne-Louise: it did not occur to Anne-Louise that Cassie might find the experience of living with her less than pleasant. When Cassie suddenly announced that a room had become vacant in a house in Putney shared by some fellow Canadians, Anne-Louise surprised herself by being offended.

'Of course I understand,' she said dismissively. 'You must go to your countrymen so you can sit around being lumberjacks and eating maple syrup.'

She walked across to the sofa which doubled as her bed, threw herself across it and picked up a magazine to indicate that the conversation was over.

She felt a sudden pang for the lost audience of Rachel, so willing to lay tributes at her feet.

Not long after Cassie was replaced by a relaxed and convivial woman from Liverpool, Hilary at the art gallery offered Anne-Louise studio space. 'I don't know if it's what you're after but you may as well have a look.'

The space was part of an old warehouse just off the Strand, not yet earmarked for renovation. Political groups had their offices there—a women's liberation centre, a committee organizing Reclaim the

Night marches—for it was still possible to rent cheap space in dilapidated buildings.

Climbing the stairs one cold bright morning Anne-Louise passed punks, women with shaved heads, young men with their lapels covered in badges. She was almost twenty-seven and felt the coming rush of thirty. She had been in London for nearly three years and could not recall where the days had fled. As she climbed, passing the young, she realized with some surprise that she no longer felt young herself. She climbed faster, telling herself that she must do something serious with her life. 'You were not destined to be a shop assistant, Anne-Louise Buchan,' she said to herself, 'even if it is in an art gallery.'

At the sixth and final floor she stopped, out of breath, then wove her way through darkened corridors as directed. Pushing open the door she saw a room flooded with sunlight, empty, waiting. She rushed to the window and tried to wrench it open but found, like the rest of the windows, it was stuck.

In the empty room Anne-Louise twirled and twirled, imagining genius pouring from her willing fingers.

She moved all her painting equipment in as soon as she could. Unlike that awful time before entering the clinic she felt entirely sober, determined to work in a disciplined but not frenetic fashion. Straight away she attempted to return to her concept of dots: on her days off she went to art galleries and drew her favourite paintings, taking her completed drawings like captives back to the studio. In the brightly lit room she tried to turn these famous scenes of London into something else, reinventing them, challenging their very structures. She knew that in Aboriginal culture the landscape itself was a kind of map and she was going to try and apply this concept to London: she was going to attempt to reconstruct the known map of London, revealing the skeleton within, the intention inherent within its well-recognized landscape. She was not yet certain how she was going to do this but it was perfectly clear to her what she was attempting: she was trying to impose the principles and concepts of Aboriginal dot art on to European art, bringing Australia to Europe, instead of the other way around. She realized as she drew that she was actually performing a colonizing act: she was going to superimpose one set of cultural reference points over another and see what came out.

Hilary occasionally asked her to dinner parties at her flat in Notting Hill. She usually invited Anne-Louise when she had visiting Australian dignitaries, men from arts funding bodies or universities, visiting painters, women come to take up Rhodes Scholarships. Hilary had established herself as a kind of unofficial Australian cultural attaché in London and was forever introducing people. She was a splendid cook and presided over these evenings with calm and grace.

On this particular evening someone from one of the Aboriginal land councils in the Northern Territory was coming. 'He's a lawyer,' Hilary said, 'white, I think.' Hilary was increasingly dealing with various government bureaucracies in her purchase and export of Aboriginal art. Anne-Louise knew that in Australia debate had begun about whether Aboriginal artists were being ripped off by rich whites, indeed whether the art should leave the country at all.

The lawyer, who was indeed white, turned out to be extremely personable. Anne-Louise was seated next to him and enjoyed the look of him, a broad, weatherbeaten Australian face of the kind she had not seen for some time.

'So, you're a painter,' he said, turning towards her.

'Only a novice,' she quickly replied.

He smiled. He appeared to be about her own age, perhaps a little older. 'What kind of painting do you do?'

She hated this question. 'Oh, I'm just experimenting at the moment. What are you here for?'

At once he began to talk about himself and she was relieved.

But later, when she was half-drunk, Anne-Louise decided she liked him. She liked his cynical Australian sense of humour, his lack of flash, the sunspots of the back of his tanned hands. She liked his unassuming presentation, the absence of suffocating politeness so familiar to her from the English. She leant closer to him.

'All right, I confess. I'm applying the principles of Aboriginal dot art to my painting,' she confided in a low voice, feeling beneficent, bursting with good news.

'Pardon?' he asked, his brow puzzled.

'You know, dot art. I'm trying to paint London through dot art.'

He put his glass down. 'But you're not Aboriginal.'

She laughed. 'I hadn't noticed.'

'No, seriously,' he said, 'how can you take dot art out of its context? It has important religious, political and social meanings to specific Aboriginal clans. It's a complex language which only its participants can comprehend. You can't simply pick it up and stick it on a T-shirt.'

She stopped smiling. 'I'm not sticking it on a T-shirt.'

'You're still hijacking something you don't know anything about,' he argued.

'Oh, come on,' she said, 'the whole history of art is one of hijacking and borrowing, of invention and reinvention. You can't impose rules and restrictions on artists' imaginations.'

He looked at her with apparent distaste.

'I see,' she said and she did see. She would have got up and left the room and never come back except that the thought of Hilary prevented her. Hilary was in fact looking over at them with what passed for curiosity on her mask-like face. With difficulty Anne-Louise smiled at her.

What a pity, Anne-Louise thought, and I was just about to ask him home. Her new flatmate was away for the weekend and Anne-Louise had already envisaged those sun-spotted hands on her high white breasts, that etched face over her own. Nevertheless, she turned her back on him, telling herself that she no longer fancied him.

The work wouldn't come, no matter how she tried. She pushed and pushed herself and it all came to nothing, no painting grew to fruition beneath her hand. Although she remained clear-eyed and calm, none of the paintings came to life, all of them resolutely refused to be born. After two months, three, six, all she had to show for her efforts was a handful of unfinished paintings. With such a powerful underlying premise to sustain her, she could not work out where she was going wrong, why she felt compelled to abandon every painting at a certain point, convinced it was lifeless and stultified. All she knew was that some essential energy was missing, the energy necessary to propel a work forward, to see it all the way home. She believed that if painting was to mean anything it must be a form of revelation, and saw that her own work offered none at all.

She was consumed with sickness and rage and even began to superstitiously consider whether it might be because she was not Aboriginal, whether she had indeed violated some secret, archaic code. But more often she grieved over her own talent, which was proving disappointing, even puny. She grieved for her mad ambition to be a genius, to create something beautiful and true. What she wanted most was to soar, to shine, to make something truthful with her own bare hands that was beyond dispute. Now, all she knew for sure was that her work was dead, and that she herself was falling into inescapable depression.

About this time Anne-Louise received a long happy letter from Rachel, who was still in France. She wrote that she was starting to paint again and, fingers crossed, her work was going marvellously, wondrously, well.

She was reading the letter when her mother called to tell her that her father had just died.

'It's a blessing, really,' her mother said, 'he would have been eighty-seven on Thursday,' she added, beginning to cry.

Anne-Louise cried too but after she had said goodbye to her mother and had stopped crying she found she could no longer picture the precise elements which made up her father's face.

RACHEL: THE WIFE OF A RICH MAN

IN Hong Kong I was frequently asked to lunches by the wives of rich men. Since I was now the wife of a rich man myself they quite naturally assumed that my time was free for lunches which lasted well into the afternoon. I resisted for as long as I could, being taken up with trying to finish some paintings for an upcoming show my gallery in Sydney had scheduled. I was rising at dawn and working late into the night, painting out my unhappiness. By then I had a studio in the surviving old quarter of Sheung Wan, a large, crumbling room in a block already earmarked for demolition. I worked in the heat inside my room without air-conditioning, the sweat between my breasts tickling as it rolled down. I had an old rackety fan which I usually kept turned off because I did not like the way its wind disturbed all the edges of my drawing paper. I wore earplugs at all times against the sound of the piledrivers and jackhammers, against the sound of the city encroaching.

When it became clear that my constant refusals to go to lunch were causing comment (for all the wives of rich men in Hong Kong were expected to perform their social duties), I reluctantly accepted. I scraped paint from beneath my nails and washed off the smell of turpentine, then selected a seldom-worn dress and took a taxi to a house on the Peak. It was considered the height of success living there, an advertisement to the world at large that money had carried these lucky dwellers to the top. I sat in the taxi as it climbed the streets, past Mid-Levels with its occupants dreaming of rising and into the territory of the risen, with their security gates, chauffeurs and housemaids. In Hong Kong even mid-career strivers employed housemaids: women and girls from the Philippines who lived in small back rooms.

I was greeted by one, who answered the door.

'How nice of you to come,' Mrs Jeremy Dowell said, coming up behind the maid. 'Imelda, take Mrs Bannister's umbrella. Please, come inside, the girls are waiting to meet you.'

She led me into a room full of wives, some heavily bejewelled. Each made a quick but skilled appraisal of my clothing before looking into my face. I immediately felt uncomfortable and gratefully accepted a glass of champagne proferred up to me by yet another maid.

'Come and meet Anne,' Mrs Jeremy Dowell directed. 'She's Australian too.'

I was taken and introduced to a large, encumbered woman who dutifully asked me which city I was from. While I answered the usual questions my eyes roamed the room: I saw Lalique crystal, wood from vanished forests, safe but expensive boardroom art.

The champagne had already gone to my head by the time lunch was announced. We were ushered into a large dining room, formally set, with white linen tablecloths and the family silver. I sat down behind my marked name card, next to the Australian woman with whom it was presumed I had so much in common. She had children at boarding school in Australia and wondered how it was going to affect them.

'Children have been going to boarding school for generations in England, Anne,' Mrs Jeremy Dowell kindly offered. 'All children get used to it.' She looked over at me. 'Now, did you all know that Rachel is an artist? I've never had an artist to luncheon before.'

All eyes turned to me, as if I were a sword-swallower or a fire-eater, a species certainly rare to Hong Kong. As I was obviously not Picasso, who was probably the only other artist they had heard of, they clearly did not know what to say to me.

'I used to draw as a girl,' Mrs Jeremy Dowell continued. 'In fact, I'm having lessons at the moment. He's a lecturer at the college, Chinese of course, but awfully well informed.'

There ensued a conversation about schoolgirl talents they had once possessed, now sadly faded. As we talked we ate chilled apple and Stilton soup, a cold chicken salad, summer pudding. We drank white wine, red, dessert wine, more champagne, until I felt gaseous and afloat. The conversation did not extend beyond the borders of upcoming charity events, money, gossip about who was having an affair with whom. The woman to my left talked incessantly about Hong Kong's finest international restaurants, about a new Australian chef she had just heard of who was cooking marvellous Australian cuisine.

'Australian cuisine?' someone interrupted. 'Isn't that a contradiction in terms?' Everybody laughed, including myself, which just goes to show how adept I had become at deception.

Saying goodbye at the door, thanking Mrs Jeremy Dowell, I lied and said that she and her husband must come over to us soon for dinner.

'Supper, dear,' she said in a helpful tone, 'here, we call it supper.'

Weeks later I heard the rumour that I was a women's libber and a socialist, for I was known to live without a maid and refused to iron my husband's shirts.

By the time I got back to Australia from France I was twenty-six and knew that if I was serious about my work I could no longer opt for safety. Although I was broke and longed to be back inside the security of the employment system, I steeled myself to jump without a safety net. In fact what I really needed after three years of living hand-to-mouth was a regular job, with a regular wage and sick pay and holiday pay. I scanned the job columns of the *Sydney Morning Herald* and frequently saw jobs I might take, except that I never applied for them. Instead I instinctively felt that another job in a magazine art department would sap my will, make me less inclined to take risks. I felt too that it would no longer be good for my painting: as I wanted to concentrate all my energy on doing real work and not fritter it away on illustrations.

In France I had taken the first tentative steps in this direction. After the summer ended, Lucy's mother had agreed to let me live in the house for the autumn and winter for a peppercorn rent. She was too busy to close up the house for winter and would have had to rely on neighbours. As long as I understood that she or friends might use the house from time to time, she was happy to have it occupied and well tended.

I loved the house, which I discovered was a converted grain mill. It was arranged in separate sections, with the kitchen and living area in a long low building and the bedrooms in a round, stone tower adjoining. I supposed this was where the actual grain was once kept and my bedroom was at the very top of this tower, accessible only by an outside staircase. I felt like Rapunzel and at night I could hear the scratchings of mice; when I slept I dreamed grains made up my pillow. My mattress was stuffed with straw and the sheets were stiff, thick cotton; through the windows in the morning I heard the sound of goat bells. The air smelt of thyme and lavender, being so far south the summers were long. During the *vendange* the smell of crushed grapes was heavy in the air and seemingly everyone in the little village at the bottom of the hill had stained purple fingers.

It was in this dry, wind-prone place that I first began to draw seriously, to paint images which did not flee. Some calm strength allowed me to hold an image in my head until I could get it down, until it assumed its inherent direction. I had never been able to finish anything before and I suddenly found my hand could not move quickly enough, my pencil was not swift enough to catch everything tumbling from my head. All at once I had shape and form before me, an imagined world I could summon at will. It was as if the grace of the body had visited me, as if some long-buried reflex had finally awakened. I could not help feeling that my time alone—eating, sleeping, walking, daydreaming—had led me forward, that while my unconscious had been unguarded, great movements had been going on unseen. I only know that I awoke as if from a long sleep and found I could capture light, earth, stillness, the dark: the whole crowded world was offered up to me.

By the time I returned to Australia I had an entire portfolio of work and a universe bursting in my head.

Before I left Europe that following October I

arranged to meet Anne-Louise in Paris to say goodbye. I was suddenly lonely: after leaving the farmhouse I had travelled in Italy for several months, seldom talking English, and I craved to see a face I knew well. I eagerly booked a hotel in Montmartre, just near Sacré-Coeur, so close we could hear the bells. I remember waiting for Anne-Louise in the lobby and when I saw her large brilliant face my heart roared. We raced towards each other.

'Rach, you look profoundly gorgeous!' she cried. 'Maturity suits you!'

I laughed and hugged her hard and was astonished to discover how happy I felt, how elated I was to see her. The instant I laid eyes on her I wondered how I had survived without her. She had put on weight and carried a new solidity, as if she were somehow more rooted. She seemed securely earthed, a live wire now grounded.

I might have known she would fly from London, even though I had sent her details about a cheap bus. She had somehow managed to smuggle from the flight five half-bottles of wine and her bag rattled all the way up the stairs. In the room she flung open the shutters, scattering the pigeons outside on the ledge, and immediately tore off the paper from the hotel glasses.

'To adventure,' she toasted. 'Here's to friendship.'

'I didn't realize you were so sentimental,' I teased. She gave me that old, characteristic look of disdain and we clicked glasses. I was reminded of how much she meant to me but, before I could speak, she turned away and leant from the window, sighing theatrically. 'Ah, don't you love the smell of Paris,' she said. 'Dog shit, traffic fumes.'

I leaned next to her on the window ledge. 'I can only smell roses,' I replied.

'Typical,' she said. 'I bet you buy all the stuff about the City of Light, too.'

I playfully knocked her elbow. 'Oh, go on, Anne-Louise, you're more of a romantic than me.'

She unexpectedly gave a bashful smile, as if I had caught her out. 'I'll admit that Paris is more beautiful than London,' she said. 'Remind me what I'm doing there again.'

'You're there because you can't speak French,' I replied.

'That's right, I forgot,' she said. 'And your French is worthy of the Academy.'

I laughed. 'My French is appalling. I still haven't mastered past tense.'

I remember we stayed in the room until we were quite drunk, then staggered out into the streets. We stood on the steep stairways of Montmartre and pretended we were in a Cartier-Bresson photograph; we rode the Metro back to the Left Bank. From St Michel we walked across the Ile St Louis and travelled back and forth across the Seine, standing in the middle of our favourite bridges. The dark river flowed noiselessly below, hardly moving. We hung our heads over the sides and stared, transfixed.

'What a perfect suicide it would make,' Anne-Louise said. 'Imagine that seamless floating.' Her arm stretched out towards the water, black and secret beneath us. I turned and saw that her eyes were glassy and dark like the water itself, locked. I didn't speak and we continued to stare in our half-drunk haze, as if we were about to discover some secret in its stillness.

Later, in a restaurant near Pont Neuf, we ate cold leeks and warm veal. As we were drinking more wine it suddenly occurred to me that Anne-Louise had not spoken about her work all evening. I put down my fork with a clatter.

'Anne-Louise! The dot art!'

She stopped chewing, her expression quite blank.

'Your great plan to paint London through dot art!'

She gave a careless toss of her shoulders. 'Oh, that. I gave it up.'

'But it was so important to you! What happened?'

She looked at me with an expression I did not recall ever seeing before, which I can only describe as malignant. It was a look of great bitterness and I knew she was challenging me not to cross some line: instinctively I pulled back.

'It was never important. It was just some passing

idea I had.' She continued to look at me and her gaze was a dare, still blazing with challenge. I dropped my eyes and finally heard her pick up her knife and fork and resume eating.

All week she dodged more general questions about her work, the one subject she had always spoken about freely. In Sydney and London we had talked about drawing and painting for days and whole nights at a time. Now, although I was bursting with discovery, I knew not to talk about my own work, instead I walked around Paris brimming with it, desperate to get back to it, wanting to shout with joy at what I had found. But I kept my mouth tightly closed and never let my rapture breathe freely.

When we said goodbye this new, dangerous space existed between us, an uncharted territory neither of us dared enter. It lay between us, murky, alive. I felt its cold rushing air as I hugged her. 'Now, write to me,' I said. 'Promise?'

'And don't forget your darlingest, oldest friend in the world,' she replied, kissing me goodbye.

I did not know that I would not see her for another three years and that when I saw her again everything would be changed.

....

MARTIN: THE COMPANY OF WOMEN

WHEN Martin left New Zealand to study in London, he often thought about finding his father. Walking down a London street he occasionally caught a glimpse of a man with a certain turn to his head, a familiar look about his eyes. Frequently Martin thought of going through official channels to find the man who had sired him before disappearing into thin air. Indeed, two days before he left New Zealand he made a visit to his mother with the express intention of finding out his real father's name.

'Ssh, Norm will hear,' she said at once, throwing Martin one of her famous freezing looks.

'I—I—I don't care what fucking Norm hears,' he shouted and she jumped.

'What's going on?' Norm called from the front room.

'Mind your own business,' his mother replied. Turning to Martin, she hissed, 'What's it to you, anyway? He never did anything for you!'

Martin let out a strangled laugh.

'What's so funny?' she asked, clearly unnerved.

'And you d—d—did everything for me, I suppose,' he said bitterly.

'Yes, I d—d—did,' she mimicked.

'M—M—Mother dear, just stop all this crap and tell me his name.'

Patricia Bannister, formerly Riley, formerly Thwaite, born Patricia Gloria Pie, continued to glare at him. 'His name was Martin James McClintock. I hope he's burning in hell,' she finally said.

'Charming,' Martin replied as he walked out. It was only later that Martin wondered why a woman who cursed a man to burn in hell would name both her sons for him.

When Martin was back in London something always prevented him from starting the search, even though he now had a name. Once he even got as far as writing a letter, which he supposed he could send to the Department of Social Security. Yet when it came to posting it Martin found he could not do it, that dread rose in him, causing his heart to crash noisily in his chest.

He found he did not want to extinguish his hopes so instead he kept them close, where they continued to flourish.

In his first year as a trader, before he left London for Hong Kong, Martin had a stroke of luck. He was allocated a client, an old woman from Birmingham, who had never played the stock market before. Martin was angry that he had been given such an unglamorous, two-bit client: she sent him notes on hideous floral notepaper thanking him in a spidery hand. One evening as he was leaving work after an exhausting day on the floor, the old woman herself appeared.

'Martin Bannister? Miss Osborne from Birmingham.'

He took the thin hand offered and waited.

'I wanted to thank you personally,' she went on, 'with that fifty thousand you made for me I've made a million pounds.'

Martin looked at her with interest. 'H—H—How?'

'I put it on a horse,' she answered proudly.

It turned out that ninety-year-old Miss Thelma Osborne, who had never bet on anything in her life, had invested her money in a share of a horse that went on to win every major race in England and Ireland. The newspapers loved the story and in every article she insisted it would never have happened at all if she hadn't trusted her life savings of two thousand pounds to one, Martin James Bannister. Although it was not the stock exchange's policy to have its traders draped across newspapers, it waived the rules for once and Martin's unsmiling face being kissed by Miss Thelma Osborne appeared on page one of the *Sun*.

Some three months later, as Martin was leaving for work one morning, a dirty envelope postmarked Suffolk, and with a return address, landed on his carpet. Inside Martin found the clipping from the

Sun with a barely decipherable scrawl in the margins. *You appear to have my eyes and my names. Are you by some act of wizardry or kismet my only surviving son?* Immediately Martin called in sick and rang British Rail to find out when the next train could take him to Walberswick in Suffolk.

It was early evening when he arrived at the tiny coastal town. A cold wind blew in off the ocean, screaming into his ears and agitating his already raw nerves. Holding the letter Martin made his way to the address written on it: there were only a few streets and he had no trouble finding the house. It was wooden, ramshackle and had probably not seen paint since it was built. The front door was slightly off its hinges and one window was missing a pane of glass, being covered instead with what looked like plastic food wrap fastened with sticky tape.

Martin stood outside for some time, the wind snapping at him. All his years of yearning rushed toward him, all his imaginings. As he waited, all his hopes escaped their confines and he almost turned and fled. In a flash he saw a pathetic image of himself with his palms offered up, his soul in a gesture of surrender.

He did not move and might have stayed paralyzed all night if some movement at the window had not startled him. Looking up, he glimpsed the briefest flash of a hand. Pushing into the wind, Martin mounted the stairs.

The old man who answered the door did not look pleased to see him. 'Who wants to know?' he asked sourly when Martin asked if there was anyone called Martin James McClintock living there.

'I—I—I do,' Martin replied. 'I have reason to believe I'm his son.'

The old man was dressed peculiarly in what appeared to be some kind of evening dress. He was wearing a bow tie and a dinner jacket of sorts, stained and fraying. In one hand he held a highball glass and a burning cigarette. The thought kept going through Martin's head, *This cannot be my father, this cannot be my father*, while the old man considered Martin with an unblinking eye, his bad-tempered expression unchanging. He did not look anything like the man in the photograph, shining and handsome.

'I believe you're speaking to him,' he said, turning his back but leaving the door open. Martin had no choice but to step inside, passing from dream to reality.

His father offered him a martini.

'I—I—I can't actually say I've ever had one,' Martin stammered.

'A martini's never had you, you mean,' he said with a sudden winning smile, pushing a glass forward. In a flash Martin glimpsed the dashing young sergeant he must have been and saw the beauty of his ruined eyes. A chill passed over him as he took the glass, knowing that his long journey had come to an end.

Over the course of two visits Martin found out that his father was a former stage actor who had spent his life appearing in productions all over England and who had also worked in America for ten years. He had even had minor roles in three Hollywood movies.

'I was once Ronald Reagan's stand-in,' he said, offering Martin another drink.

He proved to be a captivating and fluid talker, with endless charm. He did not hesitate to answer any question Martin put to him.

'Ah, your mother was a real beauty,' he told Martin that first night. 'She was like a young Elizabeth Taylor when I met her.'

'W—W—Where did you meet?' Martin asked, his head reeling from the alcohol.

'In London, just after I was de-mobbed. Another couple of chaps and myself were parachuted into Italy, behind enemy lines, to do a show. That's what I was doing you know, variety for the troops ... anyway, after we got back to London these chaps and myself got together, one had been holed up in some filthy Italian camp for two years. We were in the Coach and Horses in Soho, having our millionth drink, when this divine creature walked in ...'

As he talked, Martin McClintock seemed to grow younger, less stooped: Martin saw the debonair grace of him, the effortless elegance of his movements. He knew at once he was the type of man once described as a lady-killer. 'We went out, oh, I suppose for the next ten years, on and off. She was always wanting to get married,' he continued, straightening his shoulders. 'Take my advice, my boy. Never let any woman talk you into it.'

Ten years! Martin could not speak.

'Here I am, sixty-nine, and never been caught,' Martin James McClintock boasted.

'Why didn't you marry her when you knew she was pregnant?' Martin asked when he finally found his voice.

'What, and spend the rest of my life mowing the lawn every Sunday? Women only want children and houses—best to avoid all that . . .' He looked proud of himself.

Somehow Martin's shock finally dissolved: all he wanted was to spend years hearing all his father's stories. 'How did you know I was your son?' he asked, but his father merely smiled and touched the side of his nose. 'A—A—And why did you contact me?'

Martin James McClintock leant closer. 'Actually, I've got a little something put aside I was hoping you might do something with . . .'

It was so outrageous that Martin laughed: the old devil was stupendously, gloriously cheeky.

One morning, six months after Martin found his

father and had made him a nice tidy sum of twenty thousand pounds, he sent a telegram to his father's house enquiring about his next visit. His father did not have a telephone but usually responded to Martin's telegrams by phoning reverse charges from the local pub. Yet Martin did not hear from him that day or the next. The following weekend Martin caught the train to Suffolk.

He found the house empty, the front door open, his father gone.

'Left last week,' a neighbour said, 'didn't leave no forwarding address neither.'

Martin could not believe it: he made enquiries but his father had disappeared as mysteriously as he had arrived.

He felt outrageously cheated, and grieved in a hard, painful way totally unlike the muted grief he had once felt for his mother. Everything rightfully his had been torn from him, his life felt as if it had been shredded.

Soon after he applied for the job in Hong Kong.

After seven years in the colony, Martin was beginning to feel restless. Although he had more money than he had ever envisaged, which secretly aroused in him a searing sense of triumph, it sometimes made him feel trapped. A flat tax of fifteen per cent made it very difficult to consider going elsewhere and, anyway, whenever Martin thought of leaving, he did not know where he would go. He now owned a house on one of the outlying islands, as well as three properties in England: two townhouses in a new development in Wapping and a big house in South Kensington, one he had passed as a boy and vowed one day he would own. A Japanese family lived in it for an exorbitant rent, keeping it neat as a pin. On his occasional business trips to London Martin always made a point of admiring its beauty and bulk, its Georgian features which belonged solely to him.

On these trips, he considered moving back but was always put off by the thought of resuming some lesser job in which he would pay higher tax. Walking across Hyde Park in the chill autumn air he saw boys gathering horse-chestnuts for games of conkers, men in expensive coats walking expensive dogs. Part of him longed to take his place among them, to live a life of beauty and shape. He was beginning to wish for a wife, for a certain permanence and order. In his firm in Hong Kong he was one of two remaining 'golden bachelors' and for some time now he had felt obscurely embarrassed by this, cruelly exposed.

Each time Martin met a new woman his hopes raced. Outwardly he tried to appear ironic and detached but some part of him was still incurably hopeful. He carried with him an inchoate longing for completion which had never been met; for some wholeness which he had lost. He sincerely wanted to change his life, to leave behind the dark and dwell only in light. He yearned to fall in love, to blot out his pain and rid his life of everything cruel. While he tried to tell himself that his penchant for the whip was a kind of love play, no more remarkable than a preference for oral sex, he was sometimes paradoxically struck by distaste for his actions, a sense of shame. In truth he wished to learn new ways, gentler, more tender. Frequently now he felt intolerably lonely and had embarrassing fantasies of sitting quietly in the evenings with someone who loved him.

He was always disappointed when a woman proved a lesser creature than he had imagined, less intelligent, less giving. For a while he had been involved with an English journalist named Helen and they had even discussed living together. Ever since the debacle with Joanna he had been wary of girls moving in, but Helen appeared unusually level-headed and sincere. It took Martin some time to realize that his pay packet was as much an attraction for her as he himself was, that after marriage Helen had every intention of retiring. Martin did not want children or a dependent wife, and this only bolstered a private belief that most women went on and on about independence yet fully expected a man's money to provide them with lifetime support. In this, his father had been right.

After that first time Martin had not stopped going to prostitutes. He found he had a taste for it, for the power it granted, the licence to do anything he wanted. He remembered his father had spoken nostalgically of them: lovely Italian girls he had hired in the war, Hollywood starlets down on their luck. Martin soon heard of beautiful Russian call-girls on nearby Macau, a place which had a totally different feel to Hong Kong, less hardworking, more licentious. It was known for gambling, prostitution, drug dealing, as a destination where men with shiny new passports from obscure west African countries could enter Asia to do deals. The Russian prostitutes worked from one of the island's casinos, blonde women mostly, some of them startlingly beautiful.

Martin took to frequenting this casino, taking his pick of the women. They all seemed to be called Natalia or Natasha and appeared to him largely indistinguishable. He liked clutching one on a verandah at night overlooking the South China Sea. He felt like his father, reckless, dangerous, a man not intending to live the rest of his life playing safe. Drunk on a hot night he existed as nothing more than his senses, loosed, expanding.

Depending on which girlfriend he was with, Martin moved in and out of different circles. For a while, when he was going out with Helen, he hung out with her mainly female journalist friends at the Foreign Correspondents' Club. With Rita, an American he went out to dinner with intermittently, he mixed with public relations people. Of course, in Hong Kong it was not unusual for these circles to overlap because the actual number of Westerners was not great. Gossip was rife in such a small, tight place; private lives became the property of the public. Certain men in important positions were known for dallying with local girls, for example, for 'getting into the bamboo' and bringing well-travelled diseases home to wives. Others were known as gamblers, drunks, as lazy or corrupt men who had plenty to hide. Yet there was a singular tolerance for bad behaviour, an acceptance of Hong Kong as a place without the usual edges, a place given over to extremes.

The only male friend Martin had made in seven years was an eccentric Englishman with the peculiar name of Teddy Stumble. Teddy Stumble was famous for having personally saved two hundred thousand pounds in cash while living off tins of cold baked beans and cheap take-away noodles from dubious market stalls. He was a colleague of Martin's, the only other remaining 'golden bachelor', well regarded by the firm who had transferred him from head office in London on an enormous salary. As part of his employment package, Teddy Stumble was given a sumptuous flat in a highrise block on the Peak which, in his initial two-year contract, he had managed to turn into a hovel.

Martin was endlessly amused by Teddy Stumble, by his otherworldliness, indeed by his very obliviousness to the twentieth century. He liked the way Teddy Stumble did not notice that all businessmen in the colony had a uniform: elegant suits cut from expensive cloth, polka-dot ties in yellow or red, carefully folded handkerchiefs in a breast pocket. It cheered him to see Teddy Stumble's frayed shirt cuffs, his one unattractive brown suit and single pair of creased plastic shoes. Martin was also impressed by the fact that before he had become a trader Teddy Stumble had taken a first in history from Oxford, then effortlessly taken a second degree in theology from Trinity. He was a rare thing in Hong Kong: a voracious reader, a thinker, indeed, a scholar.

Over time Martin had developed a friendship with Teddy Stumble. They regularly took long hikes together, equipped with sun hats and water bottles, into the wild hills of outlying islands. While they never actually discussed anything of a personal nature Martin believed they shared an unspoken understanding. On these hikes they discussed St Thomas Aquinas, the speeches of Churchill, the nature of music. Martin was reminded of his younger self, a whole side of his personality the colony had all but extinguished.

The two golden bachelors walked over hills, sipping water and talking of nature. On these trips Martin dressed in his oldest clothes and felt his more elegant business-suited self fleeing. Together they sat in dirty eating houses and ate with the locals, oblivious to the spitting around them. Martin felt dirty and free, and did not mind paying for Teddy Stumble's drinks.

Teddy Stumble had never been seen with a woman, nor been known to have ever gone out with one. To Martin he seemed entirely asexual, as if he hadn't yet noticed the existence of sex, or indeed the presence of women. Martin supposed that if Teddy Stumble had a sexuality at all it would feature men, in the sense that women were not in his universe.

Martin did not give a damn: he only knew that in Teddy Stumble's blind sexless company he felt rested, and did not miss the company of women.

Martin began to feel restless in his job, to take risks in order to counteract boredom. He made a few gambles but fortunately they came good and he began to take bigger and bigger risks. He began trading in high-risk derivatives, which required he keep his nerve amidst the sharp eyes of rival traders. He took a short straddle—in essence a bet—that a leading stock market was in for a period of relative calm, and sat back to await the results. He only had to wait a couple of weeks but it suddenly seemed a long time. If he had wanted to jolt himself out of boredom he had certainly achieved it: each morning he worked with every sense on standby, his blood racing.

'Taking a big one there, Mr Bannister,' Teddy Stumble said to him one morning, bringing him a mug of Chinese tea. Teddy Stumble had a reputation for brilliance on the floor, an intuitive genius for reading the market. Martin would not have spoken to anyone else about the way he had left himself so exposed but he did not mind broaching the subject with Teddy Stumble.

'It'll be fine,' Martin assured him with bravado.

Teddy Stumble sat down. 'I trust you've hedged your bets.'

'C—C—Certainly.' Martin fervently hoped that he had hedged them enough, that his clients' money would cover any potential losses.

Teddy Stumble peered at him through thick glasses: one arm had come off his glasses and he had repaired them with masking tape, giving the impression that he was the victim of a recent accident.

'The only rule I go by, Martin, is that the market is always right,' Teddy Stumble said. 'You must never think you can beat it.'

Coming from anyone else Martin would have been offended: coming from Teddy Stumble it seemed like good advice.

When the stock market not only proved calm but began to rise, Martin's spirits rose too. On the day he cashed in his contracts he felt invincible.

'Come on, Teddy, I'll buy you lunch,' he said, grabbing his coat.

They took a ferry across the harbour to the Peninsular, one of the last remaining colonial hotels. In Gaddi's, Martin ordered the best Russian caviar with the best pure Vodka, French champagne to follow with Scottish salmon. Teddy Stumble drank and ate as if it were his last meal: he was famous for his long pockets, for disappearing when it was his turn to buy a round of drinks. Nevertheless he ate his lunch without any obvious prick of conscience, pleased to be privy to success. Martin had no idea what Teddy Stumble did with his carefully hoarded money, as far as Martin knew he owned no property, no cars, took no holidays.

Martin looked over at him now, contentedly chewing, his hollowed cheeks billowing with pleasure.

'W—W—What are we going to do with all our money, Teddy? What shall we buy?'

Teddy finished chewing then took a quick gulp of champagne before answering.

'I've just bought the old man a house in Kent,' he said. 'I don't know what I'll do with the rest.'

Who'd have thought it? Martin thought. The last golden bachelor spending his money on buying his old father a house.

He wished his own scoundrel of a father was still around to see how well he had done.

··

ANNE-LOUISE: CLOSER TO THE SURFACE OF THE EARTH

WITH a jolt Anne-Louise realized she had been at Hilary's gallery almost two years to the day. She was sitting on the tube when this realization hit and it was all she could do to remain in her seat. She felt a sick panic which washed over everything, not stopping to settle on anything in particular. Suddenly her whole life seemed to have escaped her, leading her into dried-up tributaries when she had intended to plunge headlong into open sea. In two years she had not completed one satisfactory painting, nor had any of the grand adventures she had once imagined. She had always pictured herself doing something magnificent, yet here she was on a dirty tube travelling between King's Cross and Euston.

She looked around with contempt at the other commuters. She could not bear to think she was anything like them and at the next stop flung herself from the carriage. On impulse she caught a train to Dover, then a ferry across the channel, where she rang Hilary from Paris to say she wouldn't be in. 'Where did you say you were?' Hilary asked and Anne-Louise laughed. 'I said I can't come into work today because I'm unavoidably detained on the Boulevard St Michel,' she said, and hung up. She knew Hilary would forgive her.

She spent the day imagining alternative realities for herself. She fell in love with a Marquis, who bought her a studio in the rue Dante and took her home each evening to a beautiful cottage in the forests of Fontainebleau. She painted a painting which won the Turner Prize and became the most hotly collected young artist around, feted in both Paris and London.

Sitting in a café sipping a diabolo menthe Anne-Louise vowed that she would begin afresh as soon as she got back to London.

Fortuitously, an opportunity soon presented itself. A man she vaguely knew offered her a job in arts administration, organizing shows and exhibitions to do with the Commonwealth.

'You mean the colonies,' Anne-Louise joked.

'We don't use that term any more,' the man said.

She had met him, a rather boring old fart she had believed connected to the British Council, at one of Hilary's dinner parties. It turned out that he was a big wig at the Commonwealth Institute in Kensington. Although she had no real experience it did not occur to her to question her ability to do the job.

For the first time in years Anne-Louise had surplus money, which she soon began to dispense happily.

First of all she abandoned the Bayswater bedsit and took a flat in Ladbroke Grove. It was newly renovated and she bought Turkish carpets and gilded mirrors, French chairs, an ornate hallstand. The flat was soon crammed, stamped with her style, slightly overblown though elegant. Anne-Louise liked expensive things and was a regular at the Conran Shop and other exclusive designer stores. She ran three credit cards and was soon overdrawn on every one; she wrote cheques with flourish and no forethought. She began once more to indulge her love of outlandish clothes and before long her new cupboards were bulging.

Very quickly Anne-Louise became the centre of a social group in her new job, a regular thrower of extravagant parties. She usually hired a handsome waiter and had the party catered, making sure everyone had plenty to drink. At these parties she swanned around with a cigarette and a ready quip on her lip, enjoying living frivolously and telling herself she would start painting seriously again very soon.

She infrequently sent off hastily scrawled postcards to Rachel in Australia, saying she was having profound fun. If she sometimes missed Rachel's guarded little face she also knew there was nothing to be done about it: going home to Australia would be like defeat and she was determined never to be felled.

Occasionally Anne-Louise looked up and saw the

ordinariness of London, its plain suburban people indistinguishable from the plain suburban people of Sydney and made herself look away again until her eye landed once more on the spectacular. Sometimes too she experienced London as ugly and cold but consoled herself with the thought that this was the price she had to pay for being away from everything safe and expected.

There were other things as well she tried not to think about: her fear of losing her mind, of never achieving what she hoped for as a painter. Most of the time she succeeded in assuring herself that her madness would not come again, for it had been almost two years and she had suffered no further attacks. Yet sometimes at night fear overcame her and she lay poisoned with it, her heart rocking.

These days she tried to relegate her painting to the far reaches of her mind but now and then the thought of it caught her in the chest like a physical pain. It usually passed soon enough but when it didn't she angrily got out her pencils or charcoal and attempted to draw. Sometimes she stuck it out for an hour or two but was invariably struck by a terrible lethargy. A kind of laziness came over her like sleep, stilling her hand and making her yawn. She sometimes lost hours hunched over blank paper, doodling, achieving nothing. It was always easier to get up and pour herself a drink, to walk away and do something else. Her self-discipline had entirely vanished, leaving in its wake only pain and a destructive boredom.

Anne-Louise's mother had been to England to visit her once since her father died. Anne-Louise had the distinct impression that this arms-length relationship suited her. 'You'd never get such a wonderful job in Australia,' Margaret Buchan said proudly.

Her mother belonged to an older generation of Australians who regarded England as home and she could not be shaken from the idea that it was a place of beautiful rolling countryside, superior culture, well-spoken citizens, pomp and circumstance. The Australian television soap 'Neighbours' had not long started and Margaret Buchan was horrified. 'What must they think of us!' she cried.

'I'll take you out to East Ham, darling, and you can ask,' Anne-Louise replied.

The visit was a strain: each time Anne-Louise attempted to broach any subject deeper than Royal marriage scandals or shopping, her mother attempted to cut her off at the pass. Anne-Louise wanted to speak about her father, ask questions she had long put off, to talk about her fears of going mad. She wanted to know if anyone else in the family had ever been mentally ill: she knew virtually nothing about her father's side of the family.

'There were no problems like that,' her mother said one morning in answer to a direct question, 'absolutely none.'

Anne-Louise saw her mother's mouth instinctively clench, as if she were holding words in.

'But how do you know for sure?' Anne-Louise asked. 'In the past these things were always covered up because they were considered shameful.'

Margaret Buchan unexpectedly met her eyes. 'Look, darling, you're all right now, aren't you? What's the point of worrying when you're well?'

Anne-Louise looked at her mother, so unwilling to tiptoe through the door.

'OK, let's leave it for now,' she said. 'I understand.'

For the first time Margaret Buchan looked annoyed. 'There's nothing *to* understand, Anne-Louise. All right?'

So Anne-Louise left it like her mother wanted: in the dark where she clearly felt it belonged. It did not stop Anne-Louise from waking panicked in the night, long after her mother was safely back in the warm reassuring arms of Brisbane.

Although Anne-Louise still believed she was not the kind of girl men wanted to marry, this did not prevent her from feeling that she was at least owed something. She felt it was her due to be entertained by a witty man at least once in a while and reckoned that having someone around who was fond of her was not asking too much. Yet most men she fancied did not fancy her and those who did she couldn't stand. 'He reminds me of a tapeworm,' she said to Hilary, dismissing one besotted suitor in an instant.

She had recently had a longish fling with a modestly well-known writer but he had proved to be paranoid, forever on the alert for snubs. He was completely self-obsessed, convinced that everyone was out to get him. He did not seem to notice Anne-Louise much, or even pay attention to the fact that they were supposed to be going out together. During sex he grunted and sweated over her like a pig and Anne-Louise was always relieved when the act was over. He imagined himself particularly accomplished at oral sex too and took to her most delicate parts like a starving man let loose on a pot roast, all saliva and keenly working jaws. Each time, Anne-Louise had given a thrust of her hips and a little moan as soon as she convincingly could, in an attempt to get him quickly off. She supposed it was because of other women pretending like herself that he had come to believe himself so gifted.

When they broke up she could not resist a parting shot. 'David,' she said, 'you know how you think you're such an expert at oral sex?'

He looked at her.

'I was faking.'

Anne-Louise was surprised to find that she quite liked her job, the organizing part of it especially, and that she was good at it. Since she had always been the most disorganized person imaginable, Anne-

Louise found it remarkable that she should possess any talent in this direction. As long as she kept a diary and was scrupulous about writing everything down, she found she could juggle numerous balls. What she was not so skilled at was massaging egos— Canadian painters who believed themselves important, Kenyan sculptors used to travelling first class. In her initial few months Anne-Louise had unfortunately sent one man packing, and was given a firm admonishment over the incident by her immediate boss. For the first time in her life she tried to rein herself in, to place her private feelings to one side.

The test came when she had to arrange the itinerary for a visiting artist from the West Indies. He was so pompous he set her teeth on edge within minutes of meeting him, ordering her around as if to serve him was her sole purpose on earth.

'I won't speak to the *Guardian*,' he announced loftily, 'they ran a most discourteous piece last time.' He cast his eye down Anne-Louise's proposed media interviews, ticking off those he would and would not do.

'Oh, most definitely no,' he said, sucking a Waterman pen. Anne-Louise had to stifle an urge to rip it from his self-important mouth. She had spent the best part of a week organizing the schedule he was so carefully running his expensive pen through.

She sat back in her chair and breathed calmly. 'Get me a car would you,' he ordered. 'I'm due at the Oriental Club in Stafford Place.'

Anne-Louise stood up, knowing it was her finest hour. 'Certainly, Mr Henderson,' she said graciously, walking demurely out.

Before long her self-control began to pay off and she was given the odd travel perk. She flew to Bombay to organize an exhibition, to Montreal with a group of British artists. In Montreal she came across an Australian contingent at the show and was invited to their opening. She stood around drinking many glasses of good Australian wine, making idle chat with an intense young artist.

'I'm only here for three days,' the woman said. 'I've got to fly back to Sydney for another opening.'

Anne-Louise was only half-listening. 'Oh, poor you. The tortured life of the internationally success-ful artist,' she said with heavy sarcasm but the woman did not appear to notice. Anne-Louise looked over the artist's shoulder wondering if there was someone more interesting she could talk to.

Undeterred the woman kept talking. 'It's an all-woman show at the Roslyn Oxley Gallery, two others and me.'

Anne-Louise's attention was caught: she knew the Oxley Gallery well, it was one of Sydney's most prestigious and one she had once imagined exhibiting in herself. 'I'm doing figurative work,' the woman continued. 'Rachel Gallagher, one of the other . . .'

'Rachel?' Anne-Louise interrupted.

'Do you know her work?'

She snorted. 'No, I don't "know her work", I know her.'

'Really? She's doing some interesting stuff at the moment, quite Gothic. One ...'

But Anne-Louise was no longer listening. She was thinking about Rachel and her Gothic paintings hanging in Sydney's Roslyn Oxley Gallery. She had not had a letter from Rachel in months and thought she now understood why.

Anne-Louise could not quite bring herself to write to Rachel, although she knew she should. She knew she should write and congratulate her but Rachel's success stuck in her throat, blocking out any upsurge of goodwill. It made Anne-Louise feel surly instead, causing her to ponder why Rachel should have success and not her when she believed herself to be equally, if not more, talented. She began to put it down to all sorts of things: that Rachel had somehow cleverly managed to work the system in Australia, that the very fact of her being there had given her an advantage over herself. She remembered too that Rachel had always been good at establishing contacts with the right people, going about it in a very subtle way. In fact, in her own sly way, Rachel Gallagher was ever so slightly devious and had always played her cards close to her chest.

Anne-Louise remembered all this but felt only marginally better. Back in London her life took on a new sour tone, as if she now had a bitter taste in her mouth that nothing could scour from her tongue.

When she was offered a promotional transfer not long after the successful Montreal show, she leapt at the offer with relief. The position was as administrative head for an arts centre in Hong Kong, a place she had never been. She knew very little about the colony but it did not matter: until now she had not admitted to herself how sick she was of her whole life. She was packed and ready to go within a month and barely had time for goodbyes.

Flying into Hong Kong for the first time Anne-Louise Buchan felt a seething in her blood, above her head she sensed the mustering of fate. She could not have explained it rationally but it was as if all around her something was gathering.

She could have sworn she felt the breath of destiny upon her face as the plane moved out of the heavens, closer to the surface of the earth.

....

RACHEL: THE CERTAINTY OF PAINT

HONG KONG became to me a place fraught with danger, a place of lurking violence and malignant intent. While some part of me understood that I was simply projecting my own fears on to the city, this did not make me any less scared. Terrible things kept happening to people I knew, or people I knew second-hand. One night my husband and I were invited to a party on a junk in the harbour but for some reason we did not go. That night the partying junk was hit by another vessel: a man I knew had both his legs severed above the knee, a girl I had met casually at a swimming pool was thrown overboard by the impact, struck her head, and drowned. I remembered her long graceful neck, the glide of her arms through the pool's chlorinated blue water. In the harbour's poisonous froth she must have sunk to the bottom, her long neck broken, her blond hair streaming like light. A week later the man whose legs had been severed died too, of a blood clot which targeted his shocked heart.

I wondered what stroke of fate prevented it being us; I wondered when it would be our turn. When I took elevators in tall buildings I steadied myself for the inevitable plunge, when I walked beneath construction sites I waited for the bamboo pole to pierce my flesh, the falling concrete slab to knock me to the ground. I heard of an ex-boyfriend of a woman I knew who was killed by a runaway bus careering down a very steep hill, and on New Year's Eve in Lan Kwai Fong twenty-one people were crushed underfoot, suffocating and dying help-lessly at a street party which got out of control. Most of them were young Chinese, pushed into a cul-de-sac with the crowd swelling behind them and nowhere to go.

That these incidents were meaningless and random made me fear them all the more and I began to trace a path as far as possible away from buses, crowds, elevators, boats, any room in which I could not see the door. I feared for my safety but I also feared for my mind: I was frightened and flailing, estranged in a place of estrangement. At night, lying at a great distance from my husband in our king-sized bed, my heart beat hard like a child frightened of the dark, making out shapes on the wall. I was making out shapes in the dark and all of them were monstrous, and mine.

I remember settling in effortlessly after I got back to Sydney from France, anonymous as a single fish swimming in its own school. It seemed to me that nothing had changed, that I had simply returned to some space left vacant for me. No-one seemed to have found my absence remarkable, nor my return, but merely acted as if I was as predictable as a new day. I realized how easy it is to live in one's own place, how a single drop of water becomes part of an ocean, subject to tides and the moon. Straight away a certain strenuous alertness which living in another country requires fell away from me and a sense of ordinariness, of the commonplace, returned. I grieved a little, for although I did not yet know the details of my forthcoming life in Australia, the outward form of life at least was already well known to me. I knew my place, my country, like the map of my own hand and while there was comfort in this there was also a certain flatness. Yet instinctively I felt I had done the right thing in returning: my work was there, the rocks and stones I knew best, my history, my understanding. It was only when friends acted as if I had simply been away on some kind of long weekend and supposed I was the same person who had left that I feared suffocation and wished to run away again, to reinvent myself one more time. At these moments I wrote to Anne-Louise, who seemed to understand this contradiction perfectly.

I took a cheap flat in Darlinghurst above a shop on a moderately busy road. It had a sunroom attached which passed as a studio and I began to paint at once. I painted the perfect forms of babies, icons of innocence, all I had lost, my perfection before my fall. These babies sat in the middle or on the edges of all my work, in complicated landscapes, in dark seas, in nightmarish skies. I did not call them up consciously but they came unbidden, as if to remind me of something forgotten. In this I was more like my mother than I could comfortably admit, for I recognized that these babies were a symbol for simplicity and order, an otherwise inadmissible yearning for a world without ambiguity or despair. I saw that for me paint had become my only certainty and I craved it. Every picture I made was a triumph over meaninglessness, every painting gave my life shape and direction. For the first time I realized that everything else in my life represented something I had to learn but art was something I was. I could wrest shape out of chaos through art's guiding form, through its struggle to transcend disarray and I could not understand how other people lived without this.

When I finally stood back and looked at my paintings I saw that the end result was bizarre, almost grotesque. Each painting was a point of entry into myself, a private story metaphorically told. I knew the test would come when I placed the paintings before other people: I had to find out if my story was entirely personal, or if it told everyone's story.

Before I mustered the courage to approach a gallery I set about finding myself a part-time job. I didn't want a job which had anything to do with art, not teaching, not magazines, nothing which would leech even a fraction of the creative energy demanded by my work. I wanted something mindless and mundane, some routine physical task which would not tax that part of me I used to paint. In this I was like a holy woman who kept herself apart from the world. I recognized that I would have to protect myself from interruption and diversion, from late nights and dinner parties at which I might be tempted to have too much to drink. Socializing required too much of my energy and I began to turn invitations down. I lived like a nun, sinless and pure, an empty vessel into which I poured only my work. I rose at dawn in the soft Sydney light and painted until I grew hungry. I wanted nothing else and yet I also knew I would soon be broke.

One lunchtime I was walking down Stanley Street when I saw a sign posted to the window of a Spanish restaurant. The restaurant was seeking part-time waitresses and without hesitating I went inside.

'I was wondering about your sign . . .' I said to a large woman with an apron, smoking behind the till.

'You've had experience, my beauty?' she asked as if it were only a formality and she was uninterested in my reply. She had a round, lovely face, dark, southern European, with full lips and humorous eyes.

I smiled and nodded my head, attempting to look willing and alert.

She asked if I would like a coffee. 'Sit down,' she said, indicating an empty chair.

Three coffees later I left with the possibility of a job.

Very quickly my life assumed a pattern and I settled into the regularity of days. I painted for ten or twelve hours each day and worked at the restaurant four and sometimes five nights a week. Occasionally I saw a friend for coffee or a meal but I did not feel particularly close to anyone. Instead I often felt as if I were taking part in the outward form of friendship only, as if I were merely performing some long dead ritual. I sometimes spoke on the phone to my mother in Brisbane but our conversations were cursory, without passion. It was a strange, solitary existence and I often felt as if I lived my most vital life inside my own head.

I missed Anne-Louise, for she had somehow become my one intimate friend in whose company I need say nothing, or everything. I longed to have someone to talk to about the small movements of my daily life yet I also knew there were now too many subjects she and I could not broach.

I began to wish that I could fall in love. I had my painting, a clear sense of where I was headed and yet at night my life sometimes felt empty. I wondered if it was greedy to wish for love too but I could not stop myself wanting it. Alone in my bed in the dark I dreamed of a man, a man I would recognize at once. He was faceless to me but I believed him to be out there, I believed him to be somewhere, breathing.

MARTIN: THE ILLUSION OF ANSWERS

ONE Friday night when Martin was delivered by jetfoil and taxi to the casino in Macau, he noticed some men filing into a room. The room was off one of the main blackjack rooms, or rather a door led off into what he presumed to be another room. Men were knocking on this door and being admitted singly, or in groups of two or three. Most of them cast a final look over their shoulder before entering the door, as though checking something. Martin could not see who was opening the door from where he stood, so he moved closer. It was his habit to take a stroll around the various rooms of the casino before selecting a girl, to have several drinks while he roamed around. He was not a gambler and the tables did not interest him, in fact he considered gamblers failures or fools. He could not imagine losing or winning money by such a senseless means himself and saw no connection between his own job and this. As far as he could see, gamblers were life's losers, gripped, fervent men rendered insensible. The room was hazy with smoke thick as fog, crammed with people and unbelievably noisy and Martin moved toward the door with relief.

Hovering just outside it, Martin saw a young European woman ushering a man in: she caught his eye and smiled before she closed the door. He had not seen her before, she looked young and unpeeled, unlike her older, more worn colleagues. Her small breasts were visible beneath a sheer blouse, fleshless, almost muscular. Martin took a sip of his drink and waited for the door to open again, to catch another glimpse of the girl.

When two Chinese men approached, obviously drunk, a bouncer appeared seemingly out of nowhere and skilfully steered them away. They argued loudly with him in Cantonese, red-faced, angry. Martin's attention was on them before he noticed that the door was ajar and the girl was holding it open specifically for him, giggling and beckoning him with a small finger. He looked around before moving towards her, his eyes falling involuntarily to her breasts.

Inside the room it was dark and smoky and at first he could not make anything out. As his eyes slowly re-adjusted he saw men sitting around in chairs, grouped around a kind of stage. On this stage, which was dimly lit, a girl lay trussed, her legs splayed and pulled painfully up behind her. Her arms were pulled up tightly too so that her ankles and wrists were roped together, making it impossible for her to move. She was gagged and twisting, trying to break free, and at the sight of her Martin immediately grew hard. Her eyes were wild in her head, she appeared to be trying to bite off the gag. Martin knew it must be a stage-managed act and yet the girl looked genuinely panicked, exhibiting the authentic writhe of fear. Martin smelt the unmistakable reek of it and quickly looked around: the faces of the men in the room were concentrated and tense and Martin saw that some of them were masturbating. He felt sick and aroused at once and his eyes returned to the girl. He held his breath when a man stood up and began to unbuckle his belt. The girl tried hard to move her whole body away but she was helplessly pinned. As the man got ready to mount her Martin stood up and pushed his way from the room.

He made blindly for the door, closing it too loudly behind him. Outside, he saw the bouncer leaning against the opposite wall looking at him curiously and he took a few quick breaths in an effort to compose himself. He was breathing hard as if he had run a great distance and felt soiled, close to vomiting. Breathing in, Martin walked away, telling himself to walk slowly. He passed through the gambling rooms and headed for the lifts, passing one of the indistinguishable blonde Natalias or Natashas. She smiled hopefully at him but it was all he could do to nod his head in return. He stepped into the lift alone and headed for his room, where he immediately stripped off and had a hot shower. He turned his face up to the stinging fall and pressed the palms of each hand hard into his eyes, as if he might expunge the rancid image behind them.

Martin did not take a girl that night but slept alone and all his dreams were terrible. They were filled with sensations of remorse, of mistakes which could not be rectified. He was driving a car and knocked someone down: the person was most certainly killed. He leant over the body and knew the soul inside to be inescapably gone, irretrievably lost to him. He did not recognize who the person was but grieved at the irreversible nature of his actions. At four o'clock he woke up knowing he had made some unseemly sound in his sleep and its echo was still in the room.

Martin had made a prior arrangement to meet Teddy Stumble for lunch but did not feel much like going. He had tried to sleep in the morning after his disastrous night but only succeeded in crumpling the sheets. He ate a late breakfast in his room and felt like seeing no-one, not even the good and oblivious Teddy Stumble. It seemed to Martin at that moment that Teddy was fundamentally blind to the messiness of life, the least embroiled person Martin knew. At the same time Martin wished he could be more like him, a man of no obvious needs, unencumbered. On mornings like this Martin wished for nothing more than to drop his own skin, to walk away from himself into a fresh life.

He sat in his room in an unhappy stupor until he glanced down at his watch. He was supposed to have met Teddy at the jetfoil terminal ten minutes before.

The jetfoil was late as it happened and when it finally docked, Martin watched the passengers streaming off. Locals, gamblers mostly or housewives with cabbages and flapping chickens, tourists and expatriates from Hong Kong on a flying visit for lunch. Macau was famous for these long drunken lunches, where groups of loud men and women ate copious amounts of seafood and Portuguese chicken, accompanied by endless bottles of cheap imported *vino verdi*. They regularly crashed rented jeeps on the return journey from lunch or plunged motorbikes headfirst over bridges: Martin saw in their agitated excited eyes the readiness to begin. Normally he felt this lickerish flame race up him too but today he felt depressed, and everyone struck him as offensive. When he saw the bright unblemished face of Teddy Stumble he smiled with gladness: he watched Teddy's slightly bumbling progress, his broken, unfashionable glasses, his anonymous face. Teddy Stumble looked like everyone and no-one, none of his features were in any way remarkable, except that they existed in more or less all the right places. He appeared discomfited under Martin's gaze as he dutifully waved then filed through passport control to emerge on the other side.

'Good crossing?' Martin enquired and Teddy nodded his head.

'A little rougher than I expected. Certainly quicker than the old ferry to the outlying islands.'

'Is this your first time here?' Martin asked in disbelief, for Teddy had been in the colony nine years.

'I've never had a reason to come before,' Teddy replied.

Of course he wouldn't, Martin thought. Teddy did not spend his money on lunches or expensive jetfoil trips for he was not, after all, your typical Hong Kong expat.

This had the effect of cheering Martin. He himself was not typical either and with this reassuring thought they took their place in the inevitable taxi queue, two rare men, different.

Martin directed the driver to a restaurant he knew on one of the far beaches. He had luckily booked a table, for when they arrived there was already a long queue. People stood around drinking the local beer and eating baskets of freshly baked Portuguese bread, their uncovered mostly English ears turning pink in the sun.

At lunch Teddy ate with his usual relish and concentration, not talking much and generally unconscious of the din around him. It was very hot and the restaurant had no air-conditioning, only fans which disturbed the edges of the paper tablecloth at a certain point of each rotation. The tables were too close for Martin's comfort and he was conscious that conversation could be overhead. Every now and then some vacuous remark floated towards him, reminding Martin to keep his own voice low. The place was gloriously shabby, which made a change from the restaurants Martin usually ate in, and it never failed to make him feel agreeably raffish. He was wearing an old T-shirt with the sleeves cut out, a pair of shorts and flip-flops and, as he drank, the horrors of the night before slowly left him. In the bright hot light of the restaurant, images no longer disturbed him and after two further bottles of *vino verdi* he even felt a remnant of excitement. He began to look around once more, at tables of expatriate girls, willing and waiting.

As the afternoon wore on, Martin became aware of a certain dishevelment in both himself and Teddy, of a certain absurd quality which had crept into their conversation. He somehow found himself arguing in a loud, leaking voice to Teddy Stumble about the false promises of books and their illusion of answers.

'Y—Y—You can't learn everything from books, Ted,' he heard himself saying, 'surely you can only learn from living.' He was not sure whether he believed this but was too drunk to care.

'Excuse me,' Teddy said, his broken glasses slipping awkwardly down his greasy nose, 'but that's utter nonsense. You can learn everything from books. If you arrived on Earth from Mars you could learn everything you needed to know without speaking to another living soul.'

It flitted through Martin's mind to ask Teddy if you could learn about sex from books but he stopped himself. He looked drunkenly at Teddy, full of hopeless blinking innocence and felt the air between them. 'There are some things a book can never tell you,' he said, but it came out sounding merely pompous.

Just then Martin heard a deep, commanding female voice coming from somewhere behind him.

'Amazing. Two live men in Hong Kong not talking about money.'

Martin turned in his chair and saw a woman to his right with a big, vivid face graced with impressively dark eyes. Her eyes were huge in dark sockets, and focused intently on him.

'I'm afraid we've passed on from that subject,' he heard Teddy Stumble say from across the table and the woman began to laugh. Her laugh was outrageous, immense, and Martin began to laugh too. The two of them sat there, laughing hysterically, while Teddy Stumble looked perplexed and tried to work out what was so funny.

....

ANNE-LOUISE: A CIVILIZED MAN

A S Anne-Louise looked into Martin Bannister's pale green eyes for the first time she felt a brief prick of excitement. His eyes were strangely beautiful, their centres marbled, as if covered by a fine film of cataract. He was the most beautiful man she had seen in years and she took in at once his sensuous mouth, the full curve of his upper lip. She particularly liked his voice, which sounded studied, full of careful deliberation. Indeed, it was his soft stutter which first attracted her attention before she turned her head and looked into his face.

Now that she had seen him, Anne-Louise was instantly charmed. The fellow he was with was an uninteresting looking specimen with glasses badly in need of repair and Anne-Louise immediately dismissed him.

Before she could engage the good-looking one in further conversation, the nondescript man made a silly remark. She and the good-looking man started laughing and, without even trying, her path towards Martin James Bannister was cleared.

Inevitably Martin and Teddy joined Anne-Louise and

her friends. Anne-Louise's table was made up of people from work and her flatmate Christine plus a shy twenty-one-year-old Chinese photographer she had slept with the night before. He was so cute she would have liked to have kept him but she also knew she would grow unspeakably bored. 'Move up, sweetie,' she said, shooing him a few chairs along. She patted the seat next to her so Martin could sit down.

'Tell me what a civilized man is doing amongst barbarians,' she said to him in what she hoped was an encouraging manner.

He looked momentarily taken aback but then produced a winning smile, revealing clean white teeth. 'D—D—Dispensing largesse,' he replied, quick as a flash.

'You're my kind of man,' Anne-Louise said, leaning across and patting his hand. She was drunk and so was he but to Anne-Louise their conversation from this moment seemed fluid and effortless. When she thought of it later, it seemed to her that they did not go through the usual motions of advance and retreat a man and a woman meeting for the first time invariably adopt. Instead, their mutual drunkenness conferred on them what she supposed to be an easy intimacy. Right from the start Anne-Louise was under the impression that Martin James Bannister was a soul mate.

She arranged to meet him as soon as she could. It did not cross her mind that her haste may appear unseemly, for good behaviour was not something about which she cared, or was even conscious. 'Don't you think you should leave it a few days?' asked Christine when she went to phone him the next day. 'You don't want to look too eager.'

'Why not?' Anne-Louise replied. She was not in the least dissuaded by Christine's disapproving frown. 'Christine, listen to Mummy. Girlie behaviour is not good for you.'

Christine gave her a begrudging smile. An American-born Chinese, she was the perfectly groomed area manager for all Asia's Chanel shops and more used to men choosing her.

'Now watch closely,' Anne-Louise said, picking up the phone.

They arranged to meet for a drink in Grissini's in the Grand Hyatt overlooking Victoria Harbour. When Martin walked in Anne-Louise was already sitting at the bar with a cigarette and a Manhattan. He looked entirely different: he was wearing an expensive Italian suit and looked even more handsome than before. As he sat down on the stool next to her she felt a sudden lurch of nervousness and immediately gulped down the rest of her drink.

'Don't you scrub up well,' she said a little too quickly.

'O—O—One has to set an example,' he said with a smile and his disarming stutter. 'What are you drinking?'

She told him and he gave a kind of smirk

before ordering her another. 'That's a very silly drink, Anne-Louise,' he said. She felt a spasm of embarrassment but laughed to cover it up. There was something about him to which she immediately responded: she liked his cool, detached manner, his cultivated air of superiority. It marked him out, imbuing him with a certain authority. She did not yet know what he was superior about but was curious to find out. She noticed too the way he leaned nonchalantly against the bar in a pose so apparently relaxed his body did not appear to possess a single disgruntled nerve.

'W—W—Where's the rest of your convoy?' he asked.

'I gave them the slip,' she replied, taking another large swill of her drink. She liked the fact that they could immediately talk in code, that he was as sharp-witted as herself.

'Are you always surrounded by a posse?'

It had never occurred to Anne-Louise that her predilection for large groups was in any way remarkable. 'Isn't everyone?'

He took a sip of his drink and turned his fine eyes upon her. 'No,' he said in his polished English voice. 'F—F—Frankly I can't think of anything worse.'

At that moment Anne-Louise could not either: she would forego any group for an hour alone with him. She pulled her eyes away from him and lit another cigarette.

'So, what are you doing in Hong Kong, Martin?

Escaping a bad marriage, making a million or don't you have anywhere else to go?'

He laughed. 'A little of all three,' he replied, turning towards her with what looked like real interest. 'What's your excuse?'

'I am gloriously washed up,' she declared with a theatrical sweep of her arm. Her hand happened to brush the leaves of an elaborate floral arrangement on the bar which crashed spectacularly to the floor.

'You see,' she said calmly as waiters rushed toward her from every direction, 'everywhere I go I wreak havoc.'

At dinner they continued to parry and Anne-Louise relaxed and began to enjoy herself. She drank far too much but it seemed in keeping with the spirit of exhilaration which had somehow flared up in her. She felt a great burst of excitement and laughed a lot and everything she said sounded pleasing. She felt herself growing beautiful and was ridiculously happy to be visible in Martin's marbled eyes.

They talked of London, of people they knew in common, about nothing in particular. Yet to Anne-Louise their talk seemed seamless, with no awkwardness or moments of boredom. As it grew later and later she felt her body pitching towards his, as a falling object rushes to the ground.

They went to his flat where they began to make love before they had finished their brandy. Anne-Louise was so drunk by then the room was already pulsating. When Martin leant over to kiss her she saw one perfect green eye enlarged as if magnified before she shut her own eyes and was released into her body's sweet swirling. She floated and drifted, as if moving in and out of consciousness, sensing only Martin's warm skin and his live breath upon her. Somewhere she recalled being on a carpet on the floor yet she was also adrift on some summery water, suspended and dreaming. When she felt her hands being pulled and pinned behind her back she giggled drunkenly and opened her eyes. She saw Martin's lovely face and the concentration upon it and quickly closed her eyes again. She dimly registered that he liked her restrained and struggling and her first instinct was to indulge him.

In the morning her body retained the memory of rough handling, which she acknowledged as passion's unyielding grip. She gently ran her hands up her tender stomach and breasts then raised both arms in the air. Her body remembered everything and felt galvanized.

As Anne-Louise stood alone on her balcony high above Hong Kong the next evening she knew at last why she had come. As natural light fled and a million lights beneath her bloomed she felt herself lighting up, becoming brilliant. She frantically attempted to dampen herself down but hopes she did not know she possessed had suddenly leapt into life, clamouring and calling for attention. She tried to convince herself that she was not in love, reminding herself of the long-held conviction that love was not in her life's plan. Yet escaped longings continued to race ahead of her, breaking free of every restraint.

She smoked another cigarette and considered calling Rachel, before realizing she would not know what to say. She was much too proud to admit to loosed dreams, much less before they were even realized. She hadn't even spoken yet to the recipient of those dreams and had no idea how he would receive them.

RACHEL: MY HUMAN OFFERING

MORE and more often in Hong Kong I felt myself to be dangerously teetering. Without warning my step would falter as I walked down the street and I had to remind myself to place one foot in front of the other, to compose my features into a semblance of calm. At such moments the towering buildings, the crowds of people, the noise of the traffic and jackhammers pressed upon me so that I wished to run. I went out less and less, spending all my time at the studio painting, trying to block out the roar. I was dimly aware that with my earplugs in and my door firmly locked I was also shutting out something which I wished not to hear or see.

I started to go to a room in a tall building where I paid a woman to sit and listen to me. She was English, icily reserved and scrupulously professional. Because I felt embarrassed, even self-indulgent, for a long time I did not speak and we sat together in silence. But my sense of social duty was too well developed and eventually I began to chatter aimlessly in order to fill up the spaces. I spoke of my work and my longing for order, my need to reconstruct the world. The woman merely nodded and listened, occasionally asking for clarification. Sometimes I blushed for no apparent reason, as if I were ashamed. Yet if the woman had asked me what it was exactly I was ashamed of I could not have told her.

It was as if there was a locked room somewhere in my head and in this room was everything shameful. My husband was in this room, along with parts of myself, everything that was fouled and broken.

I remember being very surprised when the first Sydney gallery I approached liked my work and wanted to discuss with me the possibility of taking part in a joint show. I was stunned, elated, and I suppose I believed my life would change completely at one fell swoop. I expected some clear division between my old hopeful painterly self and myself as a professional painter and felt as if I had been anointed, granted permission to breathe more successful air. I remember walking out of that gallery one brilliant spring day feeling like I had finally arrived. I was light on my feet, burnished, expanding, and could not remember what sadness felt like.

In the weeks leading up to my first show I was happy in the most simple way. Everything pleased me, from the bowl of spaghetti I cooked for my dinner to the one glass of good red wine I allowed myself to drink with it. When I walked out in the streets everything looked beautiful and once I happened to raise my head and the sun struck my eyes like a vision. The sun's rays fell down at perfect slants through the shivering leaves of trees and for that one shining moment I could not have requested anything more from life.

In the final days I went to the gallery to begin the task of hanging my paintings. Accompanied by the gallery director we arranged the paintings and to my surprise she considered seriously everything I said. I knew this woman by reputation and could not believe this formidable person was taking the time to talk to me. I felt myself shrinking and once or twice she asked me to repeat something.

'I like the idea of hanging them close together, without frames. What do you think, Mick?'

Her assistant Mick did not answer straight away. He was considering my paintings, naked and helpless on the wall. I was suddenly overcome by embarrassment: each painting struck me as too intimate, and I felt the cold rip of exposure. It was as if my most private self was sprawled on the wall, as if I lay pinned and dissected. It suddenly seemed barbaric that perfect strangers could come along and make any comment they liked, pronounce judgement on whether or not my human offerings were good or bad.

I must have made a move forward as if to claim myself back, for both Mick and the director turned towards me.

'Ah, I'm not sure if this was such a good idea,' I said to the floor.

The director smiled gently. 'Mick, why don't you take Rachel for a coffee. We don't have to finalize anything now.'

And so Mick and I walked out for a coffee and into our relationship, with the apparent sanction of authority, amid the protestations of my privately palpitating heart.

Mick Woodford was a painter, ambitious, gifted. His father owned a fish and chip shop in Clovelly having emigrated from England years before with the French wife he had met in the war. Mick's mother had died early and his father and elder brother looked upon him indulgently, not fully understanding him but proud of him anyway. He was not much taller than myself and looked distinctly French like the photographs of his mother, with soft brown eyes, dark skin and a finely wrought nose. 'My full name is Michel,' he told me as soon as he could. He declared his French background at every opportunity and clearly found it more inspiring than being a plain, unadorned Australian.

I found him funny and frenetic, his enthusiasms running in all directions. If straight away I knew that Mick Woodford was not the answer to my deepest needs, he was at least someone to make me feel less alone.

He was marvellous in the first days of my show, rushing out to buy the *Sydney Morning Herald* at dawn in order to vet my first review.

'It's OK,' he said as I tensely watched his face. 'It's not bad at all.'

I did not want to read it and yet I also couldn't wait: I watched as Mick put down the paper and took hold of my hands.

'Rachel,' he said softly, 'remember what I said about letting your work go? It's not just *your* work any more, it belongs to everybody. Now that you're in the public domain you can't plead special circumstances.'

I felt the blood rush to my face. 'Is it that bad?'

He smiled. 'No, of course not. It's a very respectable first review.'

I leant over and grabbed the paper from his knees, searching for my name on the page. It was a small review included with two others and my work rated only one or two lines. My eyes raced over the lines again and again trying to elaborate on their meaning. The critic wrote of 'confessional painting, undeniably female in its shape and construction. There is a self-absorbed quality to Gallagher's work and in this she belongs to that school of female artists which includes Mexico's Frida Kahlo and Australia's Joy Hester.'

I leapt up. 'What school of female artists? Frida Kahlo and Joy Hester have absolutely nothing in common! And how can a painting be undeniably female in its shape and construction for God's sake!'

Mick stood up too. 'Calm down. It's a

259

compliment to be included in the same sentence as Frida Kahlo and Joy Hester.'

I glared at him. 'It's a pretty back-handed one.'

Just then the phone rang. 'Tell whoever it is that I've jumped off the Sydney Harbour Bridge,' I shouted, heading for the door.

'Rachel!' Mick called in a pleading voice but I was already gone.

After the show closed I experienced a curious flatness. If I had thought my life would be changed forever I soon found that I was wrong. I was as anonymous as before, and eventually this came as a kind of relief. It took several months but I finally began to work again, to take pleasure in the genderless intelligence of paint. When I was at work on a painting nothing else mattered and I recognized that this was my salvation, my protection. My work was my inviolable core and inside this centre was perfect silence, free from any critical voices or eyes. Sometimes I had to struggle to make my way towards this core but once I reached it I knew I was safe. The only critical voices there were my own which sometimes threatened to engulf me. Yet I knew I could silence them through an act of will if I mustered courage and strength: the first paintings I made after the show were ineffectual and lost and I saw at once I would have to try harder.

About this time I realized it was many months since I had written to Anne-Louise. I knew she had left London and that she had a new, different life about which I knew nothing. I wondered if we had grown too far apart and then I remembered her deep, thrilling voice, her big, alive face, the way she left a trail of excitement.

There was no-one in the world like Anne-Louise Buchan and I sat down immediately to write her a long letter, to tell her of everything that had happened.

....

MARTIN: HER OWN
MASTERPIECE

THERE was some quality about Anne-Louise Buchan which attracted Martin to her straight away, some air of rebellion, a sense of escape. Her laugh was fully confident and suggested an inner recklessness, an intention to veer as close as possible to the edge. He found her more exciting than any woman he had met for some time and when she phoned him to suggest a drink he instantly accepted.

Yet she was not his physical type at all, taking up far too much space, her big face sailing before her like a prow. While he did not actively desire her, he found her presence, her intelligent eyes oddly compelling. Her spectacular laugh was a little disconcerting though, being so loud and raucous as to attract attention he did not necessarily want. He noticed it at their first meeting and it had struck him then as being wonderfully uninhibited but, in the sophisticated hush of Grissini's bar, he had to resist an urge to tell her to keep her voice down.

He divined at once that she was bright but that her talents were not being utilized. She radiated a fierce intelligence yet appeared somehow frustrated and Martin immediately wondered why.

He had not planned on ending their first evening in bed and was not sure if it was himself or Anne-Louise who initiated the first move. He knew only that they got very drunk and ended up on the floor having uneventful sex. Martin followed the familiar stirrings of his body but was tired and drunk and probably would have preferred to go to bed.

In the morning he did not feel rested and feigned sleep when he heard Anne-Louise stirring. Lying on the pillow with his eyes closed he felt as if he had been invaded. Her presence was so large, so vibrant and unpredictable that he felt overwhelmed and remained motionless, breathing deeply while Anne-Louise got out of bed and moved quietly about the room. When he heard her come out of the shower and begin to dress he risked partially opening his eyes and watching her through his eyelashes. She might be overwhelming but he was still intrigued by the sense of movement she created in the air around her.

She began to ask him out to a myriad of social events. He accepted almost every invitation because he could not quite make her out and wished to know more. There was some elusive quality to her, some sense of her attention being elsewhere. She seemed to have a million friends but adopted an off-hand manner with all of them, including himself. He was not sure if she even regarded him as a boyfriend but every now and then she surprised him by being demonstrative: leaping up to kiss him extravagantly when he joined her in a restaurant or grabbing his hand while walking down the street. It was impossible to know what she thought of him and vanity soon became part of whatever kept drawing him back.

She asked him to lunches, to parties, to junk trips on the harbour. Once she requested he accompany her to an evening in a private box at Happy Valley racecourse where she kept an entire table of conservative businessmen and their wives enthralled. Martin saw they were fascinated to see what would come out of her mouth next, whether it was an opinion on Hong Kong's archaic anti-homosexual laws ('I know you Chinese think playing with the flower in the back chamber doesn't exist, sweetie, but it does,' she said to the man sitting next to her, who giggled with embarrassment), or a story about the time in London when she almost got arrested in Oxford Street for revealing her breasts. Martin was amused to note that everyone at the table appeared torn between disapproval and admiration.

Yet even when they were alone Martin could never quite penetrate her careless veneer. He came closest when Anne-Louise was drunk, when something in her was released and she momentarily revealed a startling and unexpected vulnerability. A few times he imagined she was about to make some declaration of her feelings but he was always wrong. Once she began to tell him a story about her father

267

who had recently died and her eyes visibly clouded.

He leant across to her but she immediately drew back. 'It's all right, Martin,' she said, sitting straighter. 'I'm not about to launch into a sob story.'

He smiled at her but she had already retreated and was clearly unwilling to be coaxed.

Periodically they went to bed and Martin was surprised to discover that this was the only area in which Anne-Louise displayed passivity. She was disarmingly undemanding, following his lead at all times and asking nothing for herself. Once he gave her a few hard slaps on the buttocks with his hand and she made no response, lying inert beneath him.

He might have surmised that Anne-Louise was lacking in confidence yet could not reconcile this with what he knew of her standing upright. It was as if he could not quite make out her exact shape, like something moving fast in dark water. If he was not hopelessly in love with her, neither could he walk away.

One evening at midnight when Martin had just got into bed the telephone rang. 'I am profoundly bored,' Anne-Louise announced. 'Come and amuse me.'

For the first time he felt a flicker of irritation. 'Is this the same person who declared last week that only boring people get bored?'

She laughed. 'Probably.'

'No,' he continued, 'I—I—I can't come and amuse you.'

She gave a theatrical sigh into the phone. 'Oh, Marty why not?'

'Because I've got better things to do,' he replied, 'like sleep.'

There was a slight pause. 'Oh, well,' she said, 'I guess I'll just have to find someone else.'

Martin let her talk on for a while before telling her to jump in a taxi. The truth was that he had been bored for a long time too.

He had some chilled vodka in the freezer and when she arrived at the door he handed her a glass.

'What service,' she said approvingly, kissing his cheek.

He was determined to break through her defences and poured her another before she had even finished the first.

'Ah, the old leg opener,' she said, holding up her glass.

'N—N—Nothing is beyond me,' he replied, pouring himself a smaller nip.

She kicked off her shoes and lay her head on the back of the couch, closing her eyes. 'I am so sick of trying to explain art to philistines,' she said, her voice weary.

Martin had never been sure what her job entailed exactly because she always dismissed it with an airy wave of her hand.

'If only I was organizing corporate sponsorship for *Swan Lake*,' she said with a sigh.

'Anne-Louise,' Martin said, 'you're not making sense.' He suddenly felt cross with her.

She opened her eyes. 'I just had dinner with a real barbarian. His company has put up some big money for a new art prize and I made the mistake of thinking he might be interested in painting.' She gave a derisive snort. 'Do you know what he said? He actually said the world could go on quite happily without some wanker painting another painting. Can you believe it?'

Martin laughed. She sat up, looking furious.

'What are you laughing at? People like that should be shot.'

He laughed again. 'That's very liberal of you, Anne-Louise.'

She jumped up and stalked over to the vodka bottle, pouring herself a large glass. Still glowering at him she took a sip before launching into him again.

'I suppose you think art doesn't have a function either, except as a marketable commodity.'

'As a matter of fact I've never advised a client to invest in art,' he replied.

By now she had stopped pacing and resumed her seat. 'I bet you will now,' she said, as if with contempt. He had never seen her so obviously upset and grabbed the vodka bottle to sit down beside her.

'So, it's Anne-Louise versus mammon,' he said,

'I—I—I didn't know you were such a champion of starving artists.'

She glared at him. He topped up her glass yet again and once more she knocked it back quickly. An idea suddenly occurred to him.

'W—W—Were you ever a starving artist, my darling?'

She gave her great shout of a laugh then leaned over to tousle his hair. 'Oh, Martin Bannister, you're so sweet when you're attempting pop psychology.'

He could have sworn he saw a moment of disclosure before her well-practised social manner triumphed.

That night their conversation grew wilder and wilder, whether more ridiculous or more profound he could not tell. They talked of God and religion, of the nature of art, of the new physics, about which Anne-Louise knew a surprising amount. Towards morning she tried to explain to him some convoluted theory she had about everything in the universe being connected and how Australian Aboriginals had known this all along in concepts such as the dream-time. She was going on and on about particles being related to other particles but after a while Martin's attention began to drift. He was dimly aware that she was talking about chaos theory and how it could be incorporated into painting and how she intended to do this. By then he was sprawled on the floor staring at the whirring of the ceiling fan and made some half-serious remark about her not needing to create art because she was an original, her own masterpiece. If Anne-Louise heard him she took no notice and continued talking. As the room began to grow warmer she was still raving on about painting and connected universes. Martin closed his eyes and the last thing he saw was Anne-Louise's face lit by the sun, like a fire stoked, raging.

··

ANNE-LOUISE: THE PERFECTION WITHIN

WHEN Anne-Louise left Martin's flat that morning she was in love. As she emerged from the air-conditioned foyer into the wet, heavy atmosphere, every colour looked spectacular, the air felt voluptuous and when she raised her eyes high above the tower blocks, the mountains in the sky looked exaggerated, magnificent. A rag-and-bone man was passing slowly by, pulling his empty steel trolley and calling up to the highrise in lyrical Cantonese like an intricately composed song and Anne-Louise watched as an old Chinese woman came out of the building opposite and offered him an old burnt-out pan. His song stopped only for a moment while they haggled over price before carrying seamlessly on.

On the spur of the moment she decided to take the day off. She did not feel in the least tired and began the long descent down winding roads which would eventually lead her into Central. She waved off a taxi which had slowed down in the hope of a fare and headed towards the markets. She had always loved the sensuous heat and lush colours of Hong Kong and today everything looked even more dazzling. She wandered dreamily through the green sprout of the vegetable markets, admiring the teeming heads of lettuces, the hand-woven bamboo baskets heavy with oranges. Much of the produce was unknown to her: strange-looking grasses in bunches tied with string, long creeping weeds, unnamed fruits with skin like the hide of an animal. On the other side of the markets she emerged into the red and gold glitz of the herbal medicine shops, where the sliced and dried organs of the earth's disappearing animals lay displayed, the leaves and bark of enigmatic trees. She passed by slowly, looking at every single thing with great pleasure, filled with the sensations of love.

She remembered Martin's particular smell, strangely sweet, and how she was conscious of his breathing. She recalled the exact timbre of his voice, its soft deliberation, the way his hands had their own grace. As she walked she felt the earth beneath her, the balls of her feet, the sweep of life passing through her and unconsciously quickened her pace.

From that day on Anne-Louise hardly slept and rose every day at dawn. She had always finished breakfast by the time Christine got up and soon began to prepare Christine's breakfast too, so that it was waiting for her on the table after she had showered.

'What are you after, free rent?' Christine joked when faced with a glass of freshly squeezed orange juice, a sliver of melon and a perfectly cooked omelette.

'I am here to serve you,' Anne-Louise replied, smiling happily. She was slightly giddy from lack of sleep yet full of boundless energy. She felt unfailingly generous towards everyone and everything, over-flowing with purpose and goodwill.

'You're very chirpy these days,' Christine said to her as she drank her fresh juice.

But Anne-Louise merely smiled, keeping her secret within where it burned and raged.

She stopped smoking and began to jog up steep hills before work each day. Soon she stopped eating too and hunger only made her feel stronger. She felt com-posed of air and water, lightweight, free of the ground. During her lunch hour she shopped for clothes instead of eating, buying up dozens of silk shirts and linen skirts and dresses, small but costly items of lacy underwear. She bought mud packs for her face and took long, hot baths, she bought com-plexion powders made of the earth's clay. Alone in her bedroom she anointed herself with expensive gels and lotions, painting scented paste across her hairless thighs. Staring at herself naked in the mirror Anne-Louise unpicked herself piece by piece and found much that was wanting. She would have liked to reconstruct herself as if a painting, reassemble her muscles and bones. She imagined her intestines writhing in the dark, gaseous but empty. Above her ribcage her bosom swelled, causing her pride. She was both happy and gripped with purpose: her aim was to refine herself, to reveal the perfection she was certain she harboured within.

She went to the office earlier and earlier so that she had finished most of her work before lunch. She did not have work enough or activities enough to occupy her, and spent most of her time daydreaming of Martin. When a cigarette company contacted her about possible sponsorship she was almost grateful, for she suddenly had a battle to fight. She argued in meetings and was rude to the cigarette company executives. One of them eventually filed a complaint and Anne-Louise was invited into her immediate boss's office for a discussion. 'You can't tell a managing director that he's personally responsible for killing people,' her boss told her angrily. She could afford to say nothing for she already knew the company had taken their immoral business elsewhere.

Before long Anne-Louise's days and nights began to drift ceaselessly into one another so that only by reminding herself to look at a calendar or a clock could she see that the external world still kept to a timetable. It occurred to Anne-Louise that she might once again be losing her mind but she felt so happy, so engaged with the world that she could not believe it. She wanted only to lay Martin James Bannister down and tell him everything and for him to tell everything to her. She longed to do something difficult and dangerous, to prove herself to him in some way. She would have plucked out her heart if she could, brought him the burning entrails of stars.

Anne-Louise began to be visited by images of her dead father, to clearly hear his voice, to remember his particular smell. Lying in her sleepless bed at night Anne-Louise recalled the exact texture of her father's skin, the way he had a long fold in the flesh in front of each earlobe. It was suddenly painful to her to recognize that at thirty-two she had never been loved, that she had never risked herself, never shown her hand. She had unconsciously protected herself from harm, from loss, and was in a panic to know if she had discovered this too late. She would have rushed out to ask Martin except that she was frightened of his answer, a large part of her was still too proud, too cowering.

She started to sketch again, to attempt paintings, to write down ideas in a black Chinese bound notebook. She was never tired and sometimes wrote all night, ideas she had culled about chaos theory and quantum physics, small poems that came seamless and unbidden to her head. There was no particular order to anything she was doing yet everything she wrote or drew or painted struck her as profound. It seemed to Anne-Louise that she was attempting a kind of archeology of her life, that she was finally sorting through layers of meaning. She knew that in some way all this activity was connected with Martin, to the love he had unleashed in her which swam in her veins. She felt poised on the brink of revelation, as if she were finally about to discover some fundamental truth. She was sleepless and moving and felt herself touched by mercy.

One dusk as she was about to leave the office Martin unexpectedly called and asked her for cocktails at the bar on the top floor of the Mandarin. She had not seen him for five days and nights and had not slept or eaten anything other than a couple of boiled eggs and a few tomatoes. Going up in the lift she felt herself swaying.

She saw him as soon as she entered the bar, for the setting sun was behind him and he appeared as if in a halo. He stood up when he saw her and offered her his seat so that she then had her back to the setting sun. He ordered her a Manhattan which she drank at once and which immediately made her feel even more untied and spinning.

The sun was reflected in Martin's eyes, making them appear powerfully aflame. Without warning Anne-Louise suddenly saw that his strange, marbled eyes were not like anyone else's, that unlike other eyes he did not need to turn away from the sun. She suddenly knew that this was because they had special powers, the ability to look through human souls, as if through glass. She almost cried out but fear clamped her mouth.

Anne-Louise saw in an instantaneous, dizzying flash the terrible power within him and dared not remove her eyes from his. He seemed to her possessed, a shaman or a magician, and she did not know how she had not recognized this before. She watched his mouth move, the swing of his jaw and tried hard to concentrate on what he was saying. Her heart beat fast but she dared not move, lest she give a sign that she had divined his power.

Finally he looked away from her, casting his eyes directly into the sun. Anne-Louise tried to pull her hearing away from the voices inside her head back to the outside world, to clearly hear what he was saying. With great effort his voice slowly came back, soft and unfocused at first, like a radio not quite tuned to the station. As it grew louder and more distinct she could make out the words, that he was talking about some financial coup he had made.

Suddenly he stopped talking and looked at her. 'Are you all right?'

Anne-Louise stared at him helplessly. 'I feel a tad faint,' she said before slipping gracelessly to the floor.

RACHEL: BREATHING ANGEL AIR

I N the room in the tall building the woman asked me some questions. I did not wish to answer and my teeth came down hard, closing off any possibility of redemption. I sat in the air-conditioned room high above the city and thought of the millions of air-conditioning units all over Hong Kong sucking air from the atmosphere. They were drawing air down from the sky itself, robbing birds and plant life, stars, heaven. I imagined the hole in the sky above the city where heaven used to be. I saw myself rising up through this hole into the cold depths of space.

'Rachel,' the woman said and I looked at her. 'What do you think will happen if you talk about it?'

I did not wish her to see me cry and turned my head away.

I had been in Sydney with Mick Woodford for almost two years yet I was not in love with him. I remember thinking one day that we had somehow mistaken sexual intimacy for emotional intimacy. Because we made love, because he had charted all the most private alleyways and recesses of my body,

Mick believed us deeply connected. I was not so sure and felt as if I was only ever skimming the surface of him, of us. I was slightly ashamed of the sense I had that both of us were somehow using each other as a kind of convenience until real love surprised us.

I had grown fond of him though, even if he did have profoundly romantic notions about Women and Art which drove me to distraction. Women for him were required to be always beautiful and I considered myself lucky to have scraped in, for I knew that I only ever passed for beautiful if caught by the camera at a certain angle in a very dull light. And yet Mick was forever taking photographs of me—in the hope, I suppose, that he might catch this moment.

He had firm ideas about making love in the afternoon too, while the bourgeoisie were out at work and artists such as ourselves were free. He would fastidiously arrange his bedroom with fresh flowers and champagne and place me on the bed dressed in the black French underwear he had bought me. I remember that once he bought a small box of Turkish Delight so that we might feed each other after making love but the telephone rang and by the time he got back I had eaten them.

'Rachel!' he said in genuine outrage and I saw by his face that this was not what beautiful, erotic women wearing French underwear were supposed to do.

Every now and then Mick began an affair and I was always surprised to find that once again it felt painful. I could not honestly have said that it had to do with the loss of Mick himself, it was more to do with the wounding of my ego, the often public humiliation of his choosing someone else over me. One Christmas he went off to Italy and had a brief affair with a singer, another time he took to flying regularly to Melbourne and I inadvertently discovered he had taken up with a well-known painter much more lauded than me.

'But why?' I pleaded with him, ashamed of myself, of the pain in my heart.

'Look, Rachel, it's got nothing to do with our relationship, all right? It's just something between Kate and me.'

'But why isn't it to do with us? How can it not affect our relationship?'

He looked at me as if I were stupid, which I probably was. 'I've never made any promises have I? I don't know what's going to happen with Kate, I just have to find out.'

I did not answer his repeated messages on my answer machine when he got back one weekend from Melbourne. I did not want to know what arrangements he had come to with Kate, whether or not I was the booby prize.

As the days went by, Mick's messages grew more and more desperate. 'Rachel, I know you're there. Pick up the phone. I love you, you stupid woman. Answer me!' I knew then that things had not gone as he had hoped and that I was to be the consolation prize.

'Hello,' I said, picking up the phone. 'Didn't work out, hey?'

'It wasn't like that, you idiot. Can I come round?'

I took a deep breath. 'No, I'm working. Get lost,' I said, and hung up.

Our relationship was like that: often we would not see each other for months at a time and then we would run into each other at an opening and take up straight where we had left off. It was strangely passionless, although Mick attempted to inject as much passion as he could, or at least the outward signs of it in the form of champagne, love letters and flowers. Every now and then I got so tired of my own ambivalence that I suggested we get married, in a kind of hare-brained attempt to clear away the muck so I could see some clear shape beneath. Perhaps I thought getting married would miraculously pull from me sharp, distinct feelings, lined up like iron filings drawn to a magnet. The trouble was that I did not feel an unquenchable thirst for Mick, a longing to be with him at any cost. In my heart I knew that if I chose him it would be because I lacked the patience and the courage to wait for someone else.

Periodically Mick asked me to marry him too, most often when he could be reasonably sure I would say no. He usually asked when we hadn't seen each other for a while and he had not found anyone else exotic or famous enough.

'Why don't you ask Kate? She's much more famous than me,' I answered when he asked me again, and his French face crumpled in hurt.

'You don't know when I'm being serious, do you,' he said with genuine emotion and I looked at him, surprised. It was true that I did not know when he was being serious and perhaps that was our tragedy.

If my love life was in disarray, my working life was going better than I had ever dared hope. At the beginning of summer I learnt that I had won the *Sydney Morning Herald* Art Prize and suddenly I was the focus of attention. I was interviewed by newspapers and radio stations, I was asked to high schools to lecture to students. Even my mother rang from Brisbane to tell me my photograph was in the *Courier-Mail* with the headline LOCAL GIRL WINS ART PRIZE. I asked her to send me a copy and when it came I laughed out loud and drew a moustache on the photo. I crossed out the headline and wrote instead LOCAL GIRL ON MOON and immediately sent it off to Anne-Louise. I pictured her laughing when she opened it and remembered the pleasure contained in her spectacular laugh, how contagious it was.

I remember it was a Friday afternoon and I was at my flat in bed with Mick when the telephone rang. 'Don't answer it,' he said, nuzzling my ear. I could never stand a ringing phone and pushed him gently away.

'You just can't do it, can you,' he said as I got out of bed and started to run.

'I'm too bourgeois,' I shouted over my shoulder as I headed for the loungeroom.

'Rachel Gallagher?' I heard a voice ask.

'Yes?'

'Please hold the line.'

'Who is it?' Mick called from the bedroom.

'Oh, shut up,' I called out in reply. At the same time the director of my gallery came on the line so that she thought I was shouting at her.

'No, not you, I was talking to . . .' I began and she told me it didn't matter and to listen. I could hear the excitement in her voice and I sat down in the nearest chair.

'Rachel, you've won the Moët Chandon! Can you believe it!' and she squealed.

I sat in the chair and did not believe it.

'What's happening?' Mick called plaintively from the bed. 'Rachel?'

The Moët and Chandon Australian Art Fellowship was worth $50,000 and a year's free accommodation in a farmhouse in Epernay. I was only the second recipient of the award and had to attend several dinners and cocktail parties where I shook hands with innumerable Frenchmen. I suddenly felt like I was on a stage, as if too many eyes were looking at me. I noticed too that people began to treat me differently, in ways I could not quite put my finger on, and I was not sure that I liked the change. Mick of course was ecstatic, suddenly having someone relatively famous as his girlfriend, at least famous enough within the circles we moved in, at art openings and at parties of artists. If he was ever jealous of my success he did not show it, finding solace perhaps in the fact that if success had not come first to him, at least it had settled on someone he knew.

Not for one second did I feel torn about leaving him. I longed still for a cataclysmic love, definitive and final, and could not wait to go.

When the time came for buying my ticket to Paris I realized I could include a stopover in Hong Kong in order to see Anne-Louise. I wrote to her but she did not write back and as the time drew closer to the purchase deadline on my ticket I rang her mother in Brisbane for her number.

'She sounds very busy whenever I speak to her,' her mother warned, 'but I'm sure she'd love to see you.'

I rang off, disconcerted by some subtext in Margaret Buchan's voice, as if it held some coded message she was willing me to decipher.

When I finally reached Anne-Louise some days later she whooped with excitement as soon as she heard my voice.

'Rachel!' she shouted into the phone. 'Where are you, sweetie?'

I smiled to hear her deep, thrilling voice again. 'Didn't you get my letter?'

'Yes, yes! Congratulations, you must be breathing angel air!'

I laughed. 'I don't know about that, but I'm happy. I thought I might come and see you.'

'Come at once,' she commanded. 'We'll go on a little vacationette.'

We talked about possible destinations, about whether she could take time off. She asked me to ring her in a few days time when she would have a clearer idea.

Only after Anne-Louise had hung up did it strike me that her voice sounded strange and somehow forced, as if all the while she had been thinking of something else.

When I rang her again just a few days later she sounded inexplicably deflated. In a tired voice she said that she could certainly get time off, but that perhaps we could finalize the details about where we wanted to go once I arrived.

'Well, you know best . . .' I said doubtfully.

'Yes, I know best,' she replied but all at once I did not feel confident at all.

Two days before I left Australia tanks rolled into Tienanmen Square. As I flew into Hong Kong for the first time I already knew it to be a tributary of grief, a city howling as if from a joint mouth.

MARTIN: A PUBLIC MOURNING

SOMEHOW Martin managed to bundle Anne-Louise into a taxi and get her home, where he helped undress her and put her to bed. Her flatmate was away and before he knew it she was naked and helpless in his arms, clinging to him, weeping. The sex was over quickly and Martin slipped away as soon as he could. There had been something hysterical about Anne-Louise, some disturbing vein of mania in their frenzied coupling. She had held him too fiercely, crying out in a frightening way, so that instinctively he drew back. She appeared more fully in the moment than he was, lost in it, sometimes mumbling incoherently. He knew she was drunk but there was something else which alarmed him, causing him to be more fully conscious than he would have liked. He could not enter completely into the act, part of him remained wary and even panicked by her, of the surprising strength evident in her grip. She held him so tightly that at one point Martin struggled for air and raised his head like a drowning man. When he finally got up off the bed, Anne-Louise had collapsed into a drunken sleep, muttering words he could not understand.

When he got home he stood under the shower for a long time. He felt bruised, pummelled, and let the water spill over the back of his neck until the hot water ran out. He quickly dried himself and lay down on the bed, covered only by a sheet. He longed to fall instantly asleep but it seemed to him that he still had hands crawling incessantly over his body, that ceaseless, fervent lips were opening, seeking to suck him dry.

Martin did not ring Anne-Louise the next day, or the next. He recoiled from the thought of seeing her again yet at the same time felt curiously excited. She was like a dare, some active danger to which he felt compulsively drawn.

On the third day his dilemma was solved: he picked up the phone in his office and found it was Anne-Louise.

'Am I in your personal Siberia?' she asked and he smiled in spite of himself. 'I apologize if I did anything unseemly the other night,' she went on. 'I was profoundly intoxicated.'

Anne-Louise's voice was low and slower than usual, as if she were choosing her words with great care.

'I—I—I didn't notice, my darling,' Martin said.

She gave an odd laugh. 'How chivalrous of you,' she said. 'Now I *am* offended.'

He felt confused: she sounded much like her

usual self, only slowed down. It crossed his mind that she had taken Valium.

'Can I buy you lunch to thank you for taking me home?'

He paused. 'T—T—Today's no good I'm afraid and tomorrow I've got a business lunch . . .'

Anne-Louise interrupted. 'Dinner then? I promise I'll drink water and I won't mention chaos theory all night.'

He hesitated only briefly, having no better offers.

When Anne-Louise arrived at the restaurant Martin performed a quick appraisal. She did appear to have taken some kind of muscle relaxant drug, for her movements were slowed down considerably and all evidence of the fever with which she had gripped him was gone. He realized he had not noticed before that she was thinner than when he met her only several weeks ago, that the bones of her face had risen. He was surprised: she looked suddenly frail.

'How are you feeling?' he asked, standing up from the table, privately wondering why he had ever been frightened.

'A bit strange, actually,' she said, sitting down. A waiter helped pull her chair out but she did not thank him. Her eyes looked slightly glazed.

'Oh, yes?'

'I need a holiday. I've been working too hard,' she said. She turned to the waiter. 'Bring me some water,' she ordered in her old imperious manner. Martin immediately relaxed.

'S—S—So you were serious then,' he said, smiling.

She looked at him in confusion. 'What?'

'About drinking water.' She did not appear to be concentrating on what he was saying, even though she did not take her eyes from his.

She smiled faintly. 'I need to talk to you about something,' she said. His heart lurched, and he waited.

'What do you think of the students' hunger strike?' she asked, disarming him. 'The students in Tienanmen Square?'

He was not sure what her question meant. 'How do you mean?'

'Why is it happening now, Martin? Why has the whole thing suddenly exploded?'

He took a sip of wine. 'W—W—Well, it's been coming for a while but if you had to pin it on some specific event I suppose the death of the students' main supporter in the government triggered it off. He was seen as a liberal, their last chance of winning reform.'

She was looking at him as if he were an oracle, as if he alone knew all there was to know. 'At least that's why they started massing in the square,' Martin added, 'as a kind of wake, a public mourning.'

She continued to stare at him. 'A public mourning,' she repeated slowly.

Martin did not like the way the conversation was going. In an effort to distract her, he picked up the bottle from the cooler beside the table and offered her a glass. A waiter immediately rushed up and took the bottle from him.

'Madam?' he asked, suspending it above Anne-Louise's empty glass.

Anne-Louise did not respond and continued to look into Martin's eyes. 'I think there's another reason,' she said enigmatically, and smiled knowingly.

The dinner was over quickly, with Anne-Louise growing more and more withdrawn, smiling to herself in a way which appeared to Martin as a kind of smugness. She seemed to be holding some delicious secret to herself, one she was clearly not about to share. After a while she ceased to look so flatteringly into Martin's eyes too, as if her own private thoughts offered more nourishment. She would not be drawn either on what other reason she believed responsible for the massing of the students.

Soon after Martin finished dessert, Anne-Louise suddenly sprang from her chair. 'I'm going now, Martin,' she said and unceremoniously walked out.

As much as Martin tried to prevent it, his mind returned again and again to that trussed girl behind the door at the casino. Her image came unbidden to him at inappropriate moments, at business meetings, or even walking down the street. He remembered the writhe of her captured body, the frenzied way she had attempted escape. He put off going back for as long as he could and then one Saturday afternoon after work found himself buying a ticket to Macau. He tried not to think all the way across and was conscious only of the hot push of excitement.

At the casino he asked for his favourite room but was told it was already booked.

'I'll have the next floor down then,' he said, 'same position.'

Taking the key he was too impatient to wait for the lift and, swinging his overnight bag over his shoulder, ran up the nine flights of stairs.

Outside the window it was completely dark by the time Martin was ready. Taking a last look in the mirror, he passed his hand through his hair and inspected his teeth, then opened the door. He had already had several drinks but planned on a couple more.

After a bad meal in the casino restaurant Martin made his way to the door. The same bouncer was leaning against the opposite wall and to his surprise beckoned him over. Martin looked quickly around before crossing over to him.

'This is better place,' the bouncer said, covertly handing him a cheap, crumpled card. 'You not tell.'

Martin did not speak but immediately pocketed the card and turned away. At the door the same girl opened it, smiling prettily. 'Welcome back,' she said, standing aside to let him in.

The next morning Martin woke with a hangover. He lay in bed and recalled the slender girl forced to crawl on her hands and knees around the floor like a dog. But this time he did not feel a rush to blot out the image and instead went over every detail, again and again.

Next time he would take a camera. He might even venture into the streets, to the address on the smudged card in his pocket.

But later, when he was sitting with his eyes half-closed on the jetfoil going back to Hong Kong, he was hit by a sickening remorse. His eyes opened and he quickly looked around, feeling as if everyone knew where he had been. He felt weak and dirty and tears involuntarily filled his eyes. He turned his head to the window, blinking hard, fighting the constriction in his throat.

The telephone was ringing when at last Martin reached his front door. He was feeling bad-tempered and debated whether to let the answering machine pick it up. He made his way towards it at his own pace.

'Yes?'

'Where have you been?' Anne-Louise's voice demanded. Immediately anger burned in his chest.

'M—M—Mars,' he replied.

'Oh, I'm sorry, Martin, I didn't mean to be

rude,' she said, disarming him completely.

'I—I—I didn't realize I had to report my every movement to you, Anne-Louise.'

'Of course, you don't, you silly boy. It's just that I've got some news—my best friend is coming from Australia! She's won a scholarship to France and she's . . .'

He cut her off. 'That's wonderful my darling, but I'm afraid I can't talk now. I'll ring you back, OK?'

He put the phone down even though he was not sure if Anne-Louise had finished speaking. At that precise moment she was too much for him.

Her best friend, indeed. She had so many friends, how could she possibly tell one from another?

ANNE-LOUISE: HER BEST FRIEND'S
FACE

MOST days Anne-Louise was convinced that she was perfectly well but on others she felt decidedly strange. Luckily her well days outnumbered those on which she felt frightened and floating. On such days Anne-Louise did not feel real any more and sometimes had to inspect her own hands to see if they were in fact hers. She felt detached from the world, detached from herself, so that she often stood for hours staring at her own face in the mirror, making certain she was still there. Even so, Anne-Louise was still not sure she existed and at such moments believed she was being punished for wishing her father dead. On these days she stayed home from work, alone in her room, sometimes sobbing inconsolably, sometimes writing down every thought which came to her head. Although she felt ill, a part of her remained rational and writing notes helped ease her terror so that she sometimes believed that if she could only write *everything* down she might be saved. Yet most of the time Anne-Louise felt so well, so blissfully happy and in love, that it seemed preposterous that there might be anything wrong. She felt powerful then and could not remember the bad days. The only thing she cared about was knowing that Martin Bannister was alive in the world. She believed him to be unlike other men but did not speak of him to anyone, knowing that ears are only capable of receiving that which they have been schooled to hear.

The last time Anne-Louise made love to Martin Bannister she felt her soul shake. As he entered her, Anne-Louise's spirit rose to greet him, her whole self opened towards him. She took him in her arms and held the entire world, embracing both good and evil. She and he together became a twinned universe, balanced and spinning. As he moved inside her she let him take her soul, she let him enter her bloodstream. He was in her cells, her veins, her skin, he existed in every part of her. She was both terrified and fearless, exposing her white throat to his practised mouth, offering herself up to his plans. She gave herself to him like an Indian widow to the funeral pyre, like a willing disciple in a flaming sacrifice to God.

The very next night Anne-Louise unexpectedly got a call from Rachel. Her first instinct was to tell her everything but in the next second she could not bear to part with her secret prize. She listened to Rachel's voice and was excited to know she would soon see her best friend's face. She did not care that Rachel had won a prestigious scholarship, or indeed about anyone else. Now that Anne-Louise had private knowledge that her own time had come she felt an unspecific magnanimity towards everyone.

A few nights after Christine came back from her annual meeting with the Chanel head office in Paris, she called Anne-Louise into her room.

'Is everything all right? You're not sleeping much.'

Anne-Louise did not answer but gave a peaceful smile. Christine did not appear satisfied: her sculptured eyebrows creased and she continued to look carefully at Anne-Louise. 'You've lost an awful lot of weight, you know, honey,' she said doubtfully.

'I've been trying to. Isn't it wonderful?'

Christine was still frowning.

'Stop glowering, sweetie. I feel fine, I'm really, really happy!'

She spontaneously rushed over and gave Christine an exuberant hug: Christine reeled back in surprise.

'What are you having for dinner then?' she asked.

'Poo on toast,' Anne-Louise replied.

'Huh?' Christine said.

Anne-Louise let out an uproarious laugh. 'It's an old family joke,' she said when she had stopped.

Over the next few days Anne-Louise noticed Christine hanging around the bathroom door a lot, presumably to see if she was sticking her fingers down her throat after eating. Of course Anne-Louise would never do that: she was purifying herself from the inside out, growing cleaner by her will alone, hour by hour.

The night before Anne-Louise was due to speak to Rachel about their travel arrangements, it suddenly occurred to her that if she left Hong Kong for even a few days she would be leaving Martin. All at once she was terrified to go, frightened to be out of his vicinity. What if something happened to her? What if she wanted to reach him in a hurry and could not? It suddenly seemed too perilous to have Martin Bannister away from her. She would have to think of a plan to get Rachel to stay with her in Hong Kong, within easy reach of the man who had the ability to heal all her sorrow.

In the weeks before Rachel was due to arrive, great events began to unfold in China. Thousands of students began to mass in Beijing, peasants and workers all over the country began to rise up. Soon the students began a hunger strike and night after night Anne-Louise compulsively watched television as new camera footage came in.

Above her head a storm was gathering, a final, cataclysmic process had begun. She knew it had something to do with herself, with her physical presence in the region, with the very fact that she had come to be in Hong Kong.

She was at once terrified and exultant at her own powers and dared not speak of them to anyone.

Two days before Rachel arrived, tanks rolled into Tienanmen Square. Anne-Louise watched human bodies fall, young men and women wearing street clothes, dying.

She knew without doubt that it was because of her presence that it was happening. Great forces had been unleashed screaming in the heavens, now poised and rearing to descend.

RACHEL: INTO THE EYE OF THE STORM

ONE morning, about six months after our marriage, I woke up and realized I knew nothing about my husband. He had not seen his mother in eight years and his father was apparently missing. His first wife was gone and he had no friends of long standing. I realized I had blindly taken him at his word and had only his version of events. I had no information about him in which to place him in a wider context, no way of seeing him in the round. He was adrift from his country, a perpetual stranger in a city where the past was torn down.

I waited until he had gone to work and then I got up and began to go through his things. He kept a large wooden box in the spare bedroom in which I knew he kept old letters and other personal papers: it was always locked but I knew where he kept the key. I felt no shame and my hand did not waver as I unlocked it and pulled out everything I could find. I was looking for his past, for evidence, for witnesses, for anything which might tell me who he was.

I found at once letters from old girlfriends, letters from his first wife, which clearly showed that she had left him. My husband had told me he had left his wife: I took this new knowledge in and continued.

I saw an old tin and opened it: inside were some coins, medals, military paraphernalia, a photograph of a man in a uniform. The man looked so much like my husband I guessed it must be his father. Inside the tin too was a letter addressed to the Department of Social Security, dated several years ago, enquiring into the whereabouts of a Martin James McClintock. I was about to close the drawer when I saw at the bottom of it a package wrapped in purple satin. It was tied with a silk rope which I immediately recognized. My breath caught. I stared at the package for only a moment before leaning over to open it.

In bed at night my husband sometimes bound my wrists with that same silk rope. I hated to be bound, everything in me rebelled and yet I submitted. I submitted because I had not yet passed the stage of trying to please him. It excited my husband and I was needy enough for his approval to feel a sense of pride at eliciting such a response in him. When he whipped me with his belt I believed it would bring me closer towards satisfying him, to providing him with whatever deep and healing action he needed.

On one occasion only, my husband wound the rope around my upper chest to form a kind of harness. He pushed me onto my knees so that I was on all fours and attempted to lead me like an animal around the floor. My tears fell onto the ground as we moved. When I looked up I saw the rise and bob of his erect penis. I continued to look up, hoping to see his eyes, hoping that he would look into mine and see tears. He did not look at my face and in that instant I vowed to rise up and up until I stood at my full height, until I threw the rope from my back and shouted my defiance.

'That's enough,' I would shout and my voice would fill the world, 'that's enough, Martin. Enough!'

Months later, when I finally opened my mouth to speak in the room in the tall building, only a howl emerged. My eyes ran and my throat gasped for air and all the while the woman opposite me remained sitting quietly. Other than passing me a box of tissues she made no move to comfort me and sat silently while my pain flowed. I do not know how long I wept but it seemed to me hours before I breathed normally. I felt the air pass through my lungs again, the woollen seat cover at the back of my knees. I heard sounds, the hum of the air-conditioner, the sound of a horn far below. After a while I heard the woman moving in her chair.

'It might help you to know, Rachel, that sexual games and fantasies are rarely more than that,' she said.

'More than what?' I asked.

'More than fantasies. I don't think you should read too much into them.'

I could not tell her about what I knew, for I was

315

not yet ready to admit to myself all the terrible knowledge I had in my possession, all the damage for which I was culpable.

I could not tell her that I was no longer weeping over Martin.

When I emerged into Hong Kong airport's arrival hall for the first time I could not see Anne-Louise. The doors opened on to a large ramp sloping downwards, into a swarm of a thousand faces. I wheeled my trolley and scanned the crowd, desperate to make her out. I could not see her and I was getting to the end of the ramp, about to merge into the crowd of a thousand faces.

'Rach!' I heard and turned around but still I could not see her.

'Rachel Gallagher!' I heard again and my eyes frantically combed the faces.

'Over here, you dingbat!' she called and there she was. She stood alone in a small space she had cleared, looking very thin, holding a bottle of Veuve Cliquot.

I looked into her eyes and straight away saw the flare of madness, the burn of a fire out of control.

We walked outside into the open air and the heat immediately slapped me in the face. It was eleven o'clock at night but still the air was hot and ripe as if it were midday. It smelt of petrol and mould, heat and sweat and I felt myself to be in uncharted territory. All week I had been watching continuous CNN broadcasts revealing mayhem and I looked around me as if a great column of people might come marching down the street at any time. I don't know what I expected: civil unrest, protest riots, the closing down of the airport. All I knew was that panic and rage had been let loose and I was now in the eye of the storm.

'You still think it was safe to come?' I asked Anne-Louise and she looked at me with surprise.

'What do you think's going to happen to you?' She gazed around her with a look of wonder on her face. 'There are good reasons why all of us are here right now.'

I did not ask her to elaborate but as we walked towards the long taxi queue which snaked around two aisles, I took a closer look at her. She was walking in front of the trolley, swinging the champagne bottle at a dangerous angle. The cotton dress she was wearing practically hung off her and I could see the two wings of her shoulder blades jutting through the skin of her back. A shiver passed through me.

'Hang on. I'll just get a Diet Coke,' she said, throwing the champagne bottle recklessly on top of my luggage where it almost rolled off. I saved it just in time and looked over as she bought the drink and made her way smiling back to me. She tipped her head back and gulped it down fast.

'That stuff's full of caffeine, you know,' I said.

She laughed. 'So's this.' She unclenched her palm to reveal Nicorette chewing gum. 'I've given up smoking!'

I looked at her dubiously. 'It looks like you've given up food too.'

She ignored this. 'Oh, Rach, I've got a million profoundly wonderful things for us to do. We're going to an ancient walled village, out to a beach on my favourite island, to this really fabulous pigeon restaurant . . .'

I interrupted her. 'In the middle of protest marches?'

She looked off into the distance and something sad and dark passed across her face. I was suddenly shot through with some emotion I could not identify: pity or sentiment, a kind of tenderness for all our shared history. 'Actually I don't mind if we don't do much at all,' I said quickly, 'all I really want to do is lie on a beach. Have you booked anything?'

'No, not yet. There's plenty to do here.' She leant over and hugged me. 'Oh, it's good to see you, Rachel! I can't tell you how happy I am.'

I was happy too and yet could not ignore an undercurrent of danger. I hoped only that I had got it wrong and hugged her resolutely back.

Anne-Louise opened the champagne in the taxi and it immediately went everywhere. 'Christ, Anne-Louise!' I yelled, jumping out of the way. She was laughing and drinking from the bottle; she offered it to me.

'Come on, Miss Brizzie. Live dangerously!'

I attempted a smile. 'Drinking champagne in a taxi is not my idea of living dangerously.'

She did not stop grinning. 'Oh? And what is?'

I was tempted to tell her that coming to see her was but held my tongue. I was still hoping that things might not be as bad as I had initially guessed, that Anne-Louise might merely be overexcited. It was genuinely hard to tell with her: because she lived perpetually at full speed, more vibrant than the rest of us, it was difficult to pick the exact moment when she crossed that invisible but crucial line. I hoped that this time I would be able to judge the moment when and if it arrived.

I looked out the window, tipping back my head to witness the streaming forests of buildings, the radiance from a million lights. I had never seen a city so dense, so lit, so ceaseless in its movements. The taxi careered around corners, sped along expressways; buildings flashed by so close I could have touched flapping washing. I was jetlagged and speeding and the city passed before my eyes in an hallucinatory dream, a blinding maze of electricity and concrete.

'Astonishing, isn't it,' I heard Anne-Louise say in her deep, thrilling voice and for a moment I wondered if everything might be all right. 'I think it's the most exciting place in the world,' she said, clearly in love with it.

I looked across at her and smiled, taking the champagne bottle. 'I bet it's not as clean as Brisbane,' I said and we started laughing.

At home in her flat I discovered that Anne-Louise had purchased at least seven different varieties of cheese, pounds of red and white grapes, fresh cherries, pots of pâté and caviar. She had bought breads and biscuits, hams and smoked salmon, dozens of bottles of champagne.

'Surprise!' she cried, flinging open the front door to reveal a large room opening onto a verandah, with a table laden with food in the middle of it. 'I moved the table so we could get the best view,' she said, grabbing my bag. 'Christine's away. You can have her room.'

She rushed over to the sliding glass doors and flung them open, stepping backwards and spreading wide her arms. 'Isn't it magnificent?' she said, turning around to face the moving city with its spiral of lights. She kept her arms open in a symbolic gesture, as if crucified.

'Mine! All mine!' she cried, tipping back her head. I put my other bag down and followed her onto the verandah. I was feeling the woozy, thick-headed sensations of jetlag: I guessed it to be about four o'clock in the morning Sydney time.

'I'm very tired,' I said. 'Would you be really offended if I went to bed?'

'But I bought all that food especially for you!'

'I know, but I had about three meals on the plane. Come on, I'll help you put it away. We'll eat it later.'

She ignored me completely, pushing past me to grab a glass from the table. 'At least have some champagne before you go to bed,' she said. 'Rach?'

My eyes were nearly dropping out of my head. 'OK,' I replied, 'but only because I'm so nice.'

'That's your main problem,' she said, beginning to pour.

All that night, as I fell in and out of sleep, I heard Anne-Louise prowling ceaselessly around the apartment. I lay in bed listening to the glide of her feet, her sleepless patrol over the city and myself.

When I slept I dreamt that I was under water. I opened the door and saw all the furniture floating by, Anne-Louise drifting, drowned. My tears flowed out and mixed with the water and when I held my arm out to stop Anne-Louise's body floating away, she opened her drowned eyes and looked helplessly at me before drifting beyond my reach.

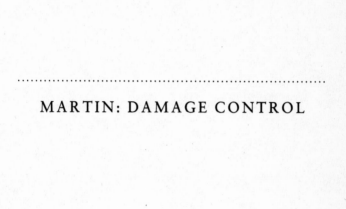

MARTIN: DAMAGE CONTROL

P ANIC broke out immediately on the stock exchange following the events in China. The market plummeted and Martin spent all week frantically carrying out damage control. He was on the telephone to an important client when his secretary Queenie Wong came into the room and stood stupidly in front of his desk.

'Hang on, Denis,' he said into the phone, then covered the mouthpiece. 'I—I—I'm busy, Queenie. Can't it wait?'

Queenie blushed and looked down at the floor. 'There is a lady to see you, Mr Bannister. I try to tell her you busy man . . .'

He saw Anne-Louise's head emerging round the door.

'S—S—Sorry, Denis, I'll have to call you back,' he said, replacing the phone.

'I know I'm being naughty,' Anne-Louise said as Queenie scuttled past her, 'it's just that you're so hard to catch . . .'

Martin leant back in his chair, exceedingly annoyed. 'I—I—I'm hard to catch because I'm snowed under. What can I do for you, Anne-Louise?'

'I wanted to ask you to dinner one night this week to meet Rachel. She's not here for long.'

He placed his hands behind his head, closing his eyes. 'Th—Th—This is not a good week. Sorry.'

'What about next week?'

The phone rang again. 'Anne-Louise, I'm really frantic. Can I get back to you?'

'Promise?'

'P—P—Promise,' he said, picking up the ringing phone.

He gave her a distracted wave as she left. As she turned at the door she ran straight into Teddy Stumble who was coming in. She made a great display of kissing him on the cheek then walked away, laughing. Teddy, of course, looked horrified and Martin couldn't help but grin.

That weekend Martin went back to the house on Macau where the girls were kept. He was stressed to breaking point and wanted to lose himself, to forget for a moment who he was. He knew by now that the activities within the house were illegal but no longer cared. He did not believe that he was taking that much of a risk anyway because he assumed the police were already in on it, knowing as he did that corruption in certain areas was an accepted way of life.

At the house, perched precariously on a hill not far from the casino, girls were brought from China and elsewhere against their will and kept in rooms.

They were bound and gagged, regularly raped, and now and then tried to escape. Most of them gave up after a while and eventually began working as prostitutes in other houses, where their eyes fast became dulled.

Martin comforted himself with the fact that he did not rape them but more or less broke them in, so that in the end they came to him willingly. He liked to believe that they favoured him over other more brutal men, that the pleasure was mutual.

Walking up to the house which appeared to be sliding down the hill, Martin felt himself to be kinder than other men: men who did things to the girls he personally regarded as reprehensible. He imagined the girls considered themselves lucky to be picked by him, for he had his own code of honour, boundaries he would not move beyond.

As he climbed the uneven stairs to the verandah, his bag over his shoulder with the camera ready, one of the released girls smiled and waved to him, as if proving his point.

First thing Monday morning Anne-Louise rang.

'I'm going to keep bugging you until you say yes,' she warned. 'Why don't you put yourself out of your misery?'

He rolled his eyes. 'I—I—I just got home. I haven't had time to think.'

'Well, let me think for you. You are coming to my place for dinner on Wednesday night at eight

327

o'clock where you will have a splendid time.'

He smiled. 'Anne-Louise, I can't promise anything. One of our directors is in town . . .'

She interrupted. 'Does that mean you have to sleep with him?'

He laughed. 'I'll try and make it, OK? That's the best I can do.'

He heard her sigh. 'Just remember, Martin, hell hath no fury like a woman scorned.'

'D—D—Don't remind me,' he said.

Her voice sounded perfectly normal, leaving him confused.

The following lunchtime Martin was having a drink with a client at the bar of the Foreign Correspondent's Club. They were in a crowd watching live satellite broadcasts of events in Tienanmen Square when Anne-Louise and her friend walked in. Anne-Louise did not see Martin for her eyes moved at once to the large projection screen in the corner, and she stopped dead. Her face was riveted, completely absorbed by the images on the screen. Even so, Martin moved his body slightly so that he was partly obscured by his client's shoulders and head. When he judged it safe he once again looked across and saw them still standing there. Anne-Louise continued to watch the screen but her friend's attention had begun to wander and she looked around, ill at ease. She seemed painfully self-conscious and had none of Anne-Louise's nonchalance. Her eyes missed nothing: clearly she was inspecting the room and everyone in it.

She was pretty in an unexceptional, unfussy way, with short dark hair and thick brows, dressed in a completely different style to the expensive silks and linen jackets favoured by Anne-Louise. She was wearing khaki trousers, well-cut but not dressed up, with what appeared to be a man's blue denim shirt: the casualness of her attire was immediately striking amidst the women's tailored business suits of Hong Kong. Martin racked his brains to remember what Anne-Louise had said about her, recalling only that she was an artist. He remembered Anne-Louise referring to her as her best friend, which at the time had impressed him as a silly thing to say.

He looked over again at the woman. At the same time she happened to glance in his direction and Martin met her eyes. Disconcerted, he immediately averted his gaze.

'Another drink to drown our losses, Martin?' his client asked.

'W—W—Why not?' he replied, risking another look at Anne-Louise's best friend.

Anne-Louise rang him late Wednesday afternoon to find out if he was coming. 'I told you I was going to bug you. Madonna needs to know how many to cook for,' she said.

'L—L—Liar,' Martin replied, 'Filipinos always cook for twenty.'

She laughed. 'All right then. *I* need to know if you're coming.'

'What's on the menu?'

'Madonna's special fish stew. It's Portuguese, I think.'

'Who else is coming?'

'Didn't your mother teach you it's bad manners to ask who else is invited?'

He told her he would try and make it by eight-thirty. 'M—M—My favourite,' he added, 'two girls.'

'Women,' she corrected before hanging up.

A few minutes before nine Martin rang Anne-Louise's front door bell. He clutched the bad Chilean wine he had bought at the last minute from the local Seven-Eleven.

Her friend opened the door. 'Just a sec,' she said, struggling with the lock on the outer security grille, 'I'm not used to these things.' He waited while she persevered, watching her inexpert fumbling.

'Y—Y—You're Rachel I assume, the other inmate?'

She laughed at him through the grille. 'I'm sorry about this. I think it's deadlocked. I'll have to get Anne-Louise.'

He was left feeling foolish on the wrong side of the gate. He waited, and after a moment he heard them giggling. They soon came into sight: Anne-Louise wearing a dressing gown with a bath towel wrapped around her hair.

'Oh, you poor baby!' she exclaimed on seeing him, and immediately burst out laughing.

He stood there smiling awkwardly while Anne-Louise ran around trying to find the key. When she finally opened the door she hugged him extravagantly. 'Free at last!' she cried, laughing wildly.

And then she stood back, still holding his hand and grabbed the hand of her friend. Standing between them she joined their hands and clasped her own over theirs.

'Rachel Gallagher meet Martin Bannister,' she announced, her voice loud and overexcited.

'Rachel is my best friend in the whole world,' she declared, 'and you are my favourite man.'

Rachel Gallagher looked at him with what could only be described as embarrassment. He noticed that her hand was sweating and she clearly felt as uncomfortable as he did.

They stood trying to avoid looking at each other, their strangers' hands forcibly locked beneath Anne-Louise's unwavering grip.

ANNE-LOUISE: A POINT OF CRISIS

A SMALL part of Anne-Louise recognized that she was going mad. A small, rational part of her mind understood everything that was happening to her and yet was not strong enough to prevent it. This rational part recognized that she was ill and knew she was behaving strangely. Yet it was as if madness was simply more compelling and she could not help but run towards its radiant conflagration. In her more lucid moments Anne-Louise even thought of opening her mouth, of telling Martin or Rachel, but when it actually came to it she could not. She wished to keep her beautiful secret deep within, to feel forever the living radiance gliding through her veins. She could not bear to part with it, and nursed her madness as if it were her prize. She knew herself to be removed from ordinary men and women, inhabiting a special place, but could not have borne to relinquish it. Walking down the street she witnessed extraordinary things: the face of a child cleaved in two, the bones of its head cruelly mismatched, the spirit of the devil moving in a feral cat who looked only once at Anne-Louise before fleeing.

Yet Anne-Louise could still hold a conversation

and her illness swept in and out like a tide. Her head would be under water and then all at once clear again, as if her ears and eyes were lifted to open air. In this way she went about the usual business of days, living concealed among the less lucky.

The thought of Martin and Rachel meeting had obsessed her and she could barely contain herself until they did. For reasons she did not fully understand this meeting became freighted with meaning, carrying a deep symbolism. It represented nothing less than the joining of her life, the meeting of the past and the future. Once Martin and Rachel met, Anne-Louise believed her life's form would finally rise, the unbroken chain linking them all would be disclosed. That all three lives were bound together she did not doubt: Anne-Louise knew herself to be at a point of crisis in a chain of events whose meaning was about to be made clear.

But until they met, Anne-Louise lived as if in a fever. She rushed everywhere and rarely sat still, dashing in and out of taxis rather than wait for buses, trains or trams. She was mad with impatience, gorged with it, and felt as if she might never rest until the fateful meeting was accomplished. At moments she was also deliriously happy and swung through the minutes and hours, pushed by the breath of private angels.

She did not wish to alert Rachel to the importance of the meeting and some instinct for self-preservation ensured that she held her tongue. It seemed critical as well not to let Rachel witness the extravagance of her feelings for Martin: if she was gripped by a mad pride she could not help it, wishing to hold close all her pleasures.

The second morning after Rachel's arrival Anne-Louise woke after perhaps an hour's sleep feeling unaccountably nervous. She lay in bed considering the best way to tell her about Martin, and when she finally heard Rachel moving about, her stomach lurched as if she had quickly passed down a steep hill. She could hear the sound of her own blood and when she swallowed her mouth felt empty.

She waited until she could wait no longer and then rose from the bed. When she opened her bedroom door, Rachel was already sitting at the table eating breakfast.

'Hello,' she said, 'did you go to bed at all? Every time I woke I heard you fossicking about.'

'I do not fossick,' Anne-Louise replied. 'Now there's a word I haven't heard for some time.' As she tied up her dressing gown she noticed that her hand was shaking.

'Tea?' Rachel asked.

'I told you, I only drink hot water,' she said and Rachel raised her eyebrows. 'I'll get it.'

In the kitchen she willed her hands to stop shaking and returned to the table with a cup firmly held.

'So, what's on the agenda for today? What

superficially amusing things have you got planned for me?'

Anne-Louise took a sip of water but it was too hot and she drew back in shock. When she had recovered she took a deep breath. Her heart was beating so fast she feared for her blood. 'I've been going out with someone,' she announced, putting the cup down.

Rachel looked at her in surprise. 'Apropos of nothing,' she said. Anne-Louise heard Rachel but her mind was suddenly confused and she could not understand.

'Well?' Rachel asked, smiling. 'Go on'.

'I've been seeing this man,' she continued. She realized the conversation was going badly wrong but it was too late to save it. Rachel was still smiling. 'And?'

'There's nothing much to tell. He's a trader but he's not the usual City type. He also likes me.'

Rachel laughed. 'Don't sound so astonished.'

Anne-Louise did not respond and got up and walked quickly to the bathroom, closing the door hard. Her heart was still beating fast and she stood with her back to the door, her head resting against it.

She was swollen with all the things she knew which Rachel and everyone else did not. Her hands were still shaking.

The morning of the meeting, Anne-Louise rose from

her sleepless bed and began to prepare herself. First she ran a bath into which she poured special oils, carefully chosen. Wrapped in a gown she retired to her room where she anointed herself with creams and lotions, turning this way and that to watch herself in the mirror. She noticed the flare of her hip, the jut of her ribs, clearly visible beneath her firm, high breasts. She saw her own bones and knew herself to be nearing perfection. Her skin was clear and pale and she could clearly trace the tributaries of her blood. The whites of her eyes had a strange, milky glow, pure and innocent.

She looked into her face in the mirror for a long time and did not break her gaze. As she looked Anne-Louise saw all her past selves lined up behind her reflection, all her lost selves jostling into view.

She dared not move and gazed down through time, into history, into the endless repetition of the future.

RACHEL: RANSACKING THE DARKNESS

ON summer nights my husband and I sometimes went down to the pool in the apartment
block where we lived. When we emerged from the
air-conditioned foyer the warm air always surprised
me as if I were stepping into it for the first time. It
was peculiarly moist against my skin and smelt of
heat, mould and incense. The nights were never still:
there was the flap of bat wings overhead, the continuous drill of cicadas, the cries of night birds. To get
to the pool we walked through what was supposed
to be a garden, past a couple of mature red hibiscus,
a concrete picnic area, a few drying wattle.

When we got to the pool and waded into the
water it was never as refreshing as I had hoped. The
warm glide of it felt only marginally different to the
outside air. I always floated on my back, the water
lapping at my ears, looking up at the sky where
heaven used to be. My husband usually swam up and
down until he tired, which was never long. He was
not a good swimmer and I watched him move
through the water, all effort and thrash.

I recall the last time we swam together. I floated
and my mind drifted, so that I no longer knew if I

was trying to forget or remember. I suppose I was trying to lull myself to sleep, for I had certainly not yet chosen to act. On dry land I lived as if only half awake, walking through days in a trance. I floated and drifted and when my husband turned and swam towards me I remember thinking that I would eventually have to wake up.

As he drew closer my first instinct was to move out of his way. Yet I did not, I remained directly in his path, floating unanchored. Just before he reached me he dived deep below the surface, emerging seconds later next to my head. He smiled at me then pushed my head under, laughing when I came up spluttering for air. Just as I got my breath, he held me under again, then again and again.

He was laughing each time I surfaced, as if it were a bit of playful fun. I gasped and flailed and for one panicked second believed I might drown. But as I fought wildly to make my way to the surface for the fifth time, he suddenly released his grip: I pushed up with all my strength to the air. I coughed and gulped, clinging to the side, too breathless and shocked to speak.

I remember him swimming on his back away from me, his head raised from the water, a benign smile on his face. I heard other people coming into the pool and someone dive-bombed just above my head, with other young men soon to follow.

As I clung breathlessly to the tiles I watched them playing rough games in the water, standing on each other's shoulders, dragging each other down by the feet. When I could breathe normally again it seemed to me that my husband's play was just like theirs and that I had dreamed my own drowning.

Later we walked back through the gardens to the lift and I clearly recall the shape of my husband's back as he walked ahead of me. I wanted to say something to him but did not know what it was.

But in bed in the early hours of the morning I suddenly woke up, fighting for breath. I was dreaming of Anne-Louise floating out of reach and gasped into the air-conditioned air, as if screaming.

By the time I had been in Hong Kong with Anne-Louise for three days I was already unhappy. When she was not short-tempered she was overheated with excitement and it seemed there was no state in between. When she was excited it caused her to become unbearably pushy, so that I felt myself to be continually dragged around by the scruff of the neck to look at Chinese religious shrines or foisted on strangers. In three days she introduced me to more people than I ever wished to meet: I accompanied her to lunches, cocktails, dinners and even breakfasts. She introduced me at all times as her best friend in the whole world, as if we were a kind of double act. She appeared delirious with happiness at my very existence but her presentation of our friendship caused everyone to look at her, and us, strangely. She was indeed my best friend but her extravagant displays only embarrassed me.

Anne-Louise of course did not notice, just as she did not notice if her bad tempers offended me. When she was not bursting with happiness she was rudely dismissive, unwittingly cruel. One morning she took me on a hazardous bus ride out of the city, insisting that we ride on the upper deck, where I hung on to the rails paralyzed with fear while the bus swung perilously fast around blind corners. On the return journey with some of Anne-Louise's friends I refused to join them on the upper deck and insisted on sitting below where at least I could not see as clearly. Anne-Louise spent the journey ridiculing my cowardice, shouting down from the top deck the whole way.

'Still got your eyes closed, Rach?' she called. 'You should have stayed in Brisbane where it's safe!'

Whenever I was away from Anne-Louise I always forgot this aspect of her personality until on meeting her again it hit me afresh. Now I found myself relegated once more to the role of the Avon Lady: the difference was that this time I knew that revealed teeth do not necessarily mean acquiescence.

One night Anne-Louise introduced me to the man she was going out with. She had not mentioned him before my arrival and spoke of him in the vaguest, most general terms so that I had difficulty in assessing his importance. I gathered that Martin Bannister was some kind of rich broker or trader, in one of those jobs about which I knew nothing except that it involved dealing in vast amounts of money.

My first sight of the man who was to become my husband did not cause my breath to catch. It struck me only that I had seen him somewhere before but I had no sense of prescience or presentiment of what was to come. It seems to me that I simply opened the door and saw a perfectly ordinary man: I took in of course that he was extremely good looking, that he appeared fully conscious and that he was standing on his own two feet. But I cannot say I heard an inner warning or even felt the briefest prick of danger.

That was yet to come.

As the end of my first week in Hong Kong neared I realized that Anne-Louise had no intention of accompanying me on a short holiday. It was obvious she had contrived to take off a day or two but no more and that she had no intention of discussing the matter further. I was relieved in a way because the idea of spending an uninterrupted week in Anne-Louise's fervid company now filled me with nothing but weariness. At least while we remained in Hong Kong she worked much of the time, leaving my days blessedly uninterrupted. I wandered idly around the streets but mostly spent hours sitting alone in her flat, thinking about France.

I was surprised to discover that I felt

apprehensive, even frightened. Inexplicably the idea of spending several months away suddenly seemed overwhelming. In a moment of panic, I even rang Mick in Sydney. 'Do you want me to join you for a few months?' he asked at once but before he had finished speaking the thought of beginning our ambivalent relationship all over again only depressed me.

If I was suddenly exhausted by being alone, it was not Mick that I wanted.

On Friday afternoon Anne-Louise burst through the door unexpectedly. 'Start packing,' she ordered. 'We're going to my favourite island. It's a short ferry ride away.'

All week I had been crossing my fingers over Anne-Louise's mental state, hoping my initial impression had been wrong. All week I had been anxiously watching her weird, high-flying happiness, her outbursts of temper, her dangerous attraction to the highest point of the swing. I knew she was overexcited yet I also believed that this time it was manageable and I had not mentioned it.

I looked at her, at the bright bloom visible in her eyes, and still I did not speak. Looking back, it strikes me as unbelievably foolish that I did not bundle her into a taxi on the spot and take her to the nearest hospital.

Yet I did not. In my stupidity I began to pack and even succeeded in convincing myself that a ferry ride to a nearby island away from the noise of Hong Kong was just what we needed. I imagined, I suppose, returning to some mindless vegetable state, lying washed by the sea, sucked back and forth by cool waves over sand.

As our taxi made its way through the streets to the ferry terminal we ran straight into a street march. Columns and columns of people passed, dressed in yellow T-shirts and carrying banners, their mouths open in mid-protest. Our taxi was banked up behind other cars and the driver began to furiously honk his horn.

'Stop it!' Anne-Louise shouted at him. 'Stop it, you stupid man!'

The driver spoke no English but wheeled around immediately in surprise. 'No good!' he shouted again and again and the noise was overwhelming: blasting horns, the shouting, the wails of chants, the roar of traffic in the main road behind us.

'Come on, let's walk,' I said, opening the door but Anne-Louise did not follow. I waited, holding the door open and when she did not emerge I bent my head to peer in. She appeared to be in a kind of trance, watching the people passing with a rapt expression, her mouth slightly slack.

'Anne-Louise,' I called and she slowly turned her head towards me.

'Look at the people,' she said. 'Just look at them, Rachel.'

I leant over the front seat and stuffed some bills into the driver's hand, then gently pulled Anne-Louise by the wrist. Even as I pulled I was only thinking of whether we would make the ferry.

With relief I watched as Anne-Louise got out of the cab. 'We'll have to run,' I said, beginning to walk fast. I headed off down the street with Anne-Louise dawdling behind, still turning her head back.

'Come on!' I yelled and she turned around with a startled look, as if she had forgotten I was there. She began to pick up speed and I waited until she caught up. We hurried the rest of the way without speaking.

On the ferry deck Anne-Louise stretched out her thin legs on a chair and watched the sun setting. Across the harbour, reflected in the windows of buildings, the sun flared, making my eyes hurt. I looked away, turning towards Anne-Louise, whose gaze was focused on one building in particular. I followed the direction of her eyes and saw a building in the shape of a pyramid. In the setting sun it glowed as if lit from within, its modernity strangely timeless.

'It looks like one of the great pyramids, doesn't it,' I remarked.

When Anne-Louise turned to me, her face had the stillness of a Buddha. Her eyes were bizarrely serene and clear, her brow uncluttered, the skin and bones of her face composed and relaxed.

'It is my burial tomb,' she announced and panic

struck me. I leapt up and stared helplessly back at the city, retreating quickly as the ferry pulled away, faster and faster.

Again I could not think, again my good sense failed me. When the ferry docked I blindly followed Anne-Louise down the ramp, still panicked and sweating. I blindly followed her off the ferry and onto a bus as night fell and I knew nothing and no-one. The hot Asian night fell deep and close, swarming with animals and insects. Trees pushed into the windows of the bus, leaves and vines wound in, frilled, dark. As the bus climbed the hill I looked back and saw the lights of the ferry as it was leaving the harbour. At once I realized that I should have forced Anne-Louise to remain on the boat while it turned around for the trip back to Hong Kong so that at least help would be within reach.

As I watched, the bus rounded a corner and the harbour was lost from sight. I swung around in the seat and all I could see out the window in front was a dense, inhabited darkness. Safety had fled, all hope of rescue and when I turned my head to look at Anne-Louise I saw that her black eyes were filled with visions and it was too late for anyone to save us.

All that long night in the room Anne-Louise had booked for us I waited for the break of day. All that long night as I removed the razor blade from the razor I used to shave my legs, the glass tumbler from the bathroom, any object from the bedroom which

Anne-Louise might take up to lance her pain, my eyes continually ransacked the darkness, searching for light. My eyes returned continually to the opened curtains, to the open door, roaming the moonless black, casting for daybreak.

In the small, close room there was only space for one bed and when we were not standing outside on the verandah, I lay down next to Anne-Louise and held her tightly. She asked me to hold her while the devils were loose in her head, while they whispered their malignant words, pushing her deep into the abyss. I held her while her body shook, while she fought them off, while her teeth rattled in her head and her eyes rolled and she let out a long, wounded moan. I was terrified of her, terrified for myself, lest her maddened hands reach for my neck. I held her but I also cowered and shook, frightened of what had been unleashed.

The room was crudely made, in a building only feet from the sea, and an old air-conditioning unit above the bed continuously clattered and hummed. 'Turn it off! Turn it off!' Anne-Louise screamed and I jumped up immediately from the bed. 'I have to get out of here,' she cried, leaping up.

Pushing open the doors to the verandah Anne-Louise stood, her head thrown back, releasing a piercing howl. 'There's no moon, there's no moon,' she said over and over. I rushed up to her, placing my arm around her shoulders and when she turned to me I saw something had broken open in her eyes, that the full wash of madness had swept in. I looked around for the moon and when I saw its slender slice, turned her face towards it. 'It's fading!' she screamed.

The air felt unbearably wet and putrid against my sweating skin, clogged and dense, stinking of smoke and the sea. The sound of my own blood pounded in my ears together with the suck of the sea and when I looked out towards the ocean's moving blackness, fires were burning on the sand. Groups of teenagers had lit them earlier for a barbeque but now in the darkness they leapt and flared like a visible hell. 'I'm burning!' Anne-Louise cried, frantically turning her head toward the fires, her hands clawing at my chest in terror. 'It's all right, it's all right,' I crooned, 'it's only some kids having a barbeque.' My eyes desperately raked the black, searching for rescue, while all the time I knew I was stranded.

'Hell is shouting in my head,' Anne-Louise cried, her mouth pulled down. 'Help me!' I took her bodily and led her back to the room, where I laid her down again on the bed. 'I am full of evil,' she said, breaking open again. 'I am dangerous. Stay away from me.'

I sat on the edge of the bed, tentatively stroking her arm, all the while fearful lest she lash out at me. Random thoughts raced through my head: where was a telephone book or even a telephone? How could I restrain her? Why had she waited till now to go mad? The night stretched out interminably and my eyes returned again to the blackness visible through the door.

'Hold me, Rachel, please hold me,' she whimpered and I lay down beside her and gently stroked her sweating forehead. She was hot and shaking and I made shushing sounds as if I were doing something simple like comforting a crying child. She had called me by name and I took this as a hopeful sign; as the night went on and on I was growing deathly tired but Anne-Louise was too scared to close her eyes and let the rot inside her head fully claim her.

'Sshh, sshh, it'll be morning soon,' I crooned. 'Don't be frightened, sweetie, the sun will be up soon and everything will be over.'

She began to cry harder. 'This is my last night alive,' she wept, her whole body convulsing.

'Oh, nonsense,' I said. 'I'm here. I'll help you.' Yet I felt frightened myself, scared that what she said would come true, that her own body would somehow betray her. In the wild, reeling night anything seemed possible; I talked on and on, as much to reassure myself as Anne-Louise. I listened to the crackle of fire and the rise and fall of the sea and tears came to my eyes. I held her and rocked her and waited and waited, sometimes crying when she did.

It was the longest night of my life.

I must have fallen briefly asleep for when I opened my eyes I saw the first brightening of day. As I watched, the shapes in the room gradually grew firmer in outline and outside the window the spray of colour slowly came into the sky. Beside me Anne-Louise lay in a deep, active sleep, groaning occasionally, her muscles twitching. As I watched her poor, stricken face, her eyes suddenly sprang open.

'I'm sick, Rachel,' she said. 'Please take me to hospital,' and my whole body unclenched in relief.

Back on the main island I took Anne-Louise in a taxi from hospital to hospital until we were finally referred to the right one. I became her interpreter, her voice, her tongue, I spoke for her because she could not. 'Yes, it's happened before,' I told Chinese doctors who could barely speak English. 'It's manageable, she just needs the right drugs.' Anne-Louise sat as if already drugged while we spoke, her eyes occasionally fixing on me. I heard the words schizophrenia, mania, psychosis and I began to grow scared. 'Look, it's not that serious. She knows what's happening to her, she was the one who asked me to bring her here.' And as I spoke, Anne-Louise appeared to sense danger and rallied. 'I just need to rest for a while. I haven't slept for a long time,' she said in a depressed, tired voice.

Finally the doctors agreed to monitor her overnight, and decide on further action from there. We were led to a public ward in another part of the hospital, filled with Chinese, and Anne-Louise lay down fully dressed on the bed. She was pumped full of something which would make her sleep and as she lay there, fighting the drug, her eyes did not leave my face once. She looked up at me in such distress that I could hardly bear to look at her, yet each time I broke her gaze she grabbed my hand so hard it hurt. She lay looking up at me as if I were her only salvation and I stroked her brow, saying over and over, 'Everything's all right now, close your eyes.'

An old Chinese woman in the next bed suddenly set up a high wail, a kind of keening which went right through me. I glanced over and saw that she had no teeth, that she was obsessively rubbing her thumb into a groove in her forehead, making it bleed. I looked away, back into Anne-Louise's eyes, which met mine unflinchingly, as if she knew before I knew myself that I was getting ready to desert her.

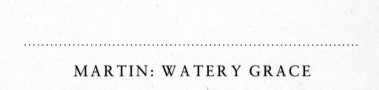

MARTIN: WATERY GRACE

MARTIN had just got in the door on Sunday afternoon after spending a couple of hours in the office when the phone rang. He picked up the beer he had just opened and walked over to the answering machine, waiting to hear who it was.

'Ah, hello, it's Rachel Gallagher here, I'm trying to contact Martin Bannister. I'm Anne-Louise's friend—we met the other night—and I was wondering . . .'

'H—H—Hello,' he said, picking up the phone. 'Martin speaking.'

He let her go through the spiel of introducing herself again so that she would not know he had been listening. 'I'm sorry to bother you, but I need to talk to you about something.'

'Oh, yes?' he asked, his curiosity nudged. She did not appear to be the type to telephone a relative stranger.

'Have you got a moment? Is this a good time?'

He took another swig of beer. 'I—I—I'm going out soon but I can spare ten minutes.' He was going nowhere but he did not particularly want her to know this.

There was a pause. 'Look, Anne-Louise is on her way over to your place,' she said. 'I don't want you to get alarmed but she's had a sort of nervous breakdown . . .'

He felt a burst of panic but did not speak. 'She's all right, I think . . . She spent last night in hospital but managed to talk her way out this morning . . .'

He interrupted. 'W—W—Why's she coming over here?'

'I have no idea, except I couldn't stop her. I just thought you should know she's on her way, that's all. You might find her a bit strange . . . Will you make sure she gets back all right? She really shouldn't have been let out of the hospital . . .'

There was a knock at the door. 'That's her now,' he said. 'I—I—I'll ring you later.'

He put the phone down and nervously drained the rest of the beer. As he headed for the door he felt the wash of dread.

In the moment it took to put his hand on the lock to open it, he realized he could have pretended to be out.

Martin saw at once that Anne-Louise was wound down, that she moved as if under water. She stood on the doorstep and turned her head towards him with a watery grace, her dark eyes filmy and translucent.

'Hello, Martin,' she said in a low, subdued voice and he immediately stepped aside to let her in.

'H—H—How are you, A—A—Anne-Louise?'

he asked, his stammer in full flight. Even though he saw she was harmless, he was irrationally frightened. She carried no weapons of war and yet he was no less scared than if she had been wielding an axe. He was immediately reminded of the drowned look his mother had acquired when she once swallowed a handful of sleeping pills and spent a week in a psychiatric ward. He had hated to visit her, to see the lost, ruined look in the eyes of all the other patients and in his own mother.

'W—W—Would you like a drink?' he offered, panic-stricken. 'A c—c—coffee?' He wanted her out of his flat, out of his sight, and had to resist an impulse to physically push her straight back out the door.

She stood in the middle of the room, her eyes unfocused. Every now and then her gaze settled on a particular object and she made a kind of bow of her head, as if in worship.

'I have come to tell you something,' she said and sat down. Her limbs fell into a chair with balletic form, her tiny feet crossed at perfect points at the ankles.

Martin sank into a chair opposite Anne-Louise, flailing in panic. He did not know how he would get her out, how to direct her from the premises and his life, how he had got himself into this mess in the first place.

'Martin, I am in love with you,' she announced calmly, her beautiful dark eyes slow moving and shining.

His heart lurched in surprise and he frantically cast around for the right answer. 'Ah, I—I—I'm very flattered, A—A—Anne-Louise,' he said. 'I—I—I think you're a wonderful person . . .'

She continued to look at him in her watery fashion, her hands stroking the arms of the chair. She was smiling, in a different place, and he was not sure if she could understand him.

'I—I—I'm very fond of you too,' he continued, stumbling on, 'but I—I— don't feel . . . I—I—I'm not in a position to . . .'

She suddenly looked at him, as if his words had pierced some barrier and the reception in her head had cleared. 'Martin, do you love me as I love you?'

What could he say? He remained sitting in his chair but a sweat broke out on his back and the water in his mouth ran dry. 'A—A—Ah, p—p—perhaps not in the same way . . . I—I . . .'

She stood up immediately. 'That's all I needed to know,' she said. 'Goodbye, Martin.'

She walked towards the door: Martin remembered that Rachel had asked him to see her safely home. He wanted to help but he wanted to get rid of Anne-Louise more and he remained motionless as she opened the door.

'Goodbye, Martin,' she said a second time.

He was on his third beer when the phone rang again. The answering machine picked it up. He stayed sitting where he was, listening.

362

'Hi, it's Rachel again. Is Anne-Louise still with you? Can you let me know? It's about . . . seven . . . no eight, on Sunday night. Can you call me? Thanks.'

He did not rise and stayed sitting in the darkened room, remembering Anne-Louise's lost eyes and the eyes of his mother, remembering all his hungry ghosts.

....

ANNE-LOUISE: A DARK PLACE

WHEN Martin told Anne-Louise he did not love her she was felled by the pain. She felt the air leave her body, all her new found calm speeding from her veins. Love rushed from her, hope, the concept of the future, the very pulse of life itself. As his words entered her bloodstream she felt life leaving, herself shrivelling up, her burdened soul fleeing from its capture. She was left as a black hole of nothingness and was amazed to find she could still stand. As her body rose from the chair she concentrated on placing one foot in front of the other, in making her way to the door. She felt herself disappearing second by second and when she reached the door was no longer sure that Martin could see her.

'Goodbye, Martin,' she called through the fog. 'Goodbye, Martin,' she called from a very long distance.

She walked out into the street and the sky was a strange metallic colour. Birds wheeled and dipped, flown in from China; she saw a giant hawk circling the birds, high above them. She walked down by the rainforest rooted to each side of the road and noted the thickened loops of vines clawing their way up the ancient trees. A canopy of webbing made the forest dark and appear wet and she lifted up her head to see if she could see the sky. Inside her own self was a dark, wet place, full of some primal slime. She looked down at her wrist and saw the throb of a vein, of something black and flowing beneath the skin. The skin, her shroud, was white and fine, stretched tight to keep all the darkness within. If she could still see herself perhaps other people might too and she stared hard into every passing face to see if she could tell.

A bus stopped beside her and without thought she climbed aboard. She walked straight past the driver down into its centre and sat looking out the window. He turned in his seat and shouted something at her in Cantonese but she did not respond. Finally he gave up and the bus took off, with Anne-Louise still staring out the window.

She got off when she saw a cage of birds, bright shiny birds swinging on polished swings. Their cages were elaborate constructions of lacquered bamboo and her eye focused on them as much as the birds. The birds were furious, she could see their hearts pumping, just as her own was slowly losing its animation. She felt her blood begin to congeal, to run heavily through the internal alleyways and chambers of her disappearing house. That her body, the house in which she dwelt, was dying she had no doubt, yet she wandered on, her eyes still searching. She was looking for a place except she was not sure where it was, knowing only she would know when she found it. She did not think of Martin Bannister again, for she could not bear it and found instead she could not think of anything. She was very tired and wished to sleep the rest of her life, to lie down for good and feel nothing again. She saw a bench and spread out full length upon it. Her vanishing self was growing lighter and freer and she closed her eyes to concentrate on the sensation. The fog in her head rose up as if to greet her and she let herself be slowly swallowed up.

When Anne-Louise awoke she did not know where she was and immediately felt frightened. She lay perfectly still for a long time while people pushed past her in the dark. She could not make out what any of them were saying and before long their babble filled her ears, her whole head. She sat up and started to sob, searching her pockets, looking for any information which might save her. 'Help me, please,' she cried out, still sitting on the bench. 'Somebody help me!' No-one stopped and she began to grow more and more panicked. The faces of the Chinese appeared evil and strange, their eyes full of burning malice. A child pointed to her but his mother quickly propelled him away: he looked over his shoulder as she dragged him by the hand. Anne-Louise got up and raced after the boy. 'Stop, please!' she called but he disappeared into the crowd. There were too many people, too many faces, too much noise. Myriad lights flickered in her eyes and she shielded her face with her hands. She was staggering now, weeping out loud, crying out in terror. She saw a doorway and stumbled towards it, huddling down inside, her arms tight around her.

'Are you all right?' she heard a voice ask and she lifted her face as if in benediction.

'Will you help me?' she pleaded, making out a European woman's face. 'Can you take me home?'

And the woman bent down and raised her up, lifting her back into life.

When Rachel opened the door, Anne-Louise fell into her arms. She clasped her fast, weeping, and felt Rachel weeping too.

'Thank God, thank God,' Rachel was saying, over and over.

'He doesn't love me,' Anne-Louise cried. 'Oh, Rachel, he doesn't love me.' Her body felt wrenched apart and Rachel rocked her.

The unknown woman remained on the threshold, holding open the front gate without speaking. She stayed while Rachel packed a bag for Anne-Louise to take back to the hospital and insisted on driving them there. 'I can't thank you enough,' Rachel said as she left the car. The woman smiled. 'I lost a good friend last year,' she said. 'Take care of her.'

As Anne-Louise walked through the doors of the

hospital for the second time she felt only relief, as if she had at last found the place for which she had been searching. As she walked into the hospital's artificial air she felt herself leaving the world of pain for good and no longer cared if she lived or died, only that the end came soon.

RACHEL: A FATAL COMBINATION

S OMETIMES when I remember that hot, surreal night when I forgot danger, forgot Anne-Louise and ultimately forgot myself, I think I was a different person. I see myself sitting in Martin Bannister's loungeroom, a willing look on my face, and feel both a poignancy and a sense of shame. My expression must surely have been one of longing, of childlike hopefulness; I was transparently naive. I believed in jumping straight in, in deep, obliterating love, in moving forwards without looking back. I was scared of being alone, weary of ambivalence and longed to rush towards a final love and slam the door. That hot night I was also out of my head with exhaustion and fear, overwhelmed by shouldering the sole responsibility of saving Anne-Louise in a strange place in which I knew no-one. By the time I reached Martin Bannister's door my nerves were bare and my heart was full of inchoate longing: it was a fatal combination, perfect in its composition, and could not have led to any other end.

Of course it is painful for me now to claim those lost, desperate actions entirely as my own, without pleading clemency for youth, for hopefulness, for circumstances. Yet as much as I might like to think of myself as being a different person then, that same person must dwell in me still, my history piled inside like archaeological layers. I am the sum of my past, a living history of want, trailing my own acts of glory and failure.

After Anne-Louise went into hospital for the second time I rang her employers to excuse her from work, saying she had some kind of virus. I was due to leave for Paris in three days time and the doctors had told me Anne-Louise would have to remain in hospital indefinitely but that when she came out she would need constant supervision. Panicked, I considered ringing her mother, postponing my flight. It also briefly passed through my mind to forget everything and catch the next plane out. Instead I rang three of the supposedly close friends she had introduced me to but each of them said they would help in any way they could except that they could not take any time off work. Then Anne-Louise's flatmate Christine arrived home from Singapore and I fell upon her with relief: although she was a stranger to me, she was someone with whom to share the burden. I tried to break the news about Anne-Louise as delicately as possible.

'I suspected as much,' Christine said at once, completely unruffled and offering me a drink. 'Poor you.' I was intimidated by her groomed control, by her perfect haircut and her unflustered, sophisticated manner. As she handed me a drink my hands were sweating, my skin was greasy from a visit by bus to the hospital in the midday heat, and I did not like my chances of being able to act coolly. Christine however did not appear in the least concerned, and I began to wonder if I had understated the seriousness of the problem.

'You know Anne-Louise might be in hospital for weeks,' I went on. 'They're quite concerned about her.'

'Oh, honey, shrinks always overreact. I had a small nervous breakdown myself once. It was heaven.'

I saw that Christine did not understand the difference between a holiday from the daily tensions of life while one wept or wallowed or ate chocolate, and what had happened to Anne-Louise.

'They're actually using words like psychosis, Christine.'

I finally had her full attention. 'Really?'

I nodded. 'Look, I'm sure she's going to be all right. It's not like it happens every month, or even regularly. The last time was years ago.'

'It's happened before?'

'Years and years ago. I'm sure it's just a case of Anne-Louise recognizing the symptoms early enough and taking preventive action. The doctors think so too.'

Christine at last looked worried. 'You know mental illness is notifiable here, or whatever the word is. By law your employer is supposed to be notified. It's a sackable offence.'

I looked at her in disbelief. She shrugged.

'Homosexuality's a crime, too.'

I took a long sip of my drink, my head racing. What if Anne-Louise lost her job? What if her name was listed on some mad person's register? And who would look after her when she got out?

'But that's barbaric!' I cried. 'Anne-Louise needs support not reprobation!'

'This is a tough city. There's no unemployment benefit or old-age pensions either. That's why you see so many old people out there wheeling trolleys and picking up trash.'

I did not care about Hong Kong's social security arrangements but I did care about what happened to Anne-Louise. 'The hospital won't notify her employers, will they? Surely they can't do that without her permission?'

Christine looked at me and shrugged again. 'Who knows?'

I felt as if I were holding Anne-Louise's life in my inadequate hands but that like captured water it was slowly escaping. I felt it running loose between the cracks of my fingers, draining fast no matter how hard I held on.

That night, from Anne-Louise's room, I watched the flicker of thousands of candles. A protest vigil was being held in the stadium which her bedroom overlooked and from her window I saw the burning of lights. It was like a galaxy of stars fallen to earth, sprinkling the ground with brilliance. Stars burned and shimmered, brighter than the lights from the surrounding buildings, hundreds of them, thousands of them, their centres quivering. I could not make out the hands which held them, only the shivering flames held aloft, human stars vying with the cosmos.

From Anne-Louise's bed high above the city the keening for the dead floated up and into my ears, a plaintive wailing. I lay trembling on her bed, washed by grief and fear, scared and alone.

The next morning I rose early to go to the hospital. Anne-Louise had asked me to bring in a few cosmetics and her special notebook. 'If you look inside, Rachel, you'll see everything is explained,' she told me, her expression grave. In looking through her things for this special notebook I found old letters of mine, with sections underlined in red pencil, the words marked with strange annotations I could not make out. Clearly everything had come to hold secret messages for Anne-Louise, the world a maze of code it was her duty to decipher. I saw strange diagrams of her family, points representing her mother, her father and herself, with words such as RETRIBUTION written in bold capitals beneath. When I finally found the notebook it was written in a tiny, indecipherable scrawl and I could not read any of it.

All the long journey on the bus I racked my

brains trying to think of what to do. Christine had been helpful but made it clear she could only remain so within certain limits: she constantly travelled and was due in Paris shortly for some important meeting she could not afford to miss. I was wary too of contacting Anne-Louise's employers in the light of what Christine had told me and was gradually coming around to the idea of ringing her mother. That Anne-Louise had specifically asked me not to was becoming increasingly irrelevant: I no longer believed I had any choice.

And then I remembered Martin Bannister. I was desperate and flailing and not thinking clearly: if I had remembered that he had already failed Anne-Louise once I would have dismissed the idea straight away. He had in fact already sent a clear message that he wished to be rid of her but I was beyond reading messages and I understand now that I was actually thinking more of myself. I wanted someone to rescue me and I made my way to Martin Bannister's door as if blind and homing, wilfully ignoring the signs.

When I entered the public ward where Anne-Louise was staying I saw her propped up in bed, surrounded by other patients. It was a tableau of adoration, with Chinese women in white gowns grouped around her, adopting various poses of worship. Anne-Louise sat amongst them in the middle of the bed, a white-gowned God, placing upon them hands of beneficence. Surprised, I stopped walking, arrested by the sight, but Anne-Louise saw me and waved me over. She was the only Western woman in the ward and as I moved towards her bed at the far end of the row, all the other women turned to look at me.

There were young women, middle-aged women and the old woman with no teeth and the bloodied brow I had seen earlier. Her forehead was bandaged now but her thumb had worn a dirty groove into the white. All the women's eyes were uniformly dull from drugs and they watched my approach with absent, unreadable expressions.

I wanted to turn and flee but Anne-Louise's face kept me walking. 'I see you've got your own fan club,' I said when I reached the bed and she looked around at the women with an expression of indulgence.

She spread her arms wide like a good hostess welcoming guests, embracing us all. 'They bring me things,' she said, dropping her arms and picking up a paper card from the bed. It was clumsily made, decorated with words in Chinese and meant nothing to me.

'It says luck is coming into my life,' Anne-Louise said. 'Lee Ling is a witch. Did you bring my notebook?'

As we continued to speak in English the women began to slowly disperse, as if buffeted. Only the witch Lee Ling remained by the bed, gazing up at Anne-Louise's face in adoration.

I handed over the bag I had packed and Anne-Louise immediately retrieved the notebook. 'Did you read it?' she asked.

'Yes, it's very interesting,' I lied but she looked at me as if this answer was satisfactory.

'Come on, let's walk in the gardens,' she said, swinging her legs out of the bed. She seemed to regard the place as a kind of hotel and I expected her at any moment to request a nurse to bring her a Manhattan. I noticed on the table beside her bed a bowl of congealed rice, obviously untouched.

'Are you eating?' I asked.

'They don't have Western food here,' she replied, unperturbed, pulling on her hospital dressing gown. I followed her outside onto the verandah and onto the lawn, where the sun immediately hit my head like a brick.

'Let's find some shade,' I said, heading for a bench beneath an enormous fig tree. Anne-Louise sat down and I could have sworn she almost looked happy. She did not appear out of place at all and indeed appeared comfortably entrenched.

'How're you feeling?' I asked.

'Oh, fine,' she said, 'except I hate the psychotherapy sessions. The doctor can barely speak English.'

'You'll have to try, Anne-Louise. It's no use bluffing your way out again.'

She looked out over the lawn. 'They said I can

go home soon,' she said slowly. 'The trouble is I can't remember where home is.'

She did not appear to remember either that I was only passing through and that I was due to leave soon. I looked at her newly unburdened face and knew I could not remind her.

I rang Martin Bannister at his office to ask if we could meet.

'I—I—I'd like to help,' he said straight away, 'b—b—but I'm really busy I'm afraid.'

I panicked. 'Can't we meet for a quick drink or something later? I'm really desperate.'

I heard him waver. 'Look, I—I—I don't know Anne-Louise very well. W—W—We've only been friends a short time . . .'

'I know, I know. I just need to talk to someone.' Christine was away again and if Martin Bannister would not help I knew I would have to ring Anne-Louise's mother.

There was a pause. 'I—I—I really don't know how I can help you . . .'

To my embarrassment a sound like a sob escaped me. My throat was closing and I struggled to open it.

'Are you all right?' he asked but I could not answer.

'P—P—Perhaps if you came around to my place,' he said, 'R—R—Rachel?'

Still I could not speak and I pressed my hand

hard against my mouth. 'Thank you, Martin,' I finally said. 'Thank you so much.'

'I—I—I can't promise anything,' he said before hanging up.

I believe now that he heard in my voice a readiness for rescue, reaching far beyond the immediate moment.

As I knocked on Martin Bannister's door that night I can no longer remember exactly what I was expecting. Did I expect him to magically make everything all right, to command that the world stand to order? He invited me in and handed me a large drink; the air inside his flat was hot and I remember that some music was playing, unknown to me. Was it Indian sitar music? Andes flutes? I no longer recall.

I sat in a velvet chair and the windows were open and the sounds of Hong Kong rushed in. For some reason the air-conditioning was not on and my hair was soon sticking to the back of my neck: although my hair was short, it felt too heavy against my skin and I remember rubbing my hand up over it again and again. I remember having two large vodka and tonics, three, four, and all my burdens and fears rising up and away from me.

I remember that we initially spoke of Anne-Louise and the problem of who would look after her. Martin Bannister declared absolutely and at once that he wanted nothing further to do with her. If warning bells should have sounded in my head they should have sounded then, but they did not. Instead I drank another vodka and we somehow began to compare Anne-Louise stories, illustrating how infuriating, how entertaining, how glorious she could be. I found myself telling him about meeting her for the first time when I was nineteen and how even then she had seemed larger than everyone else, more alive.

'She terrified us all,' I said, holding my glass up to be refilled. 'She was so worldly, so self-possessed ...'

'Sh—Sh—She delivers lines better than Bette Davis,' Martin remarked. 'When did you realize she was a nutter?'

I sat straighter in my chair. 'She's not a nutter,' I said, offended on Anne-Louise's behalf. 'She's saner than most people ...'

Martin smiled. 'I—I've had enough of nutters, th—th—thanks very much,' he said. 'S—S—Starting with my barmy mother.'

He proceeded to tell amusing stories about his once glamorous mother and how she went out with gangsters from the East End who financed her taste for fur coats and colonic irrigations. All his stories were sharp, pungent, delivered with a dashing sense of drama. His descriptions of his beautiful, doomed mother were so violently romantic and strange that it was impossible to imagine any other truth except his own. As we got drunker his stories grew more and more risqué and he told me about his first girlfriend getting caught with his penis in her mouth and his over-wrought mother trying to smash the car window.

I remember finding all his stories witty and hilariously funny, how laughing felt like release. I began to enjoy the beguiling way Martin Bannister's stutter fell unexpectedly on certain words, how his delivery of phrases sounded airily elegant. His voice was soft yet seductively dramatic and I found myself leaning towards it.

I cannot say at what point I realized that Martin Bannister was flirting with me, and I with him. I remember that the strap of my cotton dress kept slipping off one shoulder and that after a while I no longer bothered to push it back up. I remember thinking at one stage too that my mouth had dissolved into a ludicrous, drunken grin and noticing for the first time that Martin Bannister had exceptionally beautiful green eyes.

I sat in that velvet chair getting drunker and looser, freedom bursting in my veins. Everything was suddenly strange and exotic to me and I felt incredibly light, unbound. At some point Martin Bannister struck me as being unlike any other man I had met and I remember looking out the window into the blazing Hong Kong night feeling as if I had begun some startling new adventure. I was drunk but I was also slightly deranged, in my own way as derailed as Anne-Louise.

Somehow over the course of several hours, my deepest desires, my most buried wants came to rest upon Martin Bannister's person. I know that he was suddenly breathing very close to me and as his mouth came down upon my own I protested, 'I can't. What about Anne-Louise?' I tried to picture her sitting up in a hospital bed but the image kept slipping away.

'W—W—What about her?' he replied. 'She's not my girlfriend, Rachel.' I remember thinking in a drunken leap of logic that his rejection of her meant that he was free and that I could embark on whatever it was I was embarking on with a clear conscience.

But as his lips came down upon my own I felt the briefest flush of triumph. It was in this one small moment that I forgot myself, forgot Anne-Louise and the fate of our love was sealed forever over the heads of the drowning.

I remember saying goodbye to Anne-Louise for the last time. She was leaning up against some pillows in her hospital bed and looked up, giving me a small distracted smile before returning her attention to a card someone had sent her.

I remember standing very still looking at her bowed head, the remnant of the smile still on her lips.

'Take care of yourself,' I said again, leaning over to push the hair from her forehead. She looked up at me in confusion but before she could speak I turned and walked quickly from the ward.

The sound of my footsteps sounded too loud on the linoleum. 'Rach?' I heard her call in a small, panicked voice.

I will never forget that I lacked the courage to look back.

....

ANNE-LOUISE: CLEAVING TO LIFE

AFTER Anne-Louise finally found out, months after Rachel had gone, she tried to recall Rachel's face as she said goodbye. She tried to recall if there had been any sign she had missed, any gesture of betrayal her eyes had failed to see. But she had not been fully lucid at the time and Rachel's leaving slid by her somehow, so that she remembered it as if in a dream. Now that Anne-Louise was well again she tried to reconstruct the event, to will her mind to recall it more clearly. Had Rachel's hand shook as she pressed Anne-Louise's own? Had she kissed her three times just to make sure? She wished she could drag her eyes from the present back to the past, so that she could look with clear eyes upon this vital moment.

In the hospital, and for weeks afterwards, Anne-Louise had lived in a watery world, floating in and out of lucidity. It was strangely pleasant in her drug-slowed place, safe, noiseless. The outside world somehow failed to press in, so that she could look at it but not hear the full brunt of its shouting. Everything was muted, colours, shapes, her own emotions.

For weeks the days and nights slid by and she was almost happy, though that was not exactly the right word. In truth she did not feel sharply enough to be happy, but felt something quieter, perhaps satisfaction. She felt complete, unburdened, and floated on days and nights, which swam beneath her, holding her up.

But then one morning her new doctor spoke of reducing her medication, of getting her to stand unassisted on her own two feet. She felt the clutch of fear and told him she was not ready but he merely looked down at his notes and folded his glasses. 'Why don't we give it a try?' he said in perfect Oxford English. He was Chinese, young and ambitious, smarter than the last, and had lived a long time in England. Anne-Louise dimly recognized that she could no longer get away with anything.

And so, hour by hour, she was returned to the outside world, tipped from her basket even though she tried to cling on. Slowly she began to hear the world again, the roar of traffic, the rattling of the food trolley. As she slowly rose through the water her ears cleared, her vision focused, and before she broke the surface she was already anticipating entertaining visitors. She was curious to know what had happened to her life while she had been absent from it, and set about finding out.

Christine came to see her, bringing Anne-Louise's bankbooks and credit cards. 'I need money,' Anne-Louise ordered just like her old self and

Christine brought cash too, together with several outstanding bills.

'There's nothing like a Mastercard bill to shock you into sanity,' Anne-Louise quipped as her eye ran over the bill. In the weeks leading up to her hospitalization she had somehow managed to run through thousands of dollars in purchases of expensive clothes, cosmetics and gym equipment. She realized she was badly in debt and then Christine reminded her she also owed two months' back rent.

'Oh, and your mother has arranged for a private nurse to come to the flat when you get home,' she added.

'What?' Anne-Louise spluttered. 'I don't need a nanny!'

Christine shrugged. 'Apparently the shrinks think you do.'

'How did my mother get involved in this?'

'I think Rachel spoke to her,' Christine replied.

Anne-Louise could not recall any of this, only that Rachel must have known that Anne-Louise would not have wanted to involve her mother.

'Have you heard from Rachel?' she asked Christine. 'She seems to have gone missing.'

'She's rung a few times to see how you're doing,' Christine said. 'She said she's going to write to you.'

But Anne-Louise did not hear from Rachel for weeks, not a phone call, not a letter. Long after she

393

was home with the young English private nurse she kept expecting a call at any time.

She began to wonder why none came.

Anne-Louise wondered too what had happened to Martin. Of course she realized she must have completely blown her chances, for going mad in the initial stages of courtship was not usual accepted behaviour. She felt unspeakably tired whenever she thought of him, weighed down by a depression she was not confident would ever lift. Her life seemed to lie about her in ruins and she felt her soul to be irreparably bruised. For one stupid moment she had imagined she might even win the ordinary prizes: a husband, a child. As depression swept in she hated herself for her slip, for publicly falling in love. She felt embarrassed for her mad self, for what she might have said or done, for involving Martin Bannister in the first place. She wanted only to retrieve the situation as best she could and packed away her wishes so they might never spill out again.

She was not sure of the most appropriate way to approach Martin. Should she telephone him? Write him a letter? In the end she decided on a card, light in tone, hopefully witty. She practised writing a few sentences until she got it right, then dashed it off and sealed the envelope before her nerve failed her. She asked the nurse to post it.

Next she began a long letter to Rachel in France.

I'm so very sorry you arrived in the middle of my nightmare, she wrote, *and I can't thank you enough for everything you did.* She wrote about how much better she was feeling, how she even felt brave enough to continue psychotherapy and that from now on she would monitor herself closely. *This new doctor is very hopeful. He says that as long as I'm sensible I should be able to nip any problems in the bud as it were, but that it's up to me to be responsible. I only know that I never, ever want to go through that again and I'll do anything to prevent it.*

Anne-Louise wondered if Rachel's long silence meant that this time she had gone too far, if she had demanded too much beyond the bounds of friendship.

Please write, Rach. I think of you often and know that no friend in the world would have done for me what you did.

In the letter she enclosed a photograph taken during Rachel's visit. Anne-Louise had found a roll of film in her camera but did not remember taking any photos. When the film was developed there were thirty-six photographs of Anne-Louise and Rachel. In all of them her own face was transfused with happiness. She could not bear to look at it.

The photograph she sent was of herself and Rachel, their arms around one another, smiling into the lens.

One evening, not long after the nurse had left to take

up another position, Anne-Louise was surprised by a call from Martin.

'Ah, hello,' he said, sounding uncharacteristically nervous. 'I—I—I got your card.'

Anne-Louise found she could hardly breathe and could not think of one clever thing to say. All her hopes rushed back, alive and raring, and straight away she supposed him to be ringing to offer her a second chance.

'H—H—How have you been?' he asked and she found her tongue at last.

'Well, let's just say I haven't taken any personal messages from God lately.'

He laughed. 'I—I—I'm glad to hear it, although it must be disappointing not having your own hotline.'

She managed a sort of laugh, all the while waiting to discover the reason for his call. 'I'm going back to work next week,' she said while she waited.

'I—I—Is there any chance we can get together for a drink before then? I—I—I'd like to talk to you about something.'

Her heart jumped. 'Certainly,' she said at once. 'What night suits you?'

'What about tomorrow? Six-thirty at Grissini's?'

'Fine,' she replied, ringing off. When she put the phone down her hands were shaking.

As Anne-Louise walked towards Martin Bannister in Grissini's bar her mind raced over all the possibilities of what he might say. He might have discovered that he really did love her after all and want to ask how he could help in her recovery. She would allay his fears, tell him all the good news the doctors had told her, that she was most definitely not schizophrenic or psychotic and that if she ever showed the slightest signs of mania again, all she had to do was take a short course of medication.

As she walked towards Martin that night Anne-Louise summoned all her willpower, all her nerve, so that she would look as calm and indifferent as possible. She was in fact intensely nervous and tried to pull her twisting mouth firmly into line.

'Hello,' she said, kissing him lightly on the cheek. She had forgotten how good looking he was.

Martin stood up as she sat down and lifted a hand to attract the waiter's attention. It was a graceful gesture and she admired it.

'Y—Y—You're looking well,' he said, clearly nervous. 'V—V—Very well.' His eye passed quickly over her face and body so that if she had not taken half a Serapax she might have blushed. 'W—W—What will you have, Anne-Louise?' he asked as the waiter came up to the table.

She was puzzled that he did not remember that she always drank Manhattans. After they had ordered, Martin sat back in his chair and Anne-Louise saw that he was distinctly uncomfortable. She had been so busy concentrating on herself she had failed to see just how agitated he looked.

'S—S—So, how have you b—b—been?' he

began hesitantly and suddenly Anne-Louise could bear it no longer.

'What exactly did you want to talk to me about, Martin? I can see that something's troubling you.'

His glorious eyes glanced away from her, jumping from object to object round the room. 'Ah . . . I—I—I don't really know where to start. I—I—I don't want this to come as too much of a shock . . .'

She let out a snort of contempt. 'It looks like it's more of a shock to you.'

He squirmed uncomfortably in his chair before the waiter returned with their drinks to release him. When the drinkmats, the drinks, the peanuts and the swivel sticks had all come to rest, he began again.

'Y—Y—You know I met R—R—Rachel when she was here,' he started and as he spoke Anne-Louise suddenly knew what he was going to say. Some part of her had always known that she would not win love and that Rachel would, that Rachel would take Martin away from her.

As he spoke Anne-Louise watched his mouth but she could no longer hear what Martin was saying. When she stood up and made her stumbling way to the door, she was conscious of someone chasing her, of someone trying to hold her back from feeling the full force of the blow. But the blow hit her again and again, making her reel, following her into the ladies' where she stood over a toilet and retched. It hit her in the solar plexus, the heart, the head, it hit her so hard she fell to the ground.

Hanging on to the toilet seat, Anne-Louise began to sob. As she wept the realization was already settling in her that she must have known all along, that she had even somehow conspired in this very outcome. This small, knowing part remained unsurprised by the news just befallen her and it was to this part Anne-Louise knew she must cling if she decided to make her way back to life a second time.

Events moved quickly after this. She soon heard that Martin Bannister and Rachel Gallagher were to be married and, even worse, that Rachel was coming to join Martin in Hong Kong. It was more than Anne-Louise could bear and she began to make frantic enquiries about transfers. She found her feelings towards Rachel swinging wildly: one minute she hated her for what she had done and the next felt that she could not blame her. It quickly became clear to her that it was not the loss of Martin that she mourned: as the months passed Anne-Louise realized that her passion for him had been nothing more than a frenzied infatuation, too closely intertwined with her madness to have ever achieved any solid outline. It was the loss of her friendship with Rachel for which she mourned, and she felt a deep and bitter grief. When exactly had their long friendship become of little consequence to Rachel? Why hadn't it been a powerful enough presence in her life to stop her?

Anne-Louise began to obsessively go over Rachel's departure, to rack her brains for any details which might yield meaning. She wondered if Rachel felt guilty, if she regretted what she had done.

One night she sorted through all the letters Rachel had ever written her, all the old photographs of them together, from the first days in Sydney at the fashion magazine, to parties they had been to, houses they had lived in together, to the days of the bedsit in London.

She found one from their Sydney days in which Rachel was kissing her cheek. She scrawled on the back, *The kiss of Judas?* and sent it to Rachel's address in France, unsigned.

A few weeks before Rachel was due to arrive in Hong Kong to live, Anne-Louise had still not been able to negotiate a transfer. She was getting desperate and one day from a distance she saw Martin in the street and knew she would not be able to bear the sight of Rachel.

Within hours she had booked a flight to Brisbane, tendered her resignation and arranged for the removalists to come. She had no firm plans except to spend a few weeks in Brisbane with her ageing mother whom she had not seen for two years. She wanted to go somewhere noiseless, where the world still lived by old-fashioned rules but, mostly, she just wanted to get out of Hong Kong as fast as she possibly could.

On the plane flying out she sensed the flame of her life flicker dangerously, as if almost extinguished. She felt deathly tired and was not sure if she had the will to rise again.

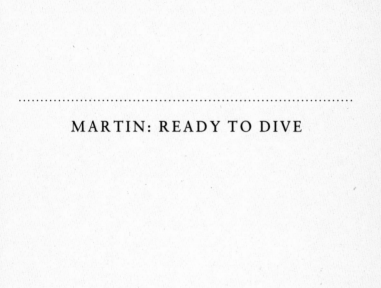

MARTIN: READY TO DIVE

THE moment Rachel Gallagher appeared at his door Martin's plans went astray. She was much prettier than he had first thought, all unwrapped, the drama of the situation making her large eyes impassioned and alive. Her whole face was animated by extreme emotion and as soon as he opened the door she began talking in a great rush. 'Thank you so much for seeing me,' she said, disarming him at once by clutching his wrist, 'I know you're busy and you've got to go out and I'll try not to take up too much time. It's just that I don't know what to do. Christine's going away and Anne-Louise doesn't want me to ring her mother and . . .'

'S—S—Sit down,' he said, moving her bodily to a chair by the window. He handed her a large drink but she did not stop talking. Everything about her was galvanized, every feature working and ablaze. Her eyes were enormous and scatter-gunned about the room, blinking furiously. He had not seen her in a dress before and it was made of something lightweight and flimsy, revealing the shape of her breasts. Martin quickly ran his eyes over her body and saw the pleasing sensuality of her limbs. He felt the shock of strong sexual attraction and immediately felt alert and excited.

As Rachel talked on, falling over words, he found her strange naked quality more and more appealing. There was a nervousness about her that was like an inexhaustible energy, some rawness which suggested vulnerability. She struck him as lacking in confidence and this lent her a softness, some sense of yielding. She had too the most alarming way of looking at him as if impressed by everything he said. She looked into his face with a complete absence of guile and he felt flattered and hopelessly ensnared.

He found himself showing off, telling stories designed to make her laugh. She laughed like a child being naughty and as the night went on his stories became more embellished and bawdy just so he could hear her laugh again. At first all she wanted to talk about was Anne-Louise but he managed to wean her away from the subject by entertaining her with further stories and pouring her extra large drinks. Soon she was completely untied and when her dress started to slip alluringly off one shoulder he knew she would sleep with him.

Just before he took her to the bedroom she made some drunken, half-hearted speech about not hurting Anne-Louise. He did not care about Anne-Louise and breathed hotly into Rachel's mouth, stifling her words.

Whenever he came to recall that first night with Rachel, Martin remembered waking to find himself in love. He was lost, completely besotted, and from that moment could not keep his mind and hands off her. They had made love several times with an intensity which astonished him and he had not felt the need to wield the strap once. In the morning all his senses were roaring so that the thought of anything extra seemed like excess. He was unbelievably happy and looked across at Rachel's sleeping face, certain that she had saved him from himself. He felt cleansed of shame, of his own worst self, of every shabby act he had committed. Lying on one arm gazing at Rachel he swore to put everything dark behind him and to dwell only in light. He wanted clean love, pure and distilled, to rest his weary head on some unsullied pillow.

When Rachel suddenly opened her eyes, his heart rocked. 'Good morning, my darling,' he said and the words came straight out, whole.

They went to dinner the following night and Rachel was due to fly out the next morning. He insisted on taking her to Gaddi's where she fed him with her fingers and he licked them clean. 'You've got beautiful lips,' she said, tracing their outline with one finger.

'So have you,' he replied. 'Our children will have m—m—magnificent mouths.'

She laughed but all at once her face grew solemn. 'I feel terrible about Anne-Louise,' she said.

'W—W—What's there to feel terrible about?' he replied, kissing her hand. 'It's not like you've run off with her husband. I—I—I barely know her.'

'That's not the point,' Rachel said. 'Anne-Louise would expect me to forego any involvement with you, even if you're not together. She's in love with you.'

He snorted. 'H—H—How can she tell? She's been out of her tree most of the time.'

Rachel cast her eyes down at the tablecloth, her face suddenly sad. 'I can't break her heart,' she said softly. 'I just can't.'

He picked up her champagne glass and placed it in her hand. 'Sh—Sh—She wouldn't know if you did,' he said. 'She's away with the p—p—pixies. D—D—Drink up.'

But she would not be cheered and the light-hearted spirit of before had completely vanished. He should have seen then that she had a tendency towards broodish introspection but all he had been concerned about was the new, free feeling in his heart and how he was going to keep it. It had seemed to Martin that he was tantalizingly close to getting everything he had ever wanted.

In bed that night he found himself making absurd demands, urging Rachel to cancel her flight and stay. At first she laughed but once she realized he was serious she raised herself up on one elbow.

'I can't stay, Martin,' she said, looking full into his face. 'I've got commitments.'

'C—C—Cancel them,' he said, pulling her towards him. She giggled and tried to pull away but he only clutched her harder. She struggled and finally broke free, sitting up with her back against the wall.

'I know the timing's bad,' she said, 'but I can't do anything about it.'

'Yes you can. D—D—Don't go.'

She looked away from him. 'Why don't we meet in Paris? Come and see me.'

'All right,' he said. 'I will.'

After Rachel left for France, her absence only added to his frenzy. Within days of her departure it seemed perfectly logical to Martin to be thinking of marriage: there were too many wild cards involved for him to feel safe, different continents and endless complications. He saw that the situation required some large, dramatic action and on the fifth day after she had left he went out and bought a first-class ticket to Paris.

As he emerged from the arrivals hall at Charles de Gaulle he knew he had not made a mistake. Rachel's waiting face was suffused with love and he swept her up and held her.

'I'm going to follow you everywhere,' he said.

He immediately waged a campaign to get her to come back to Hong Kong, to abandon her scholarship or whatever it was.

'W—W—What are you worried about? That

your feminist sisters will stone you? S—S—Scholarships are a dime a dozen, Rachel. It's this that's hard
to come by.'

He knew she was a painter, she had shown him
colour transparencies of her work but, privately, he
did not think them very good. He could not understand why she would not jump on the next plane
back with him and the more she resisted the more
he wanted her.

He would not give up trying and one afternoon
when they were in bed he took another tactic. He
began talking about risk, how all was lost unless
one was prepared to risk in life. 'W—W—Why
don't you jump for once?' he asked but she did
not answer.

'You know how we have access to the sea?' he
continued and she looked at him, puzzled. 'B—B—
Because one man got inside a diving suit and lowered
himself into the ocean. Everyone thought he would
drown.'

She listened, smiling enigmatically.

They talked as Martin had rarely talked before, as if
words were suddenly sufficient. He talked about his
failed mother and the father he had found only to lose
again and it seemed to him his tongue had broken free
of its restraints. They made love often and not once did
he bind her hands or use his belt. He was pleased that
he still felt a powerful excitement which when dis-
charged always left him satiated.

410

He felt an almost religious purity and once after they had made love tears came into his eyes. He had tasted redemption and Rachel kissed his eyelids, holding him close, weeping too.

He went back to Hong Kong and had to make do with the telephone. He wrote Rachel letters and sent her postcards with messages either metaphoric or direct. *Are you ready to dive?* he wrote and she wrote back, *Is there an expiry date?* After two months he could stand it no longer and negotiated another three weeks off. In the farmhouse in Epernay he saw at once that Rachel was lonely and that she was wavering. By the time he flew back to Hong Kong for the second time they had set a date for the wedding.

They were married in the mayor's office in the Hôtel de Ville in Epernay four months later. The ceiling was adorned with blue and gold angels and the mayor had donned his mayoral robes for the occasion. It was a surprisingly long ceremony in formal, old-fashioned French and Rachel did not understand a word. Martin indicated each time she was expected to make a response and her assent came out sounding timid and flat. When it was over they were handed an elaborate scroll which was their marriage certificate, rolled up and tied with a blue ribbon.

Afterwards they went to a nearby restaurant where they ate duck and drank champagne and Martin could not imagine feeling unhappy again.

411

In the afternoon they retired very drunk to a large bedroom in the town's best hotel where Martin pushed Rachel onto the bed and began to undress her. He noticed that she had bought new creamy silk underwear, hand sewn with delicate lace. She was wearing stockings with suspenders and as he snapped them free he suddenly felt possessed by a fierce familiar urge. Rolling her over he grabbed a handful of her silk knickers and could not resist pulling the fabric up hard so that she winced. When they ripped, Rachel cried out, 'Martin, stop it!' But he did not stop for he found he could not help himself. 'Say sadomasochism, Rachel, say it!' He pulled tighter, the fabric ripping, and with a gasp Rachel said the word. As he entered her he saw that she was crying and he began to thrust even harder.

When he woke feeling sick some hours later he saw Rachel sitting in a chair by the window. He wanted to say something but he could not read her expression. He felt suddenly disoriented, for she looked like a stranger.

Martin made sure it did not happen again and the only thing which spoilt their honeymoon after that was Rachel going on and on about Anne-Louise. Finally, one night over dinner when she brought up the subject of the photograph Anne-Louise had sent for the millionth time, he exploded.

'Y—Y—You're talking about a mad woman!

Y—Y—You can't expect rationality from the insane!'

She looked angrily at him. 'She's not insane—that's just a cop-out!'

'S—S—So you think believing yourself possessed by the devil is normal?'

She glared at him. 'Keep your voice down!'

He realized they were having their first fight and his face softened. 'I—I—I really don't understand you, Rachel. Y—Y—You weren't married to Anne-Louise, for Christ's sake.'

Her eyes glazed over with unshed tears. 'She was my best friend,' she said, trying to control herself.

'I—I—I don't see the point of being so involved in each other's lives anyway,' he went on, once he saw she was in control of herself.

'I know you don't,' she said. 'Men's and women's friendships are different.' She looked away from him. 'Oh God, I hope she doesn't crack up again over this. What if she commits suicide?'

Martin let out a moan of exasperation. 'N—N—Now you're being melodramatic. Anne-Louise has got better things to do than top herself over us. Sh—Sh—She's not the type.'

Rachel's eyes looked dangerously close to being overrun again but she attempted a watery smile. 'No, she's not, is she,' she said with obvious fondness.

All at once Martin felt jealous.

Within months of Rachel's return to Hong Kong

Martin knew he had made a mistake. With a sick and panicked feeling he suddenly realized that just like his first wife, Rachel was not the person he had thought she was. He found he could not stand the way she harped on about giving up the scholarship, as if her work were the most important thing in the world and no-one else was doing anything of value. He could not stand the way she professed independence and yet was perfectly happy to eat extravagant dinners and to go on holidays paid for by him, to live in an expensive apartment paid for by his company. He could not stand how she complained about being stuck in Hong Kong and when he asked how she was going to support them if they left she did not answer and always left the room.

Suddenly she no longer looked at him as if yielding herself up and was no longer impressed by everything he said. Overnight her face appeared to him to be clenched and suspicious, her mouth pulled down unattractively at the corners. They began to argue and at moments he hated her for misrepresenting herself, for not being what he wanted.

It seemed to Martin that he had fallen in love with Rachel as if falling asleep and that he had woken to find he did not know of whom he had been dreaming.

He began going back to the house in Macau. If Rachel knew she did not protest, never once enquiring into his regular absences. He wanted to strike out at something, anything, himself: he wanted to obliterate pain from his very centre. When he beat a girl all his rage was loosed, all the suffering choking inside him. He raised the whip again and again and with each fall some distress was freed, rushing from him like hard, expelled breath.

Whenever he got a girl to photograph him with another she never objected. When he later came to look at the prints he paid to be developed at a special place he knew in Wanchai, the girls were frequently smiling. It never took him long to come.

Martin began to withdraw from Rachel, to push her away as if pushing away his own pain. It seemed to him that very quickly their relationship disintegrated so that within six months he could not see her as anything but the enemy. Whenever they did have sex he was physically rough with her, frequently taking up the strap or hitting her with his open hand and tying her wrists with rope. When he came home he requested that she refrain from speaking for at least an hour while he gathered his thoughts. As soon as he stepped into the flat he headed for the spare bedroom and closed the door so that he did not have to look at her. Instead, he took out the photographs, listening to his wife moving about just the other side of the door. When she began to cry in bed at night he made no move to comfort her and waited until she had stopped.

The night Christine called to tell them the news

about Anne-Louise he did not need to look at Rachel's face to know everything was over.

'We killed her,' she cried out in an hysterical voice.

'Oh, for fuck's sake,' he said, leaving the room.

Not long after, Martin came home one evening and Rachel had disappeared. It was an eerie re-enactment of his first wife's desertion but this time he did not rush to the telephone to find out where his second wife had gone.

Instead he was relieved to discover that he carried no remnant of love. He went into the kitchen to pour himself a glass of wine.

On the kitchen bench he saw a pile of shredded photographs and knew straight away what they were.

RACHEL: EVERYTHING THAT
WAS MINE

ONE of the last things I did before leaving Hong Kong for Sydney was to tear up the photographs. After the removalists had dismantled my hopes, taken down my books, my prints, the wedding presents from the cupboards, I went and got the key to open the wooden box. As I walked through the flat for the last time I went from room to room flinging open every door, looking for everything that was mine.

In the spare room, I found the key and unlocked the box. Reaching into the bottom, I lifted out the square of purple satin tied with the silk rope which Martin had used to bind me.

Before opening it, I dropped to my knees and stared at the purple square for a long time. It seemed to me even before I opened it again to be a symbol of my shame, a physical representation of everything that was fouled and mine. I knew that in some way the package belonged to me as much as Martin, that what the rope held was also mine.

My hand shook as I picked it up and the purple cloth fell away from the photographs. I saw again Martin's face as it looked when he raised his hand, when he was about to cause pain. I saw the faces of bound young women, their mouths biting down on cloth, their eyes broken open with fear. There were dozens and dozens of photographs, of different women, some struggling, some making pathetic attempts at a smile, all of them trussed and bound. My husband was in every photograph, striding them or else bending over some woman, forcing her mouth down.

I did not know who had held the camera or where the shots were taken, only that evil was inside my door. All my own sins rushed in to break upon my head, all my betrayals, all the pain which I had caused but failed to see. In looking at the photographs I finally understood my own complicity, how I had lived blocking my ears and blinding my eyes to Martin's activities, to Anne-Louise's devastation, to everything I did not wish to know.

I felt the full force of my failures upon me, bowed my head and cried.

Later, when I at last stood up and got ready to leave, I took the photographs into the kitchen and laid them out on the bench. As I looked at them in the clear light coming through the window I considered whether to send them to the police or to a newspaper but I did neither. In my last act of denial, I took them in my hands and tore them up: I was not thinking of Martin but of myself. As I ripped, it seemed to me that I was shredding the last vestiges of my own innocence and that when I had finished I would no longer be able to wilfully close my eyes again.

I left the pile for my husband to see, and then I walked out.

Sometimes now, all these years later, I wonder what happened to Martin. We did not speak again and I divorced him effortlessly by mail under undemanding Australian divorce laws. We had only one or two friends in common and every now and then I heard that he had changed jobs or that he had a new girl-friend. I know he lives in Hong Kong still, that place so good at forgetting.

I remember his stutter, some broken quality he had about him and how when he first loved me his face had the openness and sincerity of a child. I sometimes wonder if there was something I could have done to keep that look there, to quell forever his need to raise his hand.

Mostly though I understand there was nothing to be done. In our beginning was our end and we simply walked ahead until we reached our inevitable destination.

As for myself, I am burdened with remembering. I carry my memories, the past's heavy stones, knowing I can never lay them down. Everytime I think of Anne-Louise, I am forced to remember the moment I thought I had usurped her. I know now I was jealous of her insouciance, her blithe, careless charm, and when Martin's lips approached mine I thought I had won. All my heaviness fell away from me, all my watchfulness and caution and in that moment I believed myself more weightless than her. I see now that for a long time I wanted her talent for life for myself and that when Martin Bannister chose me I mistakenly thought I had claimed it.

I remember when we were young playing Anne-Louise's favourite record about the faithlessness of men over and over. As we danced I pretended I was just like her, witty and unnoticing. I smoked pink cigarettes like her and drank Manhattans and even lowered my voice when I sang. I see now that I wanted nothing less than to leave myself behind. In my memory we are always laughing as we dance, unable to imagine harm befalling us. Anne-Louise's feet are light on the ground and we are dancing with the abandon of the young, still believing everything is redeemable.

When I try to imagine Anne-Louise wading out that night into the deep of the Brisbane River, her pockets weighted with rocks, her blood with its freight of alcohol, I can never picture her face. I can never think of her deciding that life was not after all some marvellous, open-ended adventure, of Anne-Louise being too sad to strive. The nearest I get is remembering her despair in the darkness on the island, when all her carelessness had deserted her. Then I think that on the night she died she must have been so tired of carrying her load that all she wanted was for the water to lift her up, to stream like the river itself, dumb to memory.

I wonder if at the final moment she truly felt weightless for the first and last time in her life.

I often imagine I see her. On buses I catch a glimpse of her striding along the street, in crowds I see the back of her head. Once, when I was home in Brisbane visiting my parents for the first time after her suicide, I was walking past a café in the Valley mall when for a split second I saw her sitting at a table. The air left my lungs and my knees collapsed beneath me, so that I feared I might faint. My first instinct was to rush up to her so that she might look upon me again with the full blaze of her attention, so that she might focus her dark eyes once again on mine and forgive me.

But I knew it was not her and kept walking. As I turned the corner tears rose in my eyes and I leant against the nearest wall and wept.

She was my friend, my dear, dear friend.